the battles of
bridget lee™

THE MIRACLE CHILD

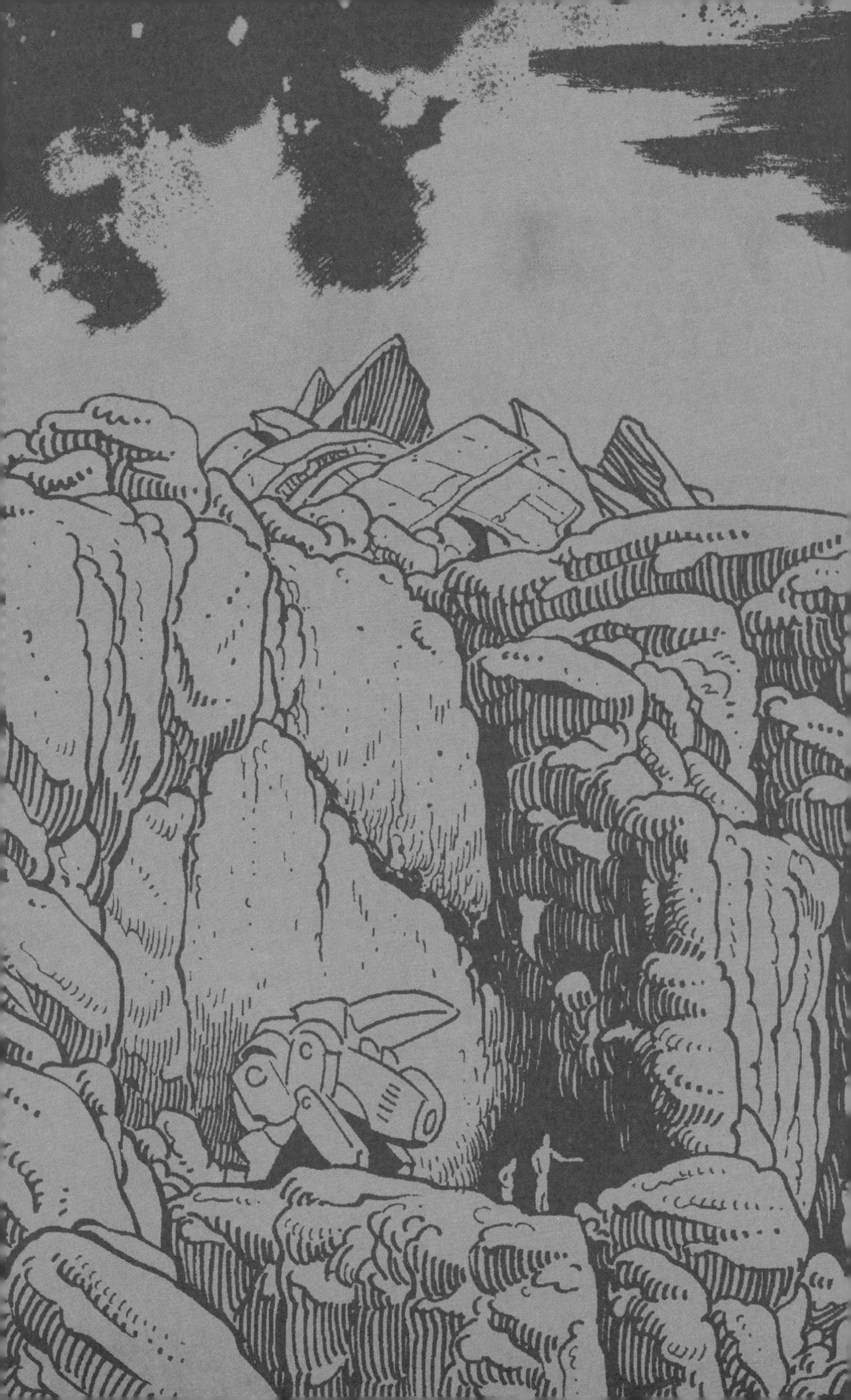

the battles of bridget lee

THE MIRACLE CHILD

ETHAN YOUNG

DARK HORSE BOOKS

President & Publisher
MIKE RICHARDSON

Editor
SPENCER CUSHING

Assistant Editor
KEVIN BURKHALTER

Designer
BRENNAN THOME

Digital Art Technician
CHRISTIANNE GOUDREAU

Special thanks to my editors, Spencer and Kevin, for making this series possible.—EY

DarkHorse.com

First edition: May 2018
ISBN 978-1-50670-500-2
10 9 8 7 6 5 4 3 2 1
Printed in China

Published by Dark Horse Books
A division of Dark Horse Comics, Inc.
10956 SE Main Street
Milwaukie, OR 97222

THE BATTLES OF BRIDGET LEE: THE MIRACLE CHILD

NEIL HANKERSON Executive Vice President TOM WEDDLE Chief Financial Officer RANDY STRADLEY Vice President of Publishing NICK MCWHORTER Chief Business Development Officer MATT PARKINSON Vice President of Marketing DALE LaFOUNTAIN Vice President of Information Technology CARA NIECE Vice President of Production and Scheduling MARK BERNARDI Vice President of Book Trade and Digital Sales KEN LIZZI General Counsel DAVE MARSHALL Editor in Chief DAVEY ESTRADA Editorial Director CHRIS WARNER Senior Books Editor CARY GRAZZINI Director of Specialty Projects LIA RIBACCHI Art Director VANESSA TODD Director of Print Purchasing MATT DRYER Director of Digital Art and Prepress MICHAEL GOMBOS Director of International Publishing and Licensing KARI YADRO Director of Custom Programs

To find a comics shop in your area, visit comicshoplocator.com

International Licensing: 503-905-2377

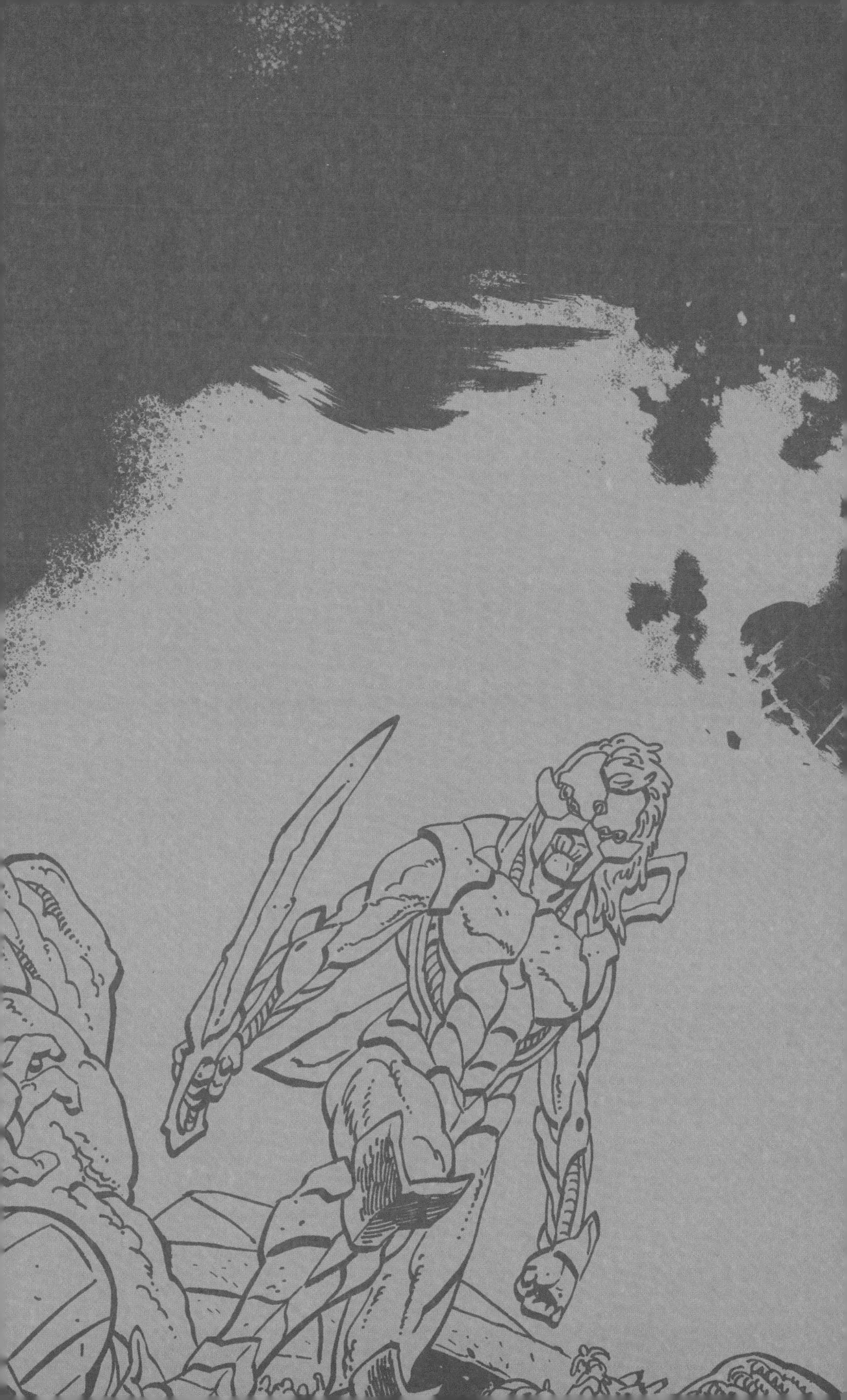

Seven years after the death of her husband at the hands of alien invaders known as the Marauders, Bridget Lee is still haunted by her loss. As the Chief Nursing Officer at Farfall, a remote human outpost, Bridget watches over the orphans left behind by the war.

After years of silence, the Marauders have begun locating and raiding outposts, and they set their eyes on Farfall. Led by a craven general named Half-Face, the alien invaders intend on capturing the orphans for unknown purposes.

With the help of her friends, Bridget defeats Half-Face. But the destruction of their home forces them to relocate. Everyday continues to be a struggle for survival, but one questions still looms large: Who is helping the Marauders locate the outposts?

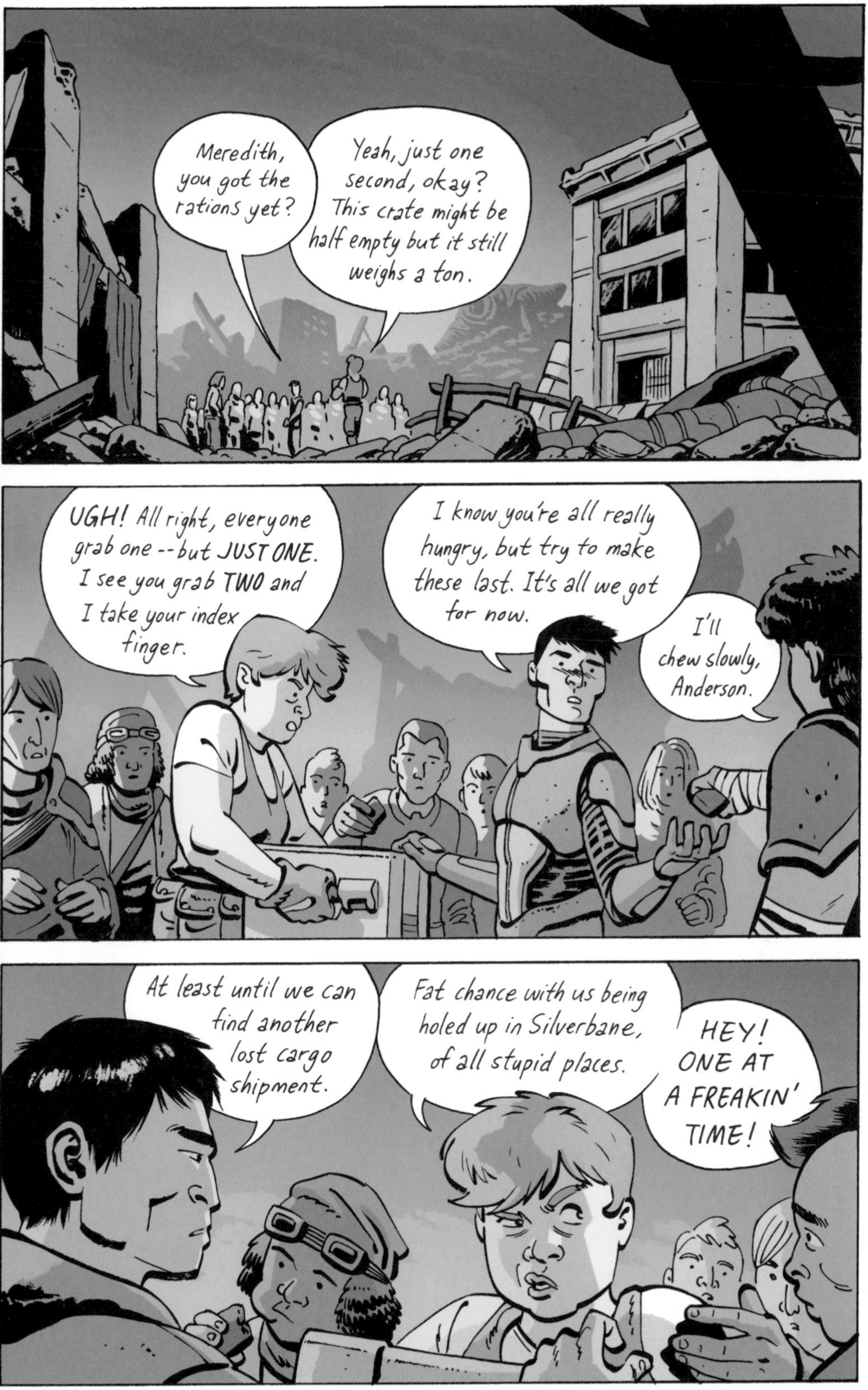

Meredith, you got the rations yet?
Yeah, just one second, okay? This crate might be half empty but it still weighs a ton.
UGH! All right, everyone grab one -- but JUST ONE. I see you grab TWO and I take your index finger.
I know you're all really hungry, but try to make these last. It's all we got for now.
I'll chew slowly, Anderson.
At least until we can find another lost cargo shipment.
Fat chance with us being holed up in Silverbane, of all stupid places.
HEY! ONE AT A FREAKIN' TIME!

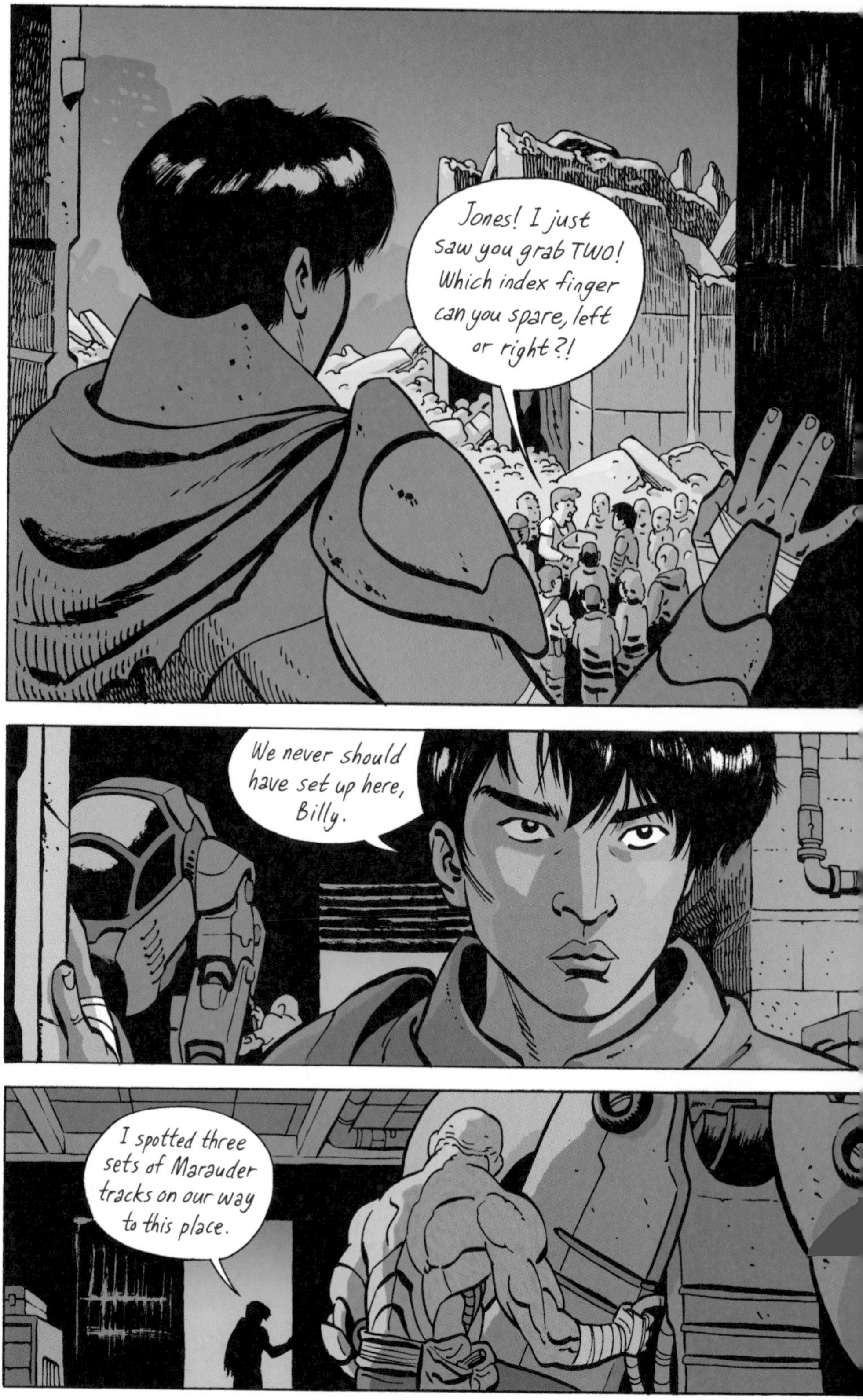
Jones! I just saw you grab TWO! Which index finger can you spare, left or right?!
We never should have set up here, Billy.
I spotted three sets of Marauder tracks on our way to this place.

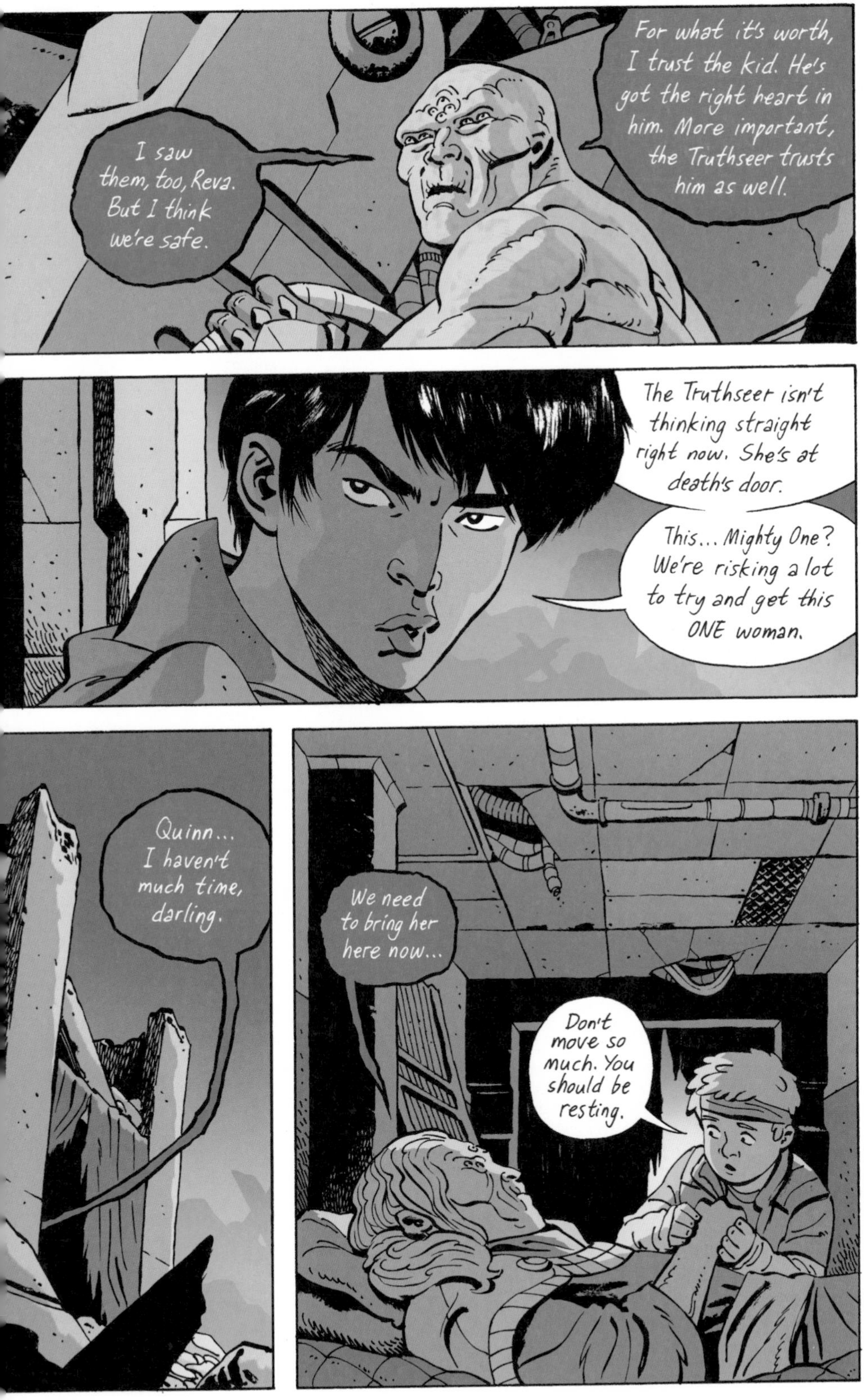

I saw them, too, Reva. But I think we're safe.
For what it's worth, I trust the kid. He's got the right heart in him. More important, the Truthseer trusts him as well.
The Truthseer isn't thinking straight right now. She's at death's door.
This... Mighty One? We're risking a lot to try and get this ONE woman.
Quinn... I haven't much time, darling.
We need to bring her here now...
Don't move so much. You should be resting.

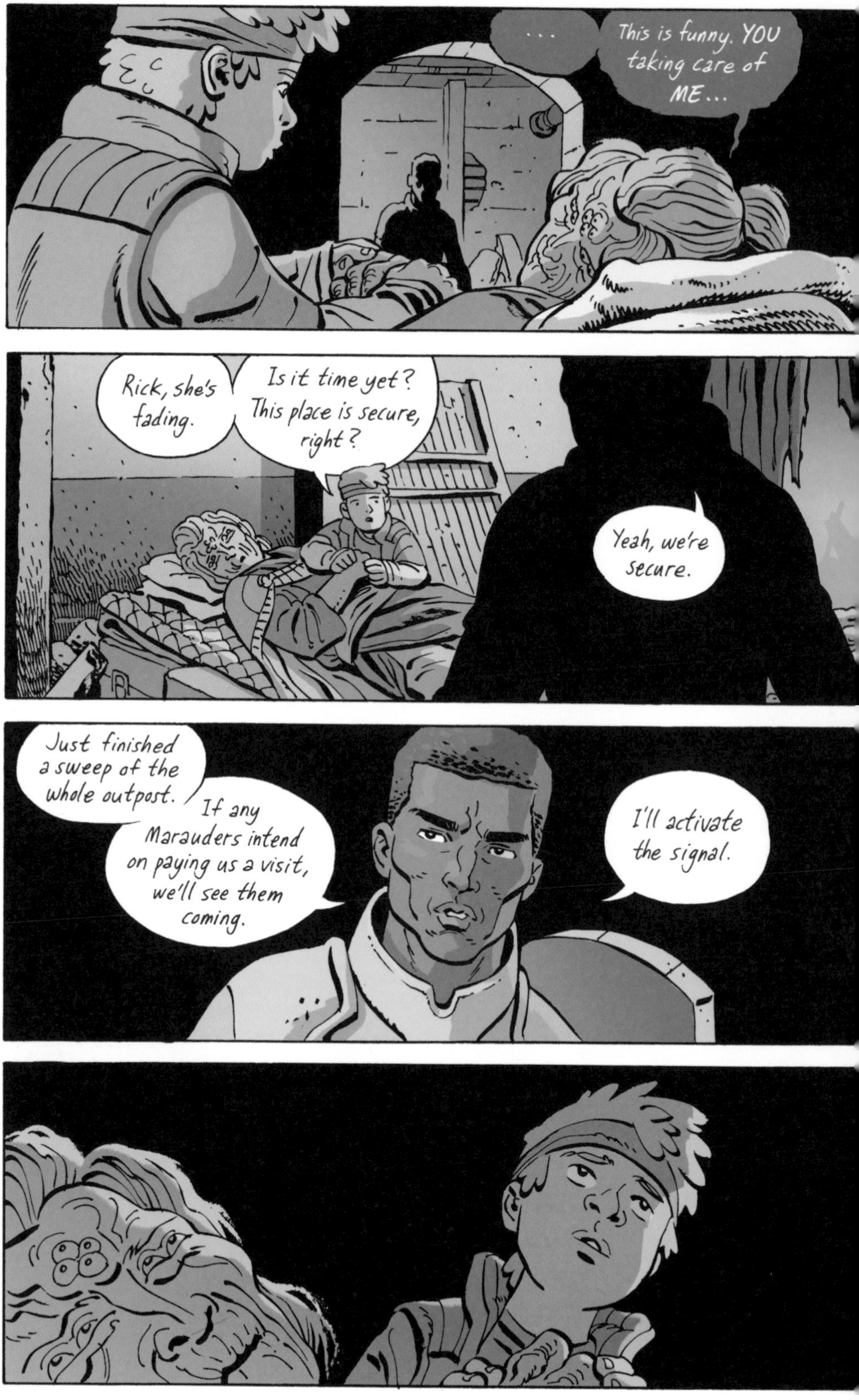
...
This is funny. YOU taking care of ME...
Rick, she's fading.
Is it time yet? This place is secure, right?
Yeah, we're secure.
Just finished a sweep of the whole outpost.
If any Marauders intend on paying us a visit, we'll see them coming.
I'll activate the signal.

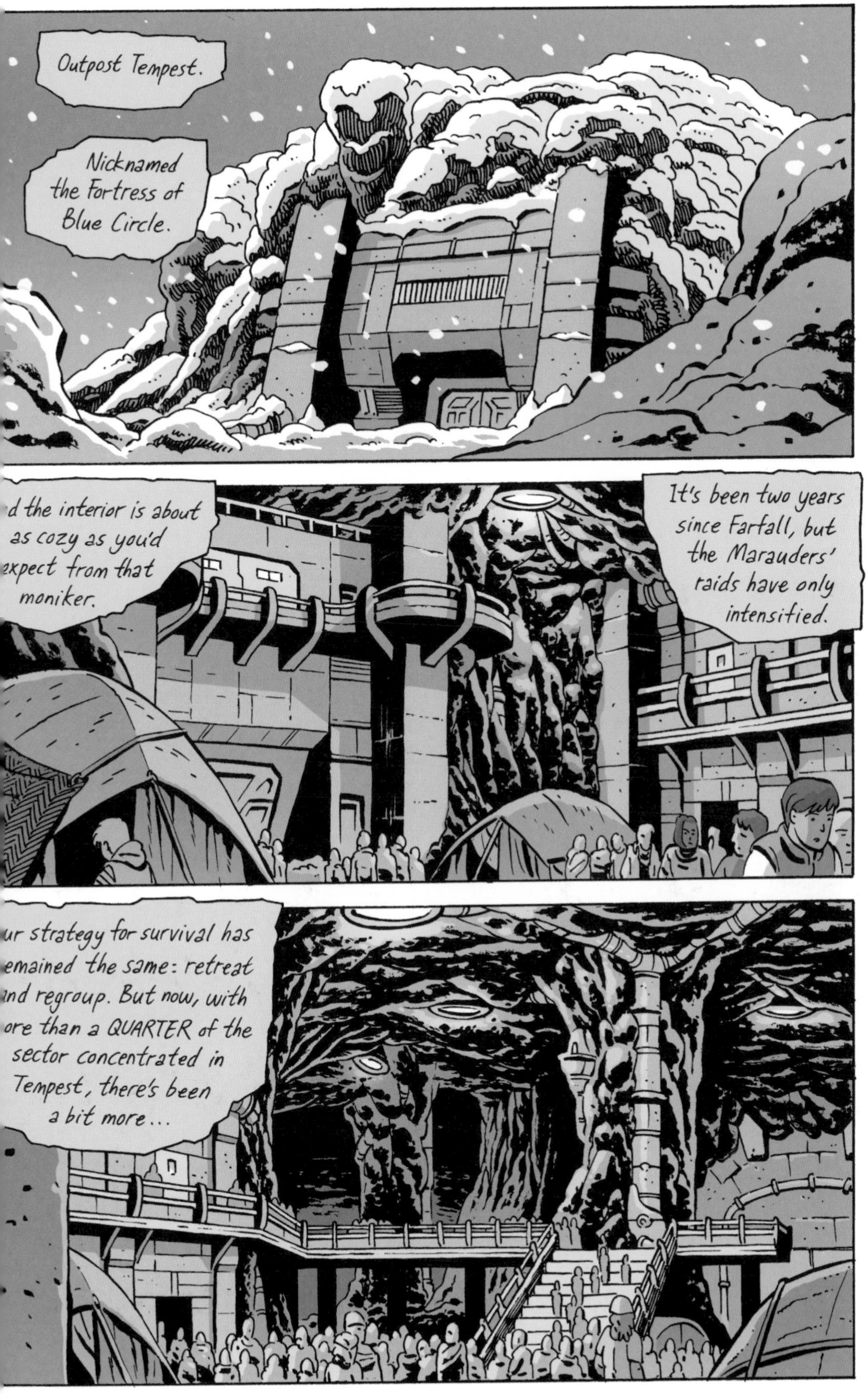
Outpost Tempest.
Nicknamed the Fortress of Blue Circle.
d the interior is about as cozy as you'd xpect from that moniker.
It's been two years since Farfall, but the Marauders' raids have only intensified.
ur strategy for survival has emained the same: retreat nd regroup. But now, with ore than a QUARTER of the sector concentrated in Tempest, there's been a bit more...

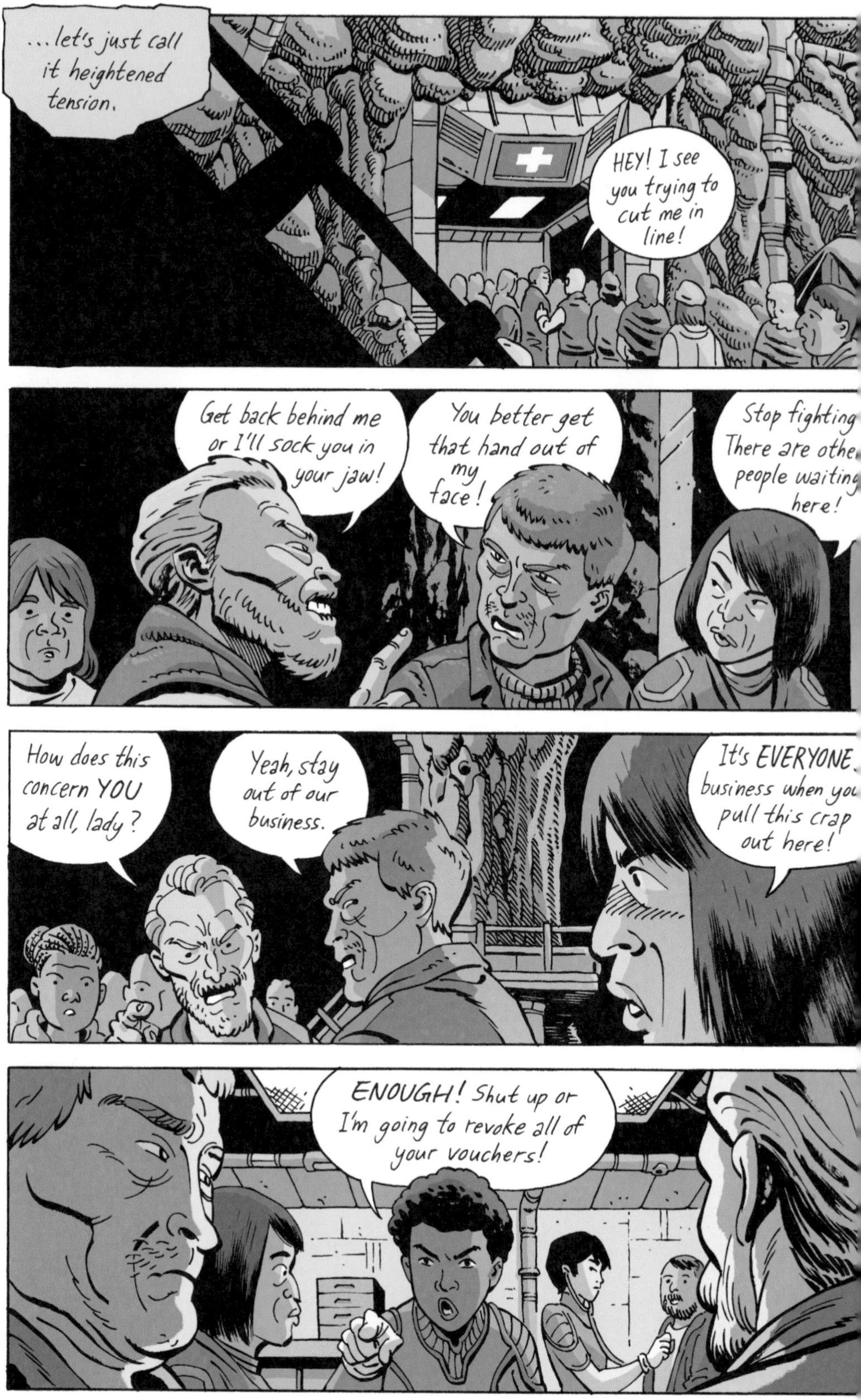
...let's just call it heightened tension.
HEY! I see you trying to cut me in line!
Get back behind me or I'll sock you in your jaw!
You better get that hand out of my face!
Stop fighting There are othe people waiting here!
How does this concern YOU at all, lady?
Yeah, stay out of our business.
It's EVERYONE business when yo pull this crap out here!
ENOUGH! Shut up or I'm going to revoke all of your vouchers!

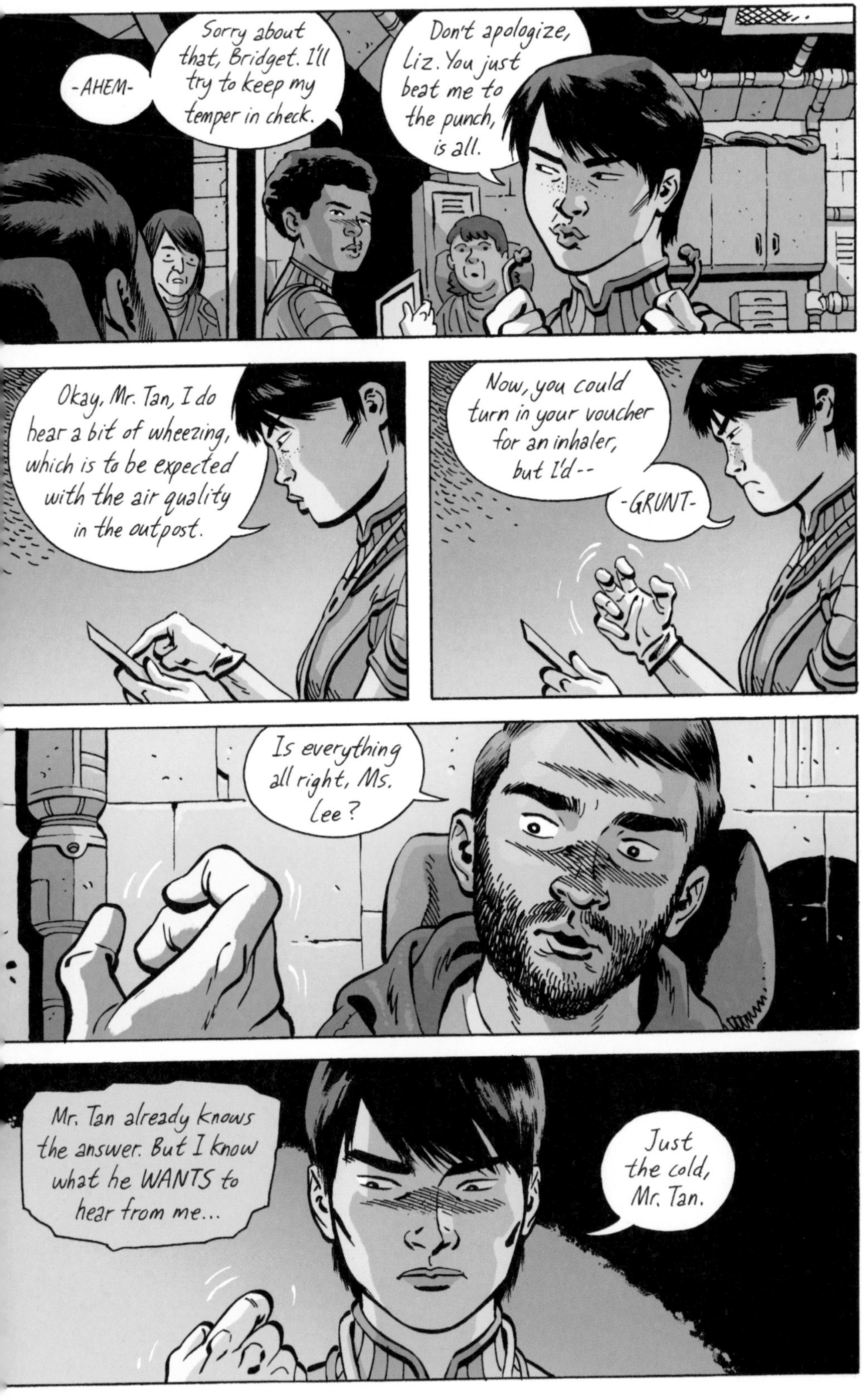
-AHEM-
Sorry about that, Bridget. I'll try to keep my temper in check.
Don't apologize, Liz. You just beat me to the punch, is all.
Okay, Mr. Tan, I do hear a bit of wheezing, which is to be expected with the air quality in the outpost.
Now, you could turn in your voucher for an inhaler, but I'd--
-GRUNT-
Is everything all right, Ms. Lee?
Mr. Tan already knows the answer. But I know what he WANTS to hear from me...
Just the cold, Mr. Tan.

See, our adventures at Farfall have grown to the level of MYTH lately. "The brave outpost that fought back the Marauders."

...and HALF-FACE was, like, TEN feet tall. Right, Jane?

TALLER, I think, Elliot.

And the children are assigning almost all the credit to ONE person...

And Bridget smashes the watchtower on top of him. She didn't even break a sweat.

Sterling, that story doesn't make sense. It's missing too many details.

Yeah, how can one woman take down the Marauders all by herself?

Well, we all chipped in. Plus, Bree was the brains behind the plan. But BRIDGET, she went toe-to-toe with HALF-FACE, and kicked his ass!

Bree? The security officer?

Yeah, she was our engineer back at Farfall.

Normally, I'd put a stop to all these TALL TALES about me but for the moment it serves as a valuable distraction.

14

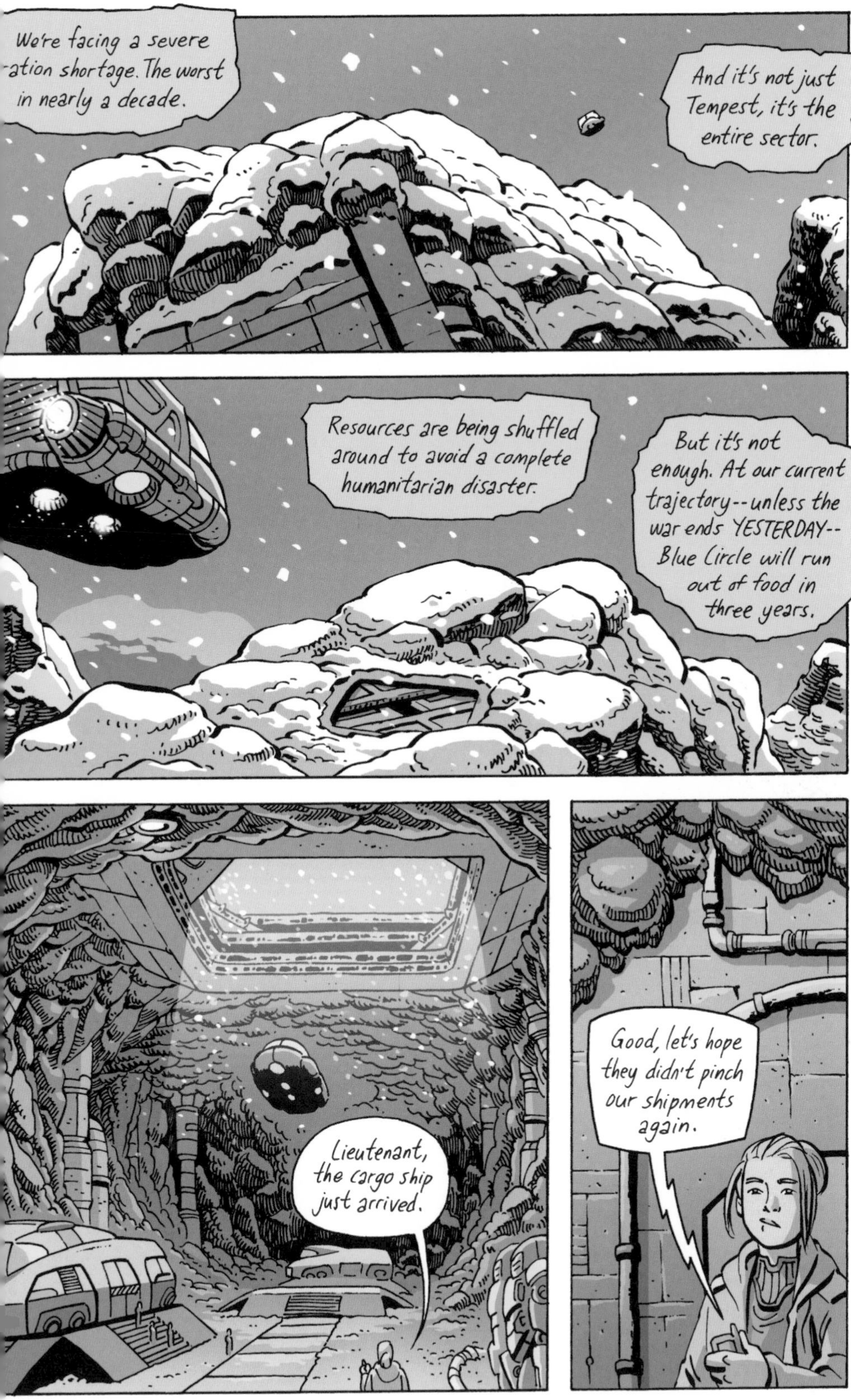
We're facing a severe -ation shortage. The worst in nearly a decade.
And it's not just Tempest, it's the entire sector.
Resources are being shuffled around to avoid a complete humanitarian disaster.
But it's not enough. At our current trajectory--unless the war ends YESTERDAY--Blue Circle will run out of food in three years.
Lieutenant, the cargo ship just arrived.
Good, let's hope they didn't pinch our shipments again.

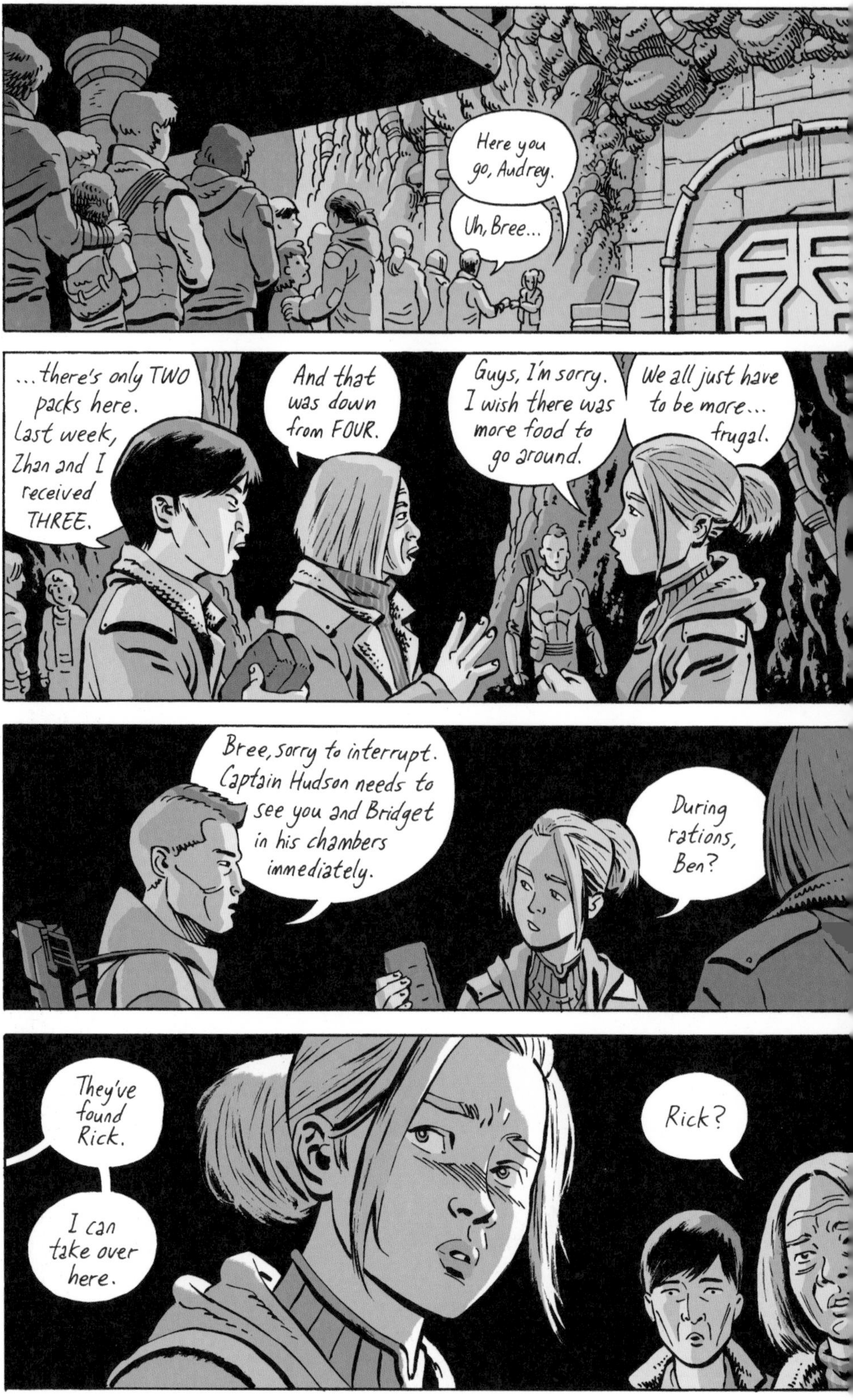
Here you go, Audrey.
Uh, Bree...
...there's only TWO packs here. Last week, Zhan and I received THREE.
And that was down from FOUR.
Guys, I'm sorry. I wish there was more food to go around.
We all just have to be more... frugal.
Bree, sorry to interrupt. Captain Hudson needs to see you and Bridget in his chambers immediately.
During rations, Ben?
They've found Rick.
I can take over here.
Rick?

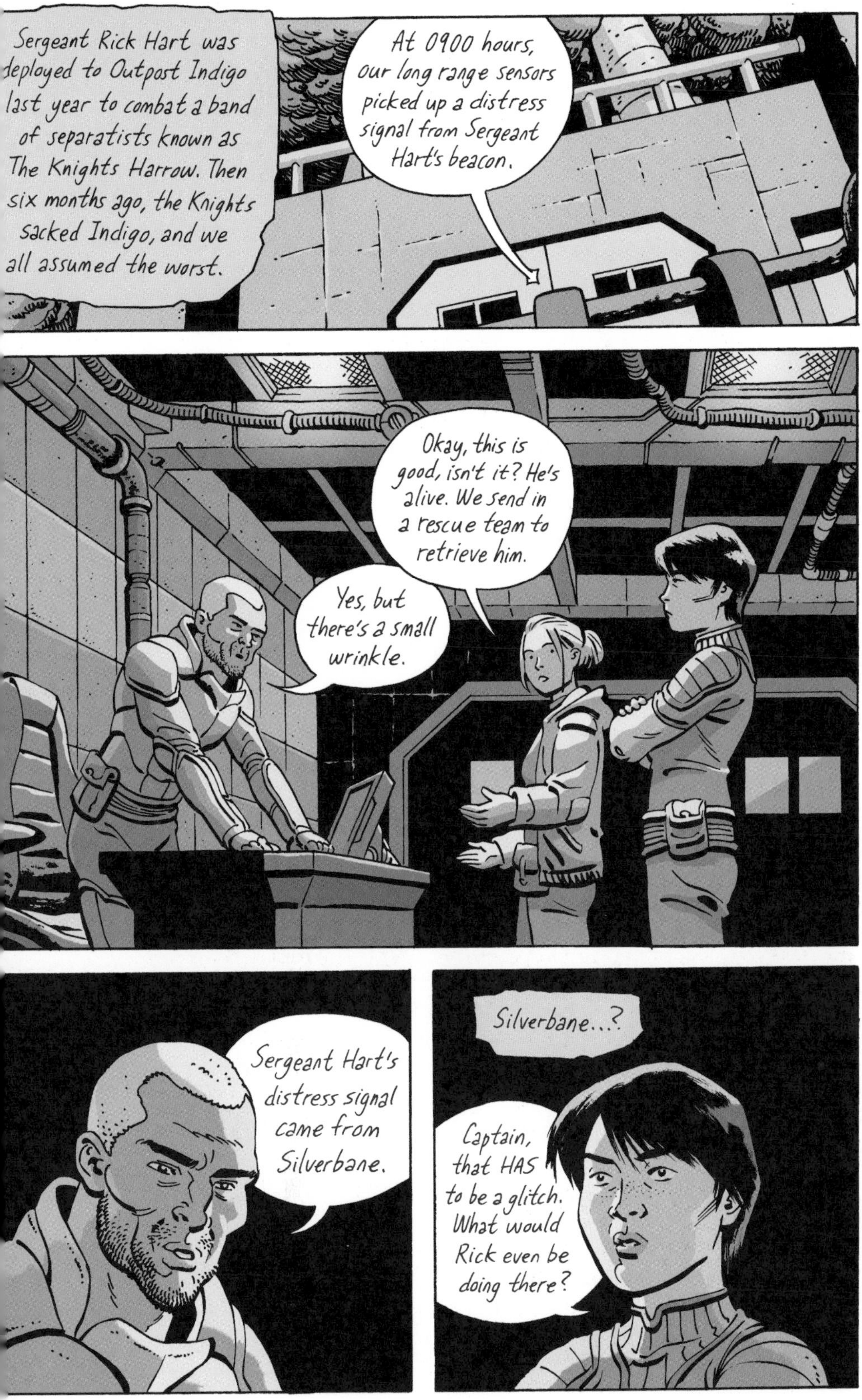
Sergeant Rick Hart was deployed to Outpost Indigo last year to combat a band of separatists known as The Knights Harrow. Then six months ago, the Knights sacked Indigo, and we all assumed the worst.
At 0900 hours, our long range sensors picked up a distress signal from Sergeant Hart's beacon.
Okay, this is good, isn't it? He's alive. We send in a rescue team to retrieve him.
Yes, but there's a small wrinkle.
Sergeant Hart's distress signal came from Silverbane.
Silverbane...?
Captain, that HAS to be a glitch. What would Rick even be doing there?

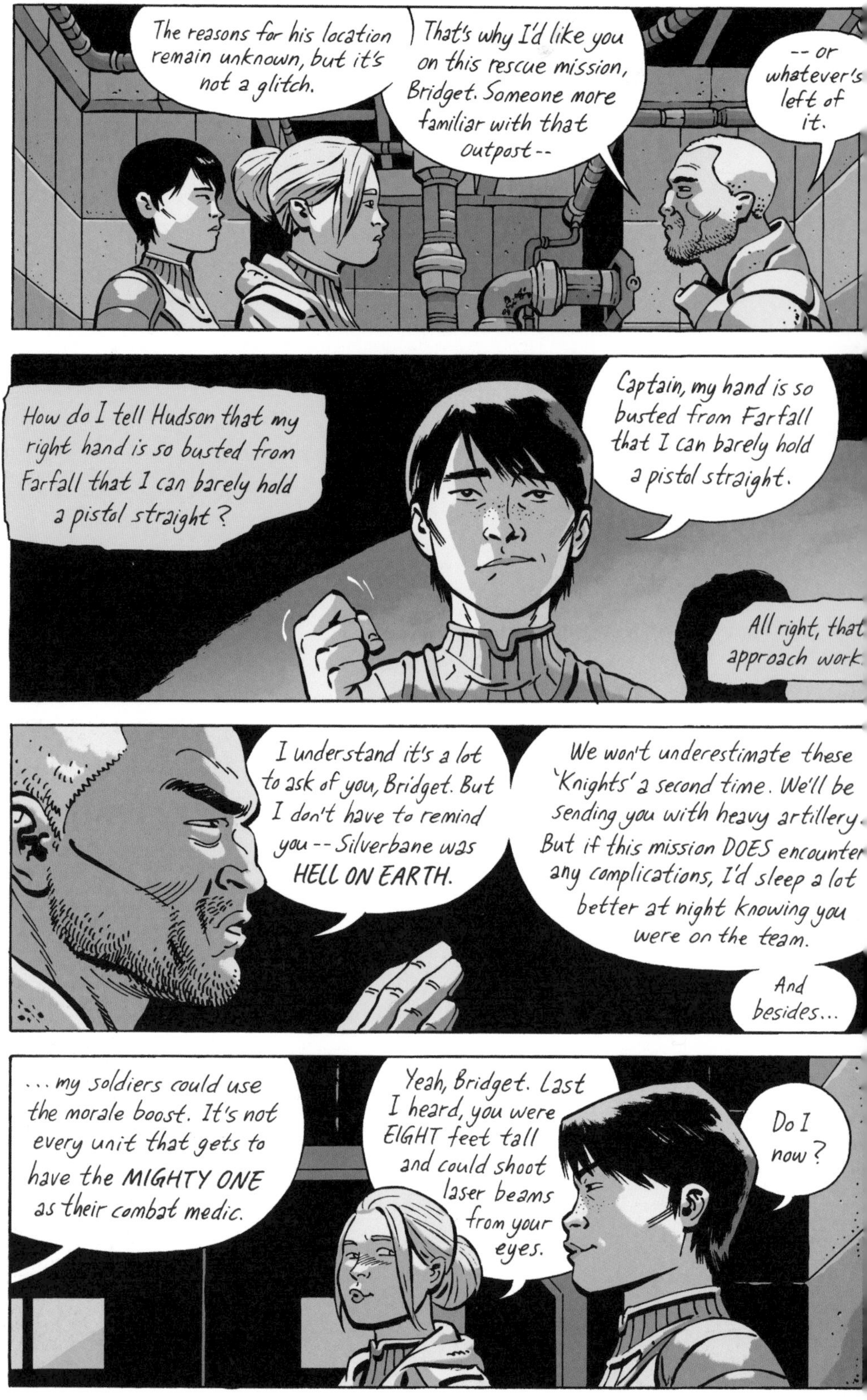

The reasons for his location remain unknown, but it's not a glitch.
That's why I'd like you on this rescue mission, Bridget. Someone more familiar with that outpost--
--or whatever's left of it.
How do I tell Hudson that my right hand is so busted from Farfall that I can barely hold a pistol straight?
Captain, my hand is so busted from Farfall that I can barely hold a pistol straight.
All right, that approach work
I understand it's a lot to ask of you, Bridget. But I don't have to remind you--Silverbane was HELL ON EARTH.
We won't underestimate these 'Knights' a second time. We'll be sending you with heavy artillery. But if this mission DOES encounter any complications, I'd sleep a lot better at night knowing you were on the team.
And besides...
...my soldiers could use the morale boost. It's not every unit that gets to have the MIGHTY ONE as their combat medic.
Yeah, Bridget. Last I heard, you were EIGHT feet tall and could shoot laser beams from your eyes.
Do I now?

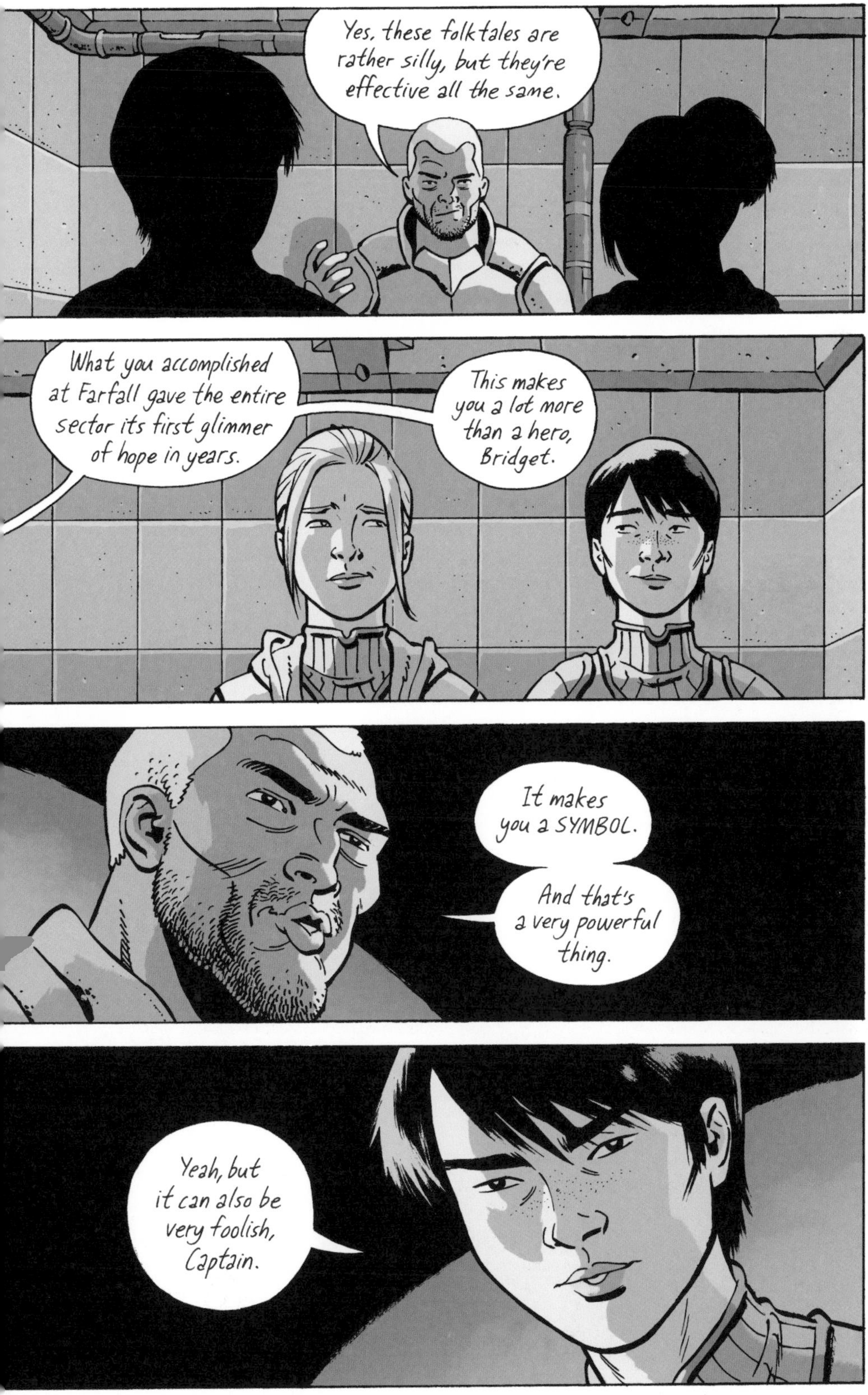
Yes, these folktales are rather silly, but they're effective all the same.
What you accomplished at Farfall gave the entire sector its first glimmer of hope in years.
This makes you a lot more than a hero, Bridget.
It makes you a SYMBOL.
And that's a very powerful thing.
Yeah, but it can also be very foolish, Captain.

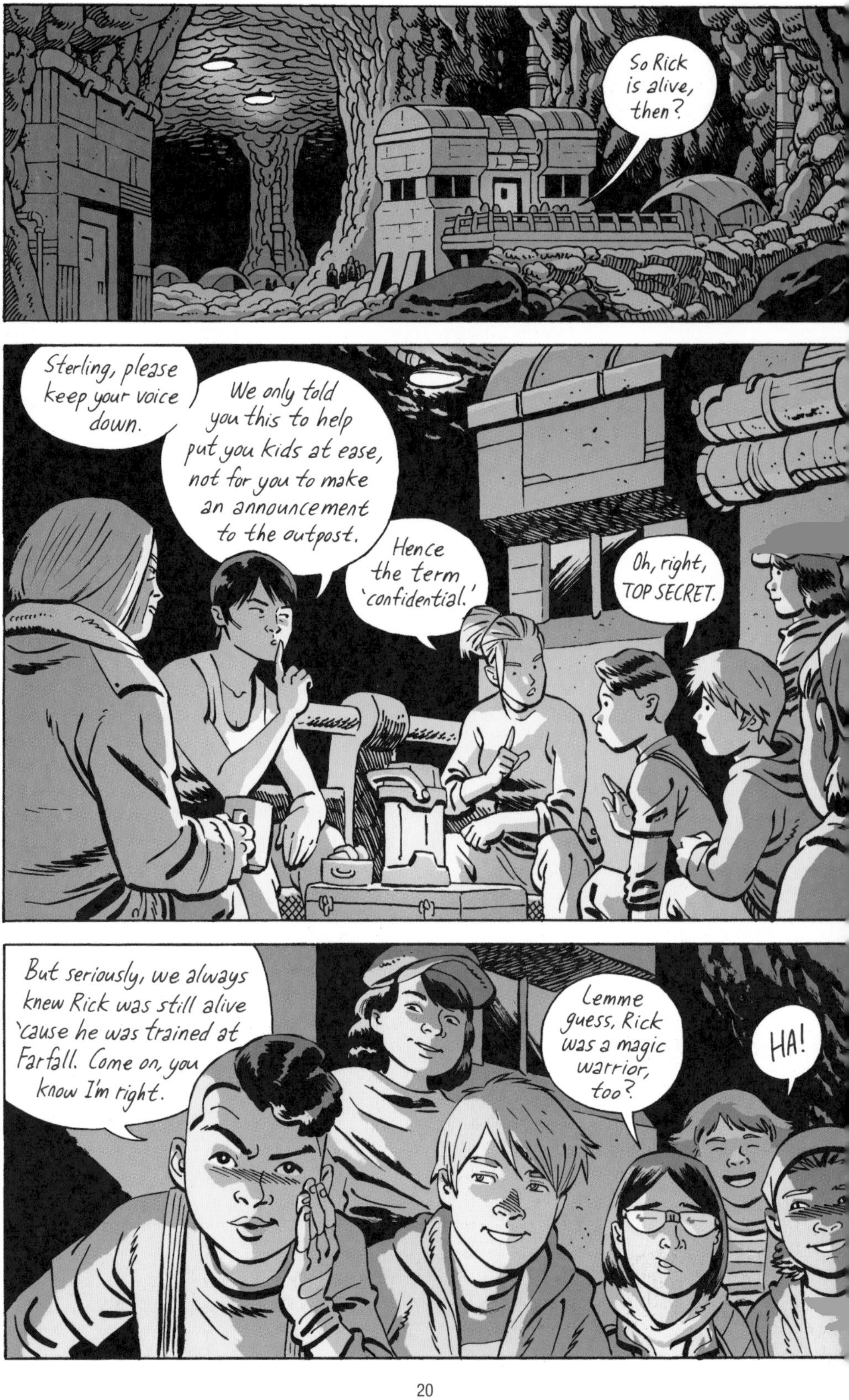
So Rick is alive, then?
Sterling, please keep your voice down.
We only told you this to help put you kids at ease, not for you to make an announcement to the outpost.
Hence the term 'confidential.'
Oh, right, TOP SECRET.
But seriously, we always knew Rick was still alive 'cause he was trained at Farfall. Come on, you know I'm right.
Lemme guess, Rick was a magic warrior, too?
HA!

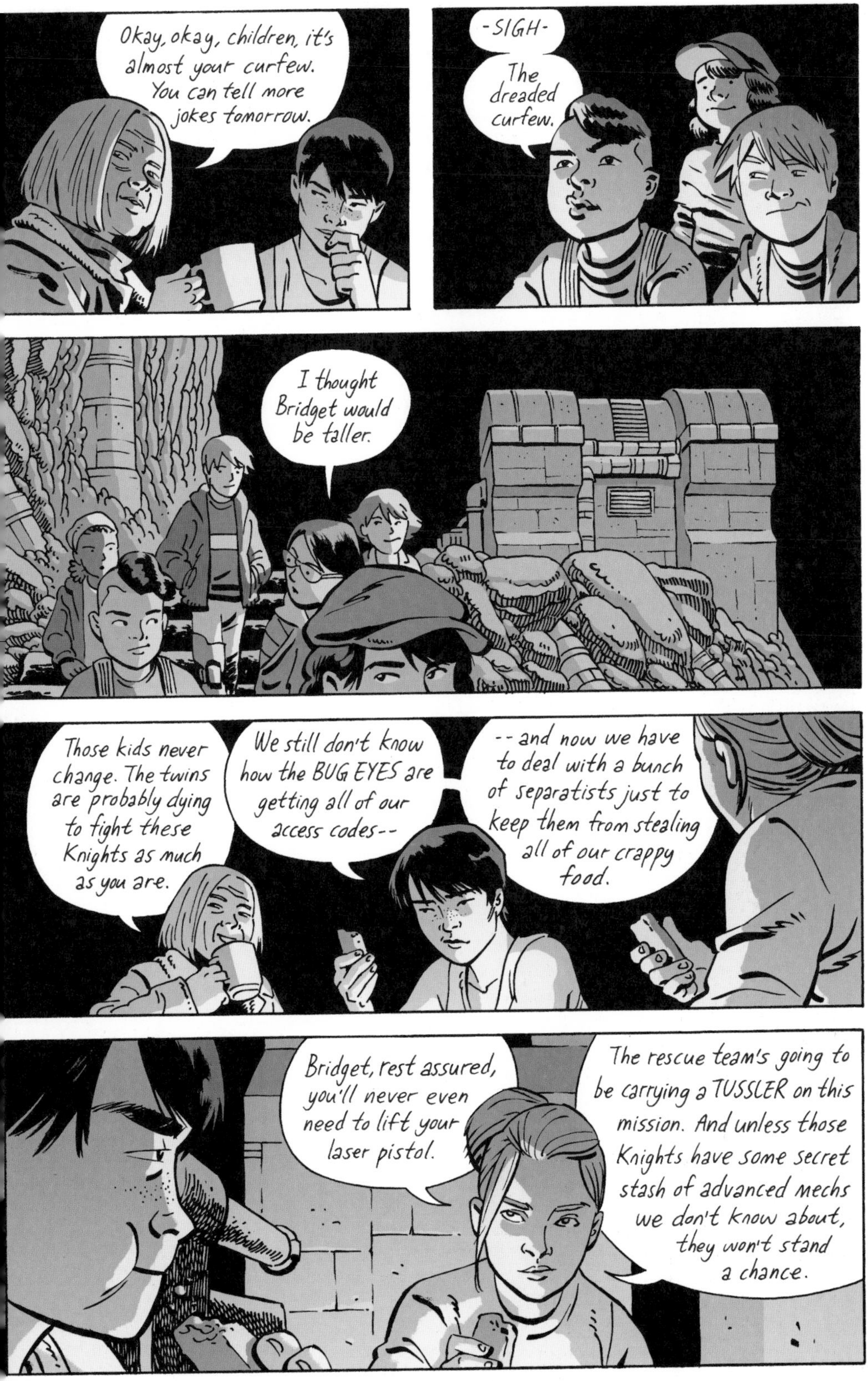
Okay, okay, children, it's almost your curfew. You can tell more jokes tomorrow.
-SIGH-
The dreaded curfew.
I thought Bridget would be taller.
Those kids never change. The twins are probably dying to fight these Knights as much as you are.
We still don't know how the BUG EYES are getting all of our access codes--
--and now we have to deal with a bunch of separatists just to keep them from stealing all of our crappy food.
Bridget, rest assured, you'll never even need to lift your laser pistol.
The rescue team's going to be carrying a TUSSLER on this mission. And unless those Knights have some secret stash of advanced mechs we don't know about, they won't stand a chance.

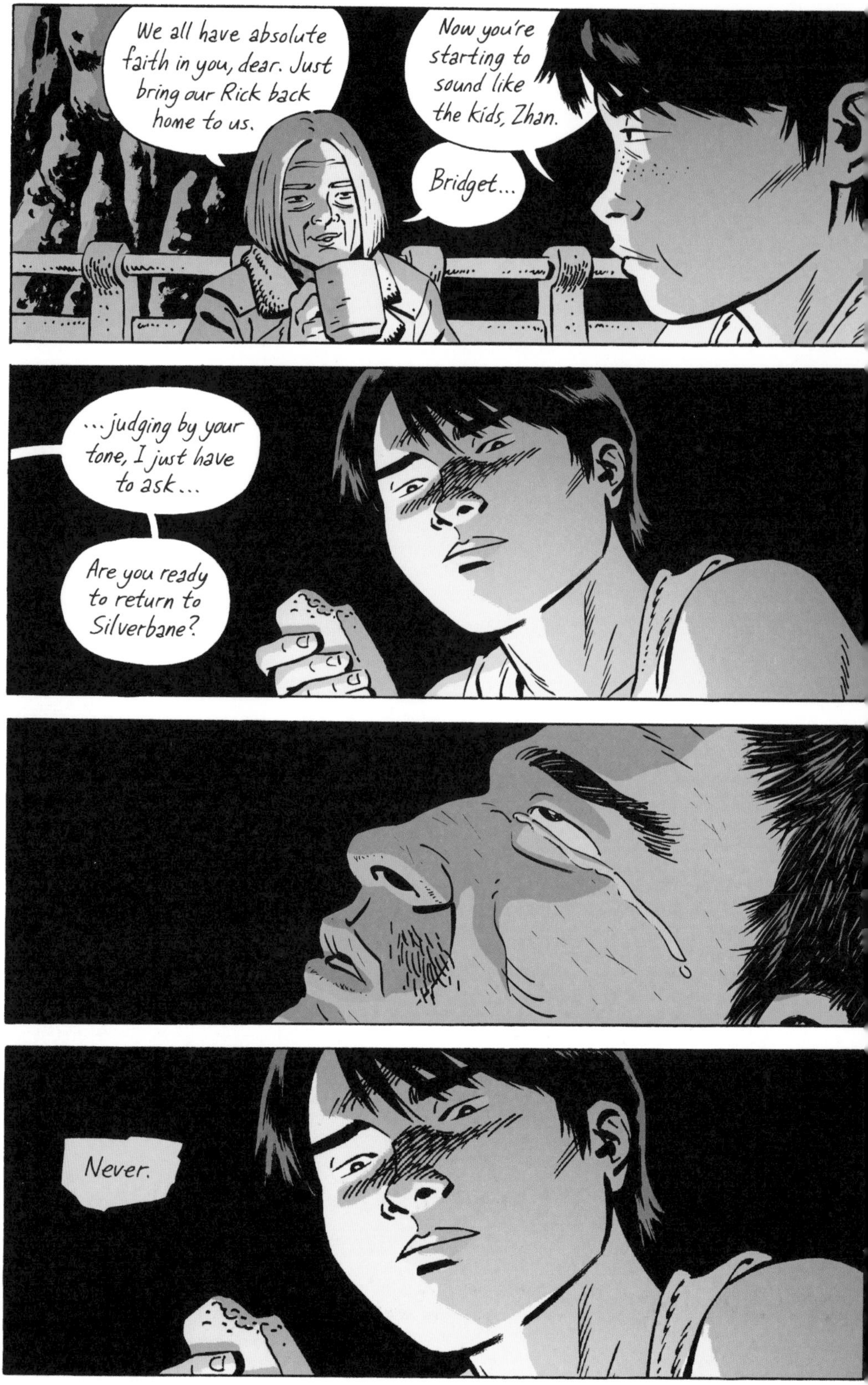
We all have absolute faith in you, dear. Just bring our Rick back home to us.
Now you're starting to sound like the kids, Zhan.
Bridget...
...judging by your tone, I just have to ask...
Are you ready to return to Silverbane?
Never.

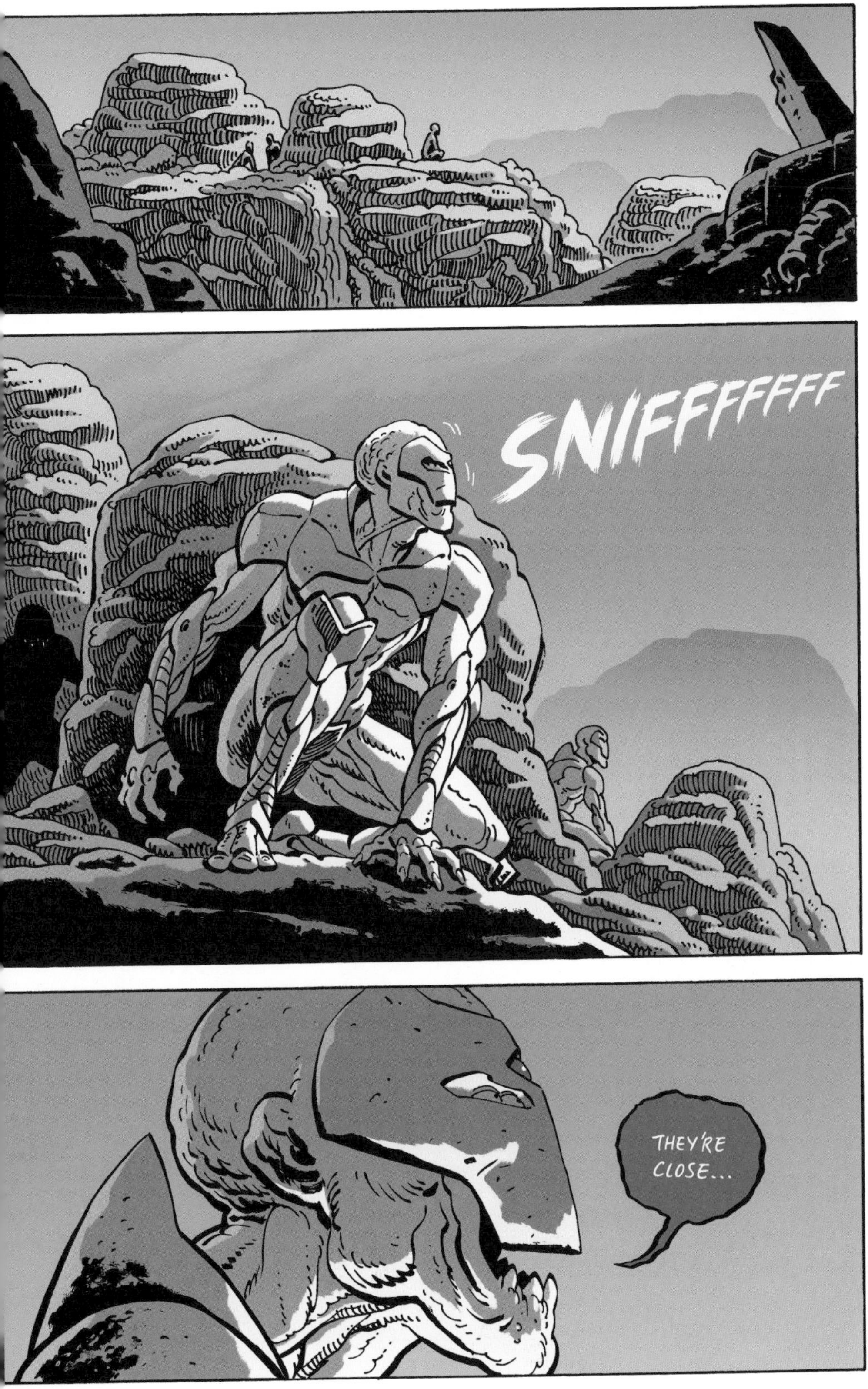
SNIFFFFFFF
THEY'RE CLOSE...

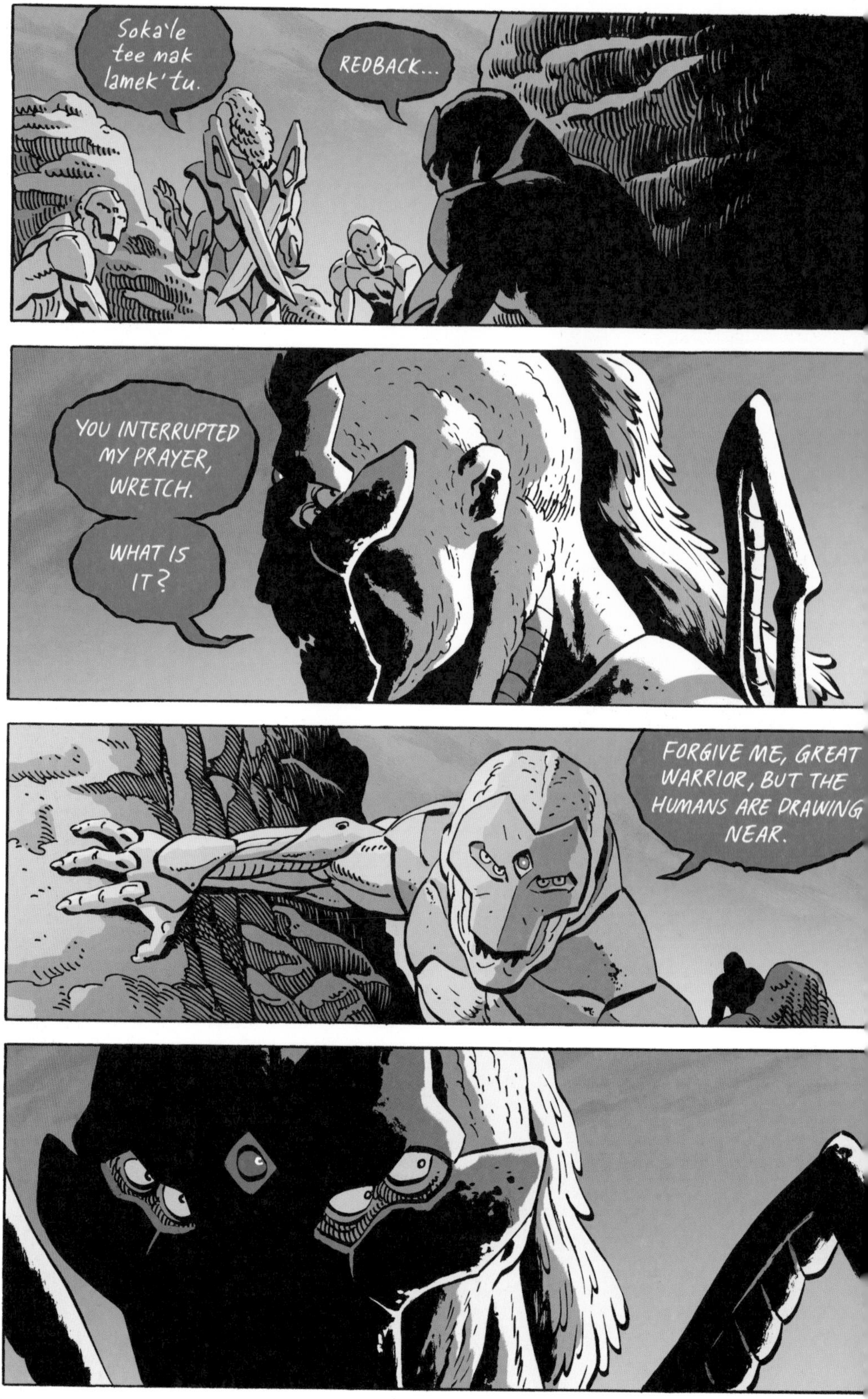
Soka`le tee mak lamek'tu.
REDBACK...
YOU INTERRUPTED MY PRAYER, WRETCH.
WHAT IS IT?
FORGIVE ME, GREAT WARRIOR, BUT THE HUMANS ARE DRAWING NEAR.

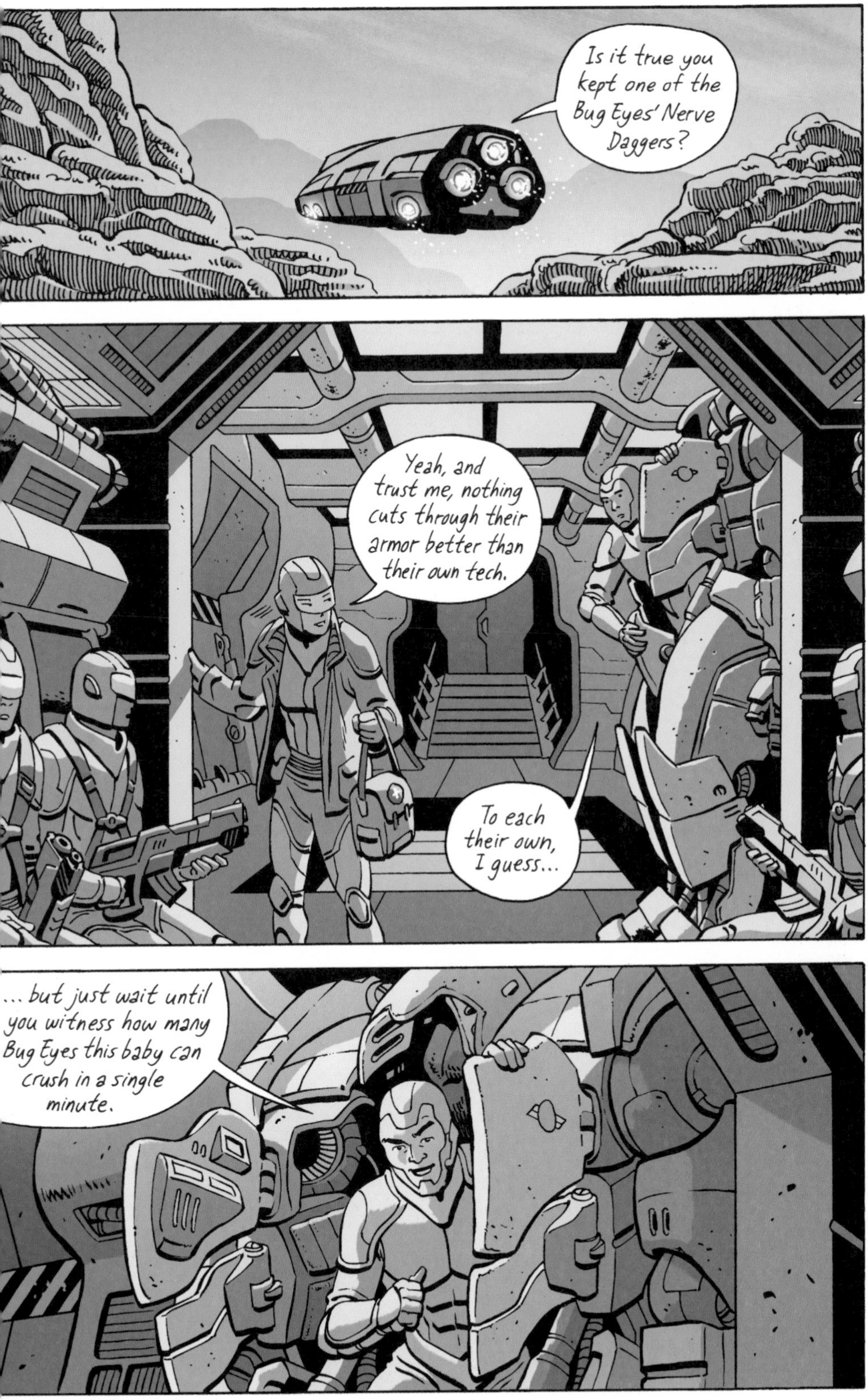
Is it true you kept one of the Bug Eyes' Nerve Daggers?
Yeah, and trust me, nothing cuts through their armor better than their own tech.
To each their own, I guess...
... but just wait until you witness how many Bug Eyes this baby can crush in a single minute.

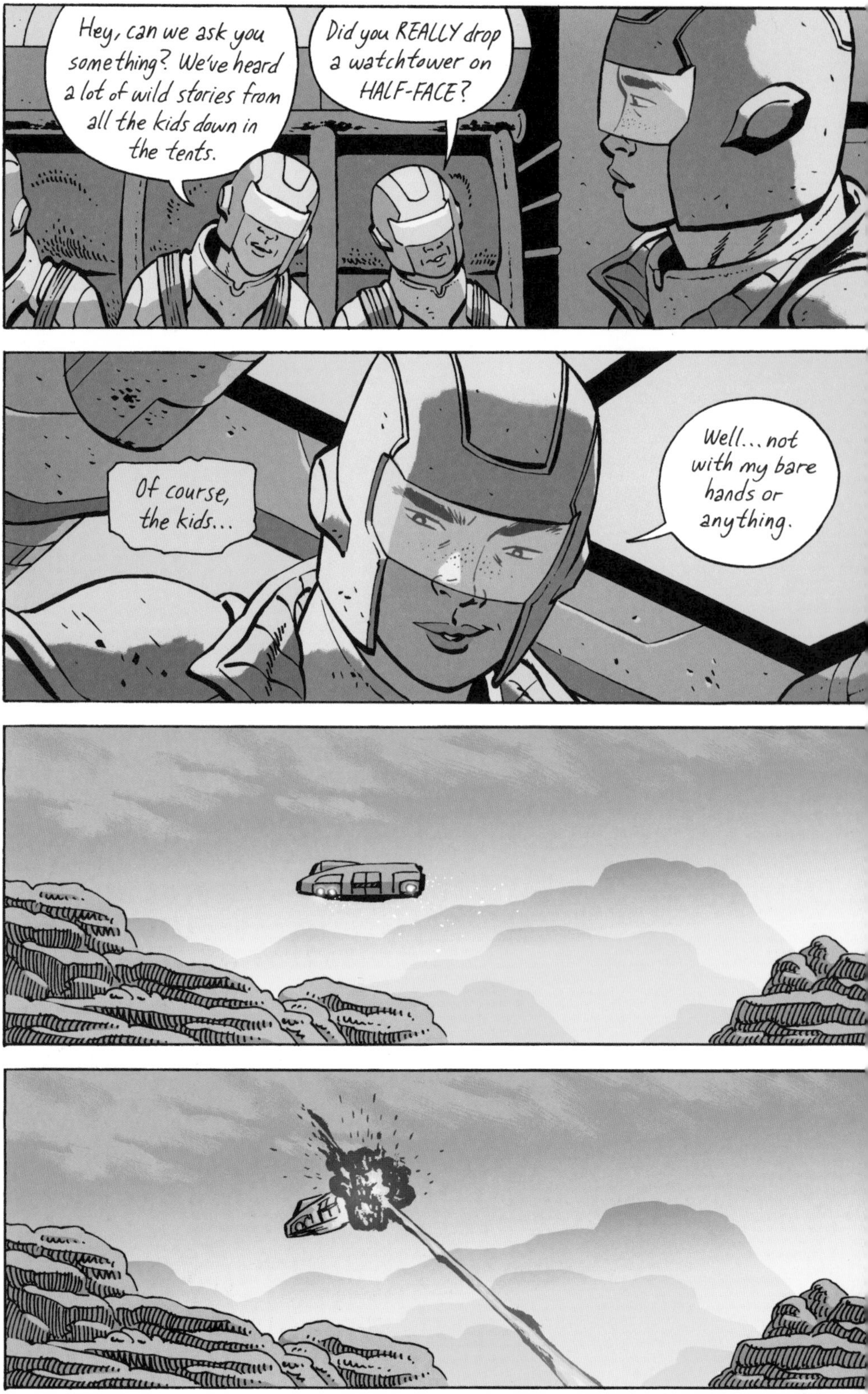
Hey, can we ask you something? We've heard a lot of wild stories from all the kids down in the tents.
Did you REALLY drop a watchtower on HALF-FACE?
Of course, the kids...
Well... not with my bare hands or anything.

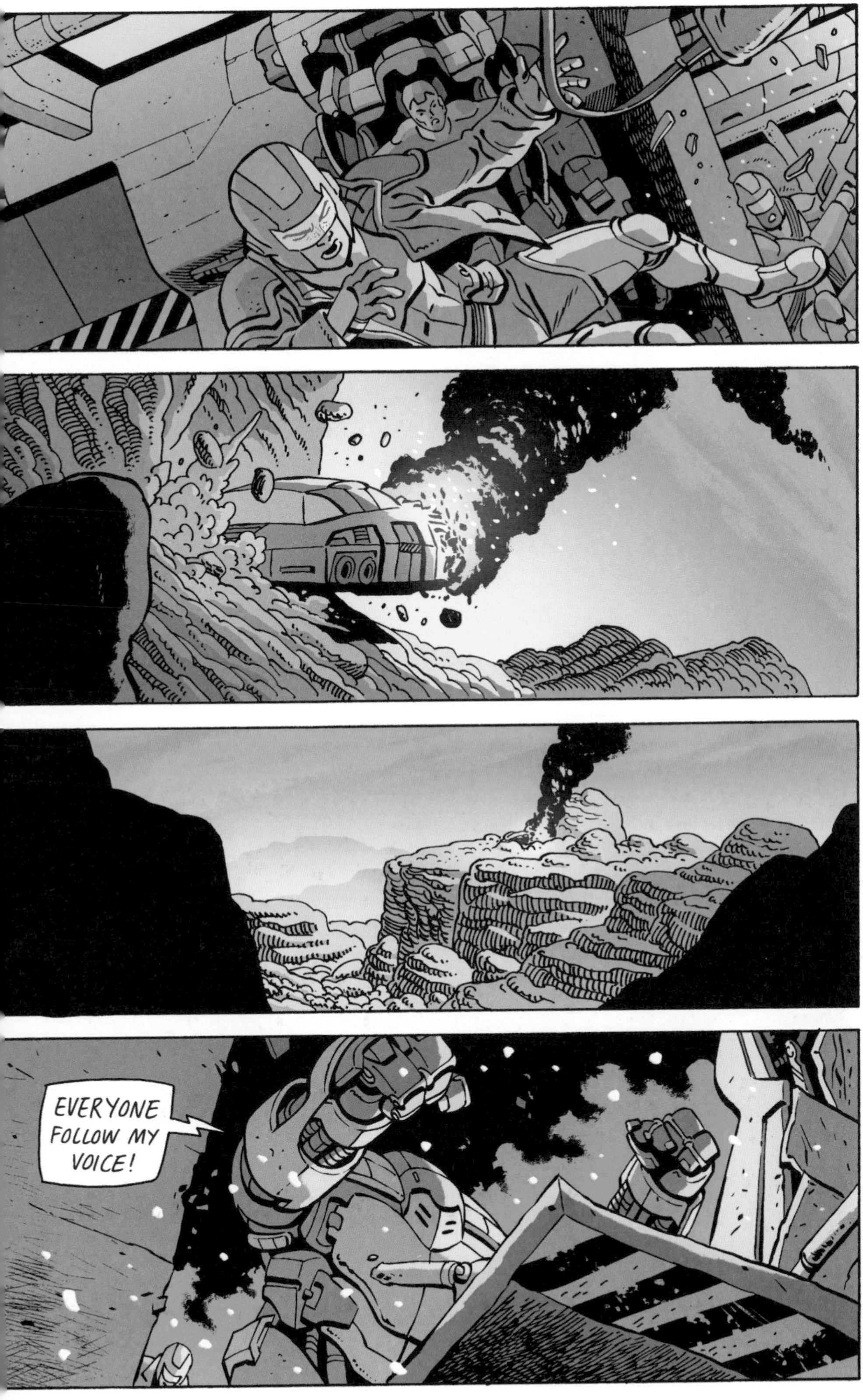
EVERYONE FOLLOW MY VOICE!

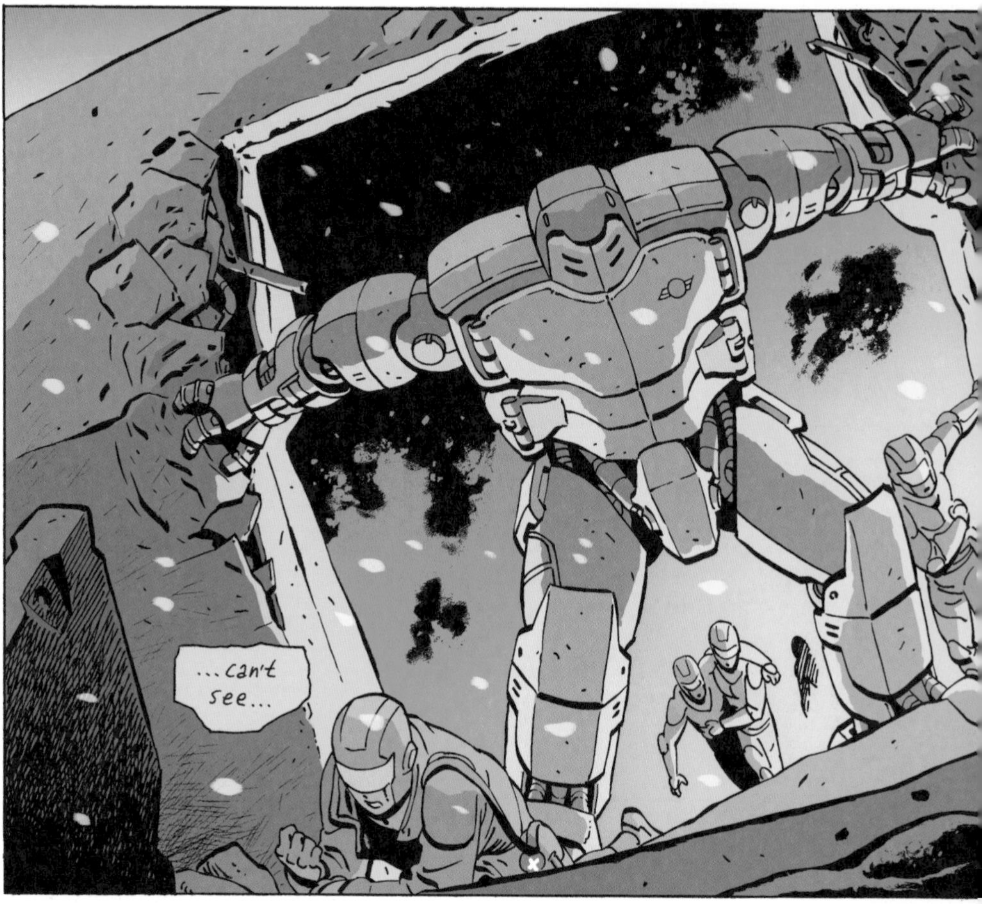
...can't see...
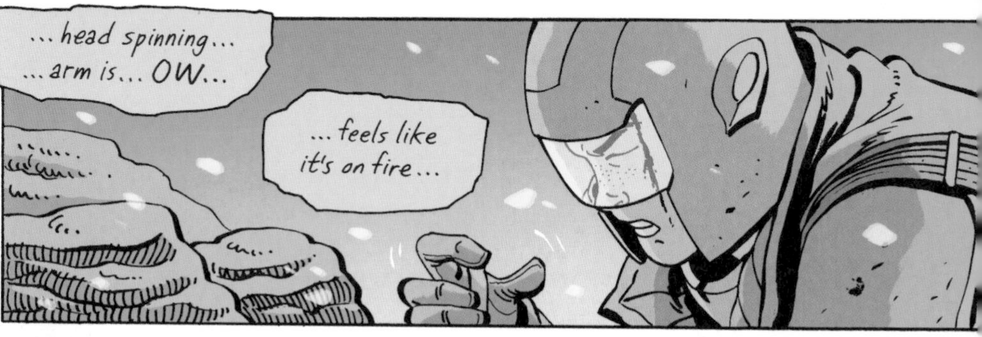
...head spinning... ...arm is... OW...
...feels like it's on fire...
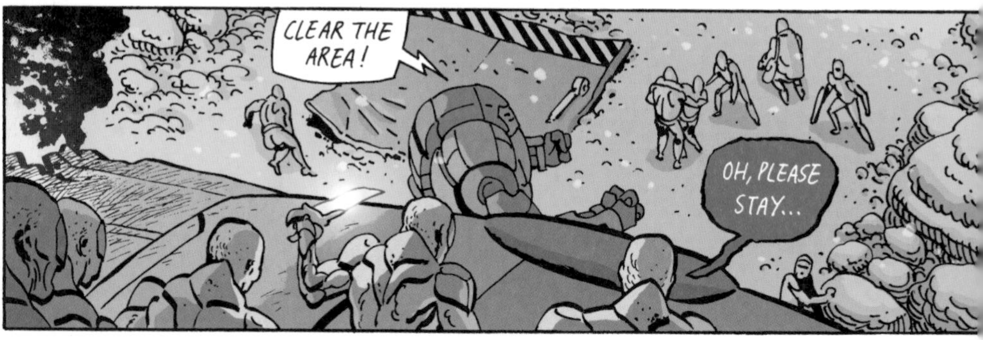
CLEAR THE AREA!
OH, PLEASE STAY...

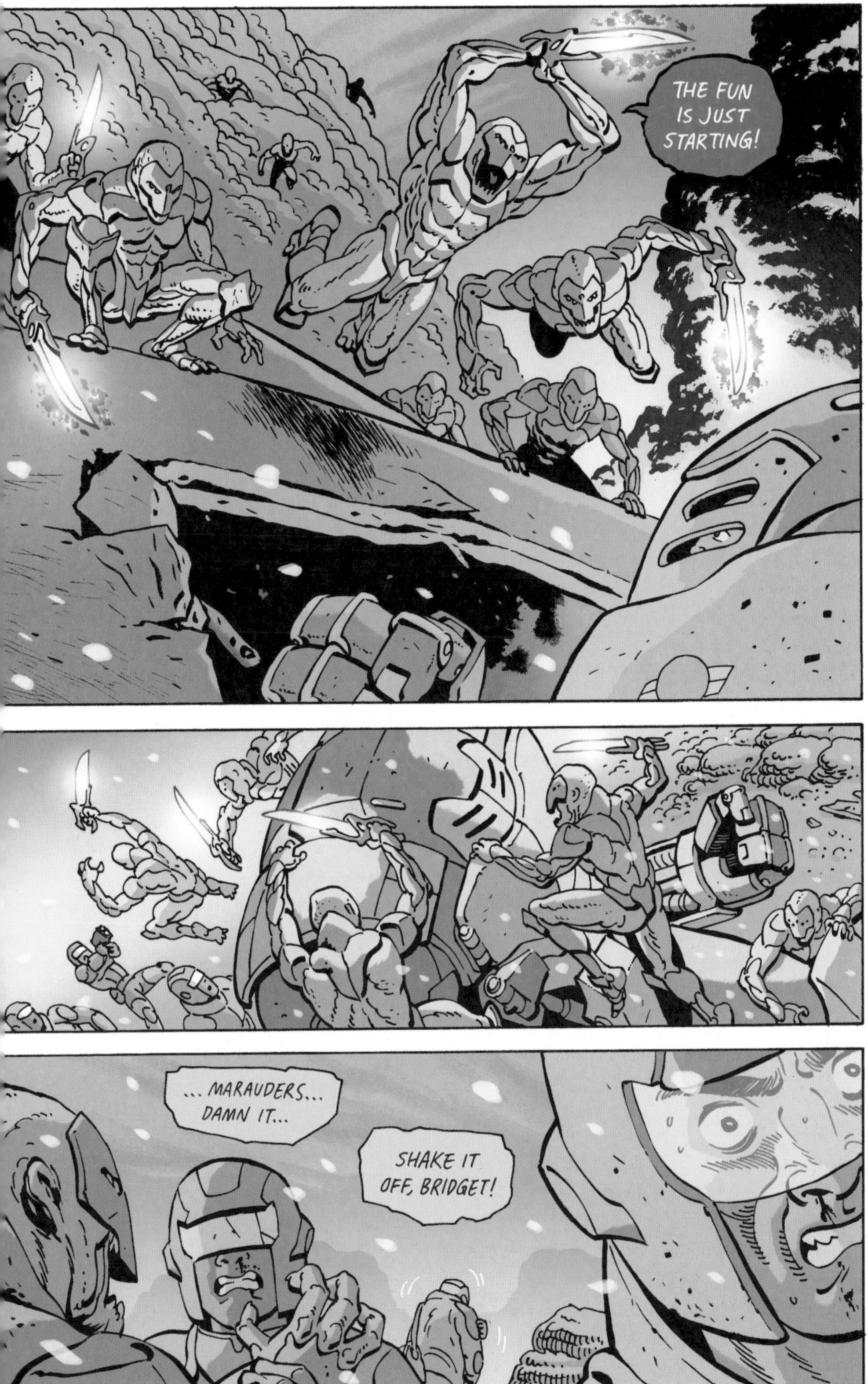
THE FUN IS JUST STARTING!
...MARAUDERS... DAMN IT...
SHAKE IT OFF, BRIDGET!

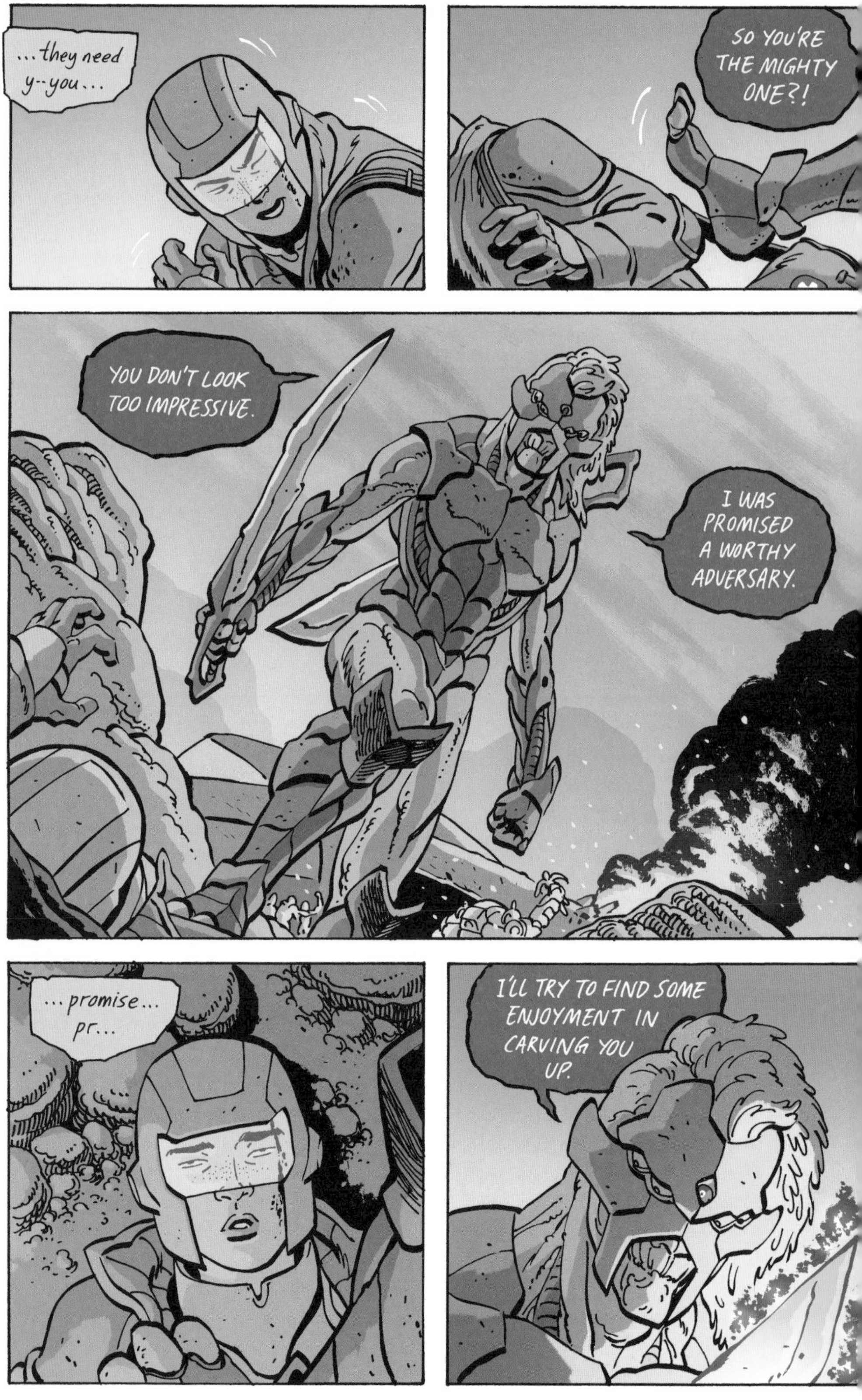
...they need y--you...
SO YOU'RE THE MIGHTY ONE?!
YOU DON'T LOOK TOO IMPRESSIVE.
I WAS PROMISED A WORTHY ADVERSARY.
...promise... pr...
I'LL TRY TO FIND SOME ENJOYMENT IN CARVING YOU UP.

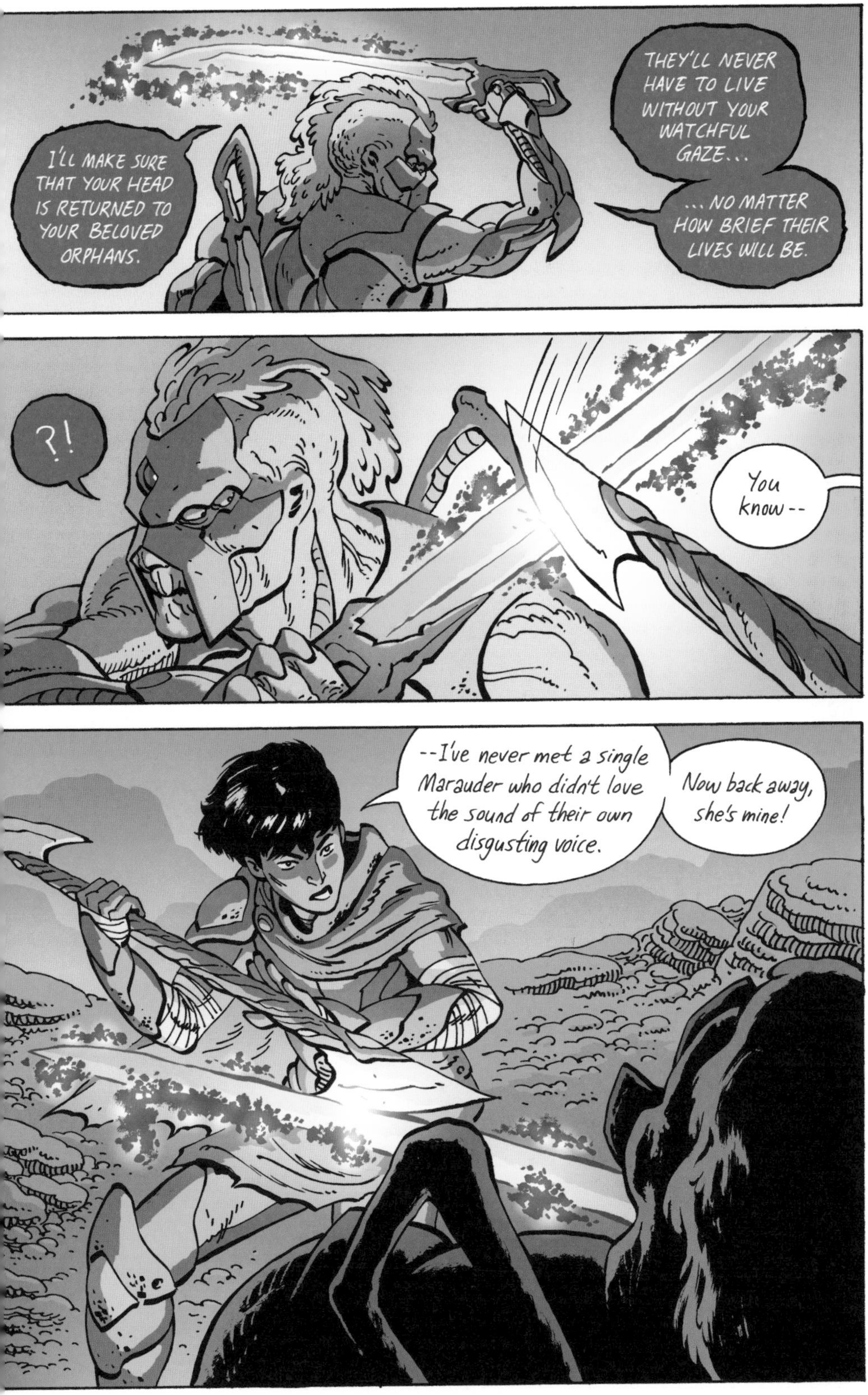
I'LL MAKE SURE THAT YOUR HEAD IS RETURNED TO YOUR BELOVED ORPHANS.
THEY'LL NEVER HAVE TO LIVE WITHOUT YOUR WATCHFUL GAZE...
...NO MATTER HOW BRIEF THEIR LIVES WILL BE.
?!
You know--
--I've never met a single Marauder who didn't love the sound of their own disgusting voice.
Now back away, she's mine!

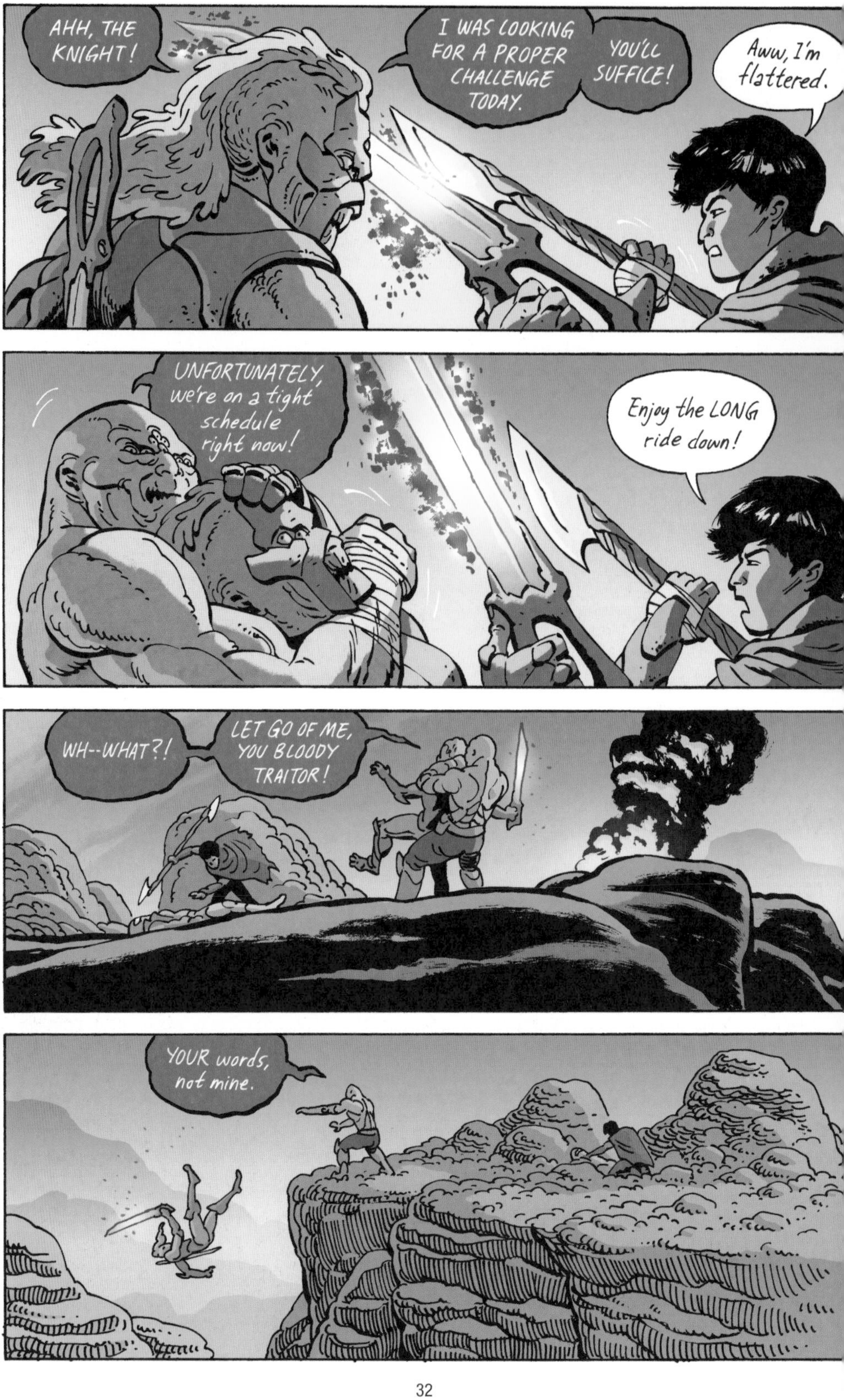
AHH, THE KNIGHT!
I WAS LOOKING FOR A PROPER CHALLENGE TODAY.
YOU'LL SUFFICE!
Aww, I'm flattered.
UNFORTUNATELY, we're on a tight schedule right now!
Enjoy the LONG ride down!
WH--WHAT?!
LET GO OF ME, YOU BLOODY TRAITOR!
YOUR words, not mine.

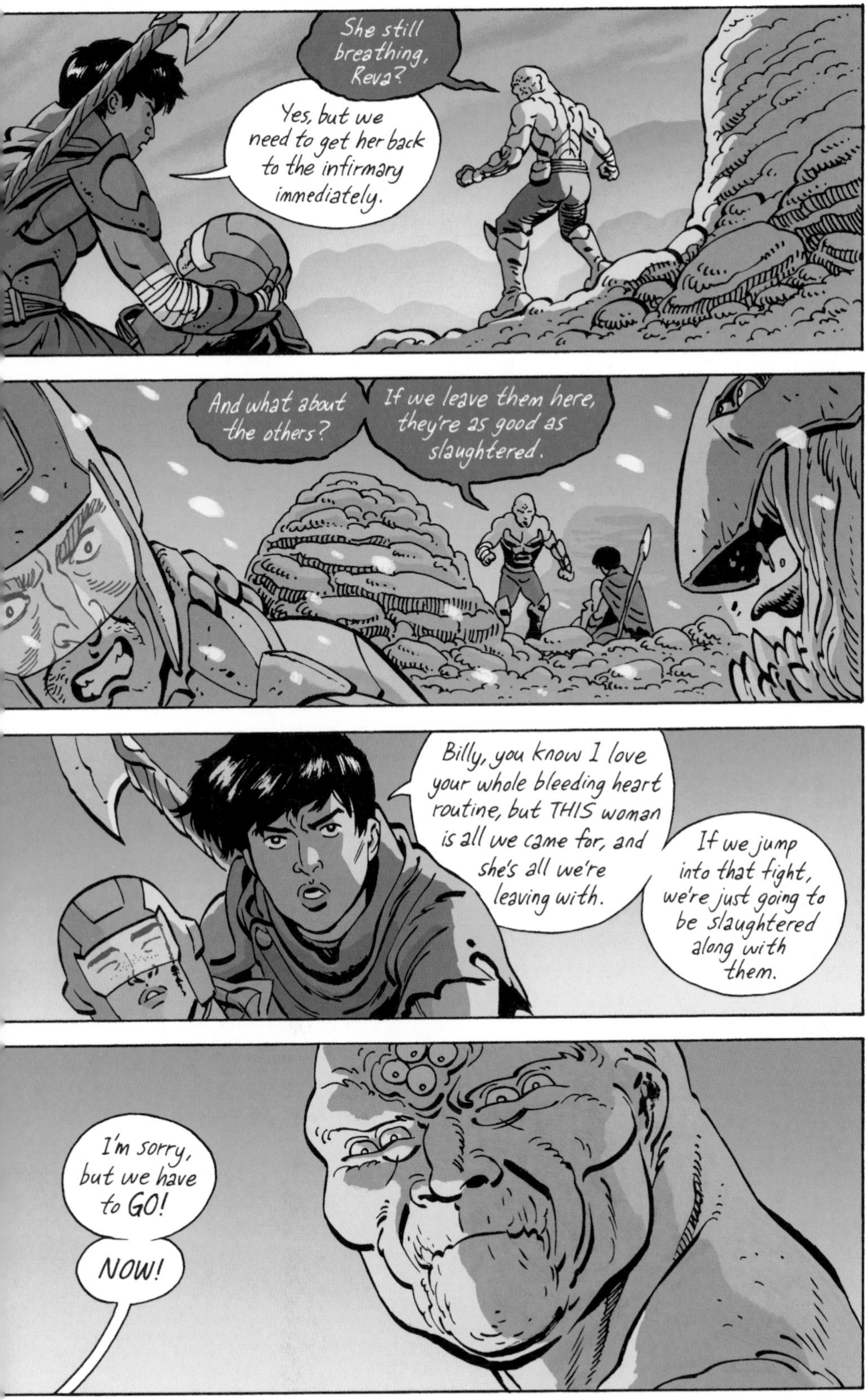
She still breathing, Reva?
Yes, but we need to get her back to the infirmary immediately.
And what about the others?
If we leave them here, they're as good as slaughtered.
Billy, you know I love your whole bleeding heart routine, but THIS woman is all we came for, and she's all we're leaving with.
If we jump into that fight, we're just going to be slaughtered along with them.
I'm sorry, but we have to GO!
NOW!

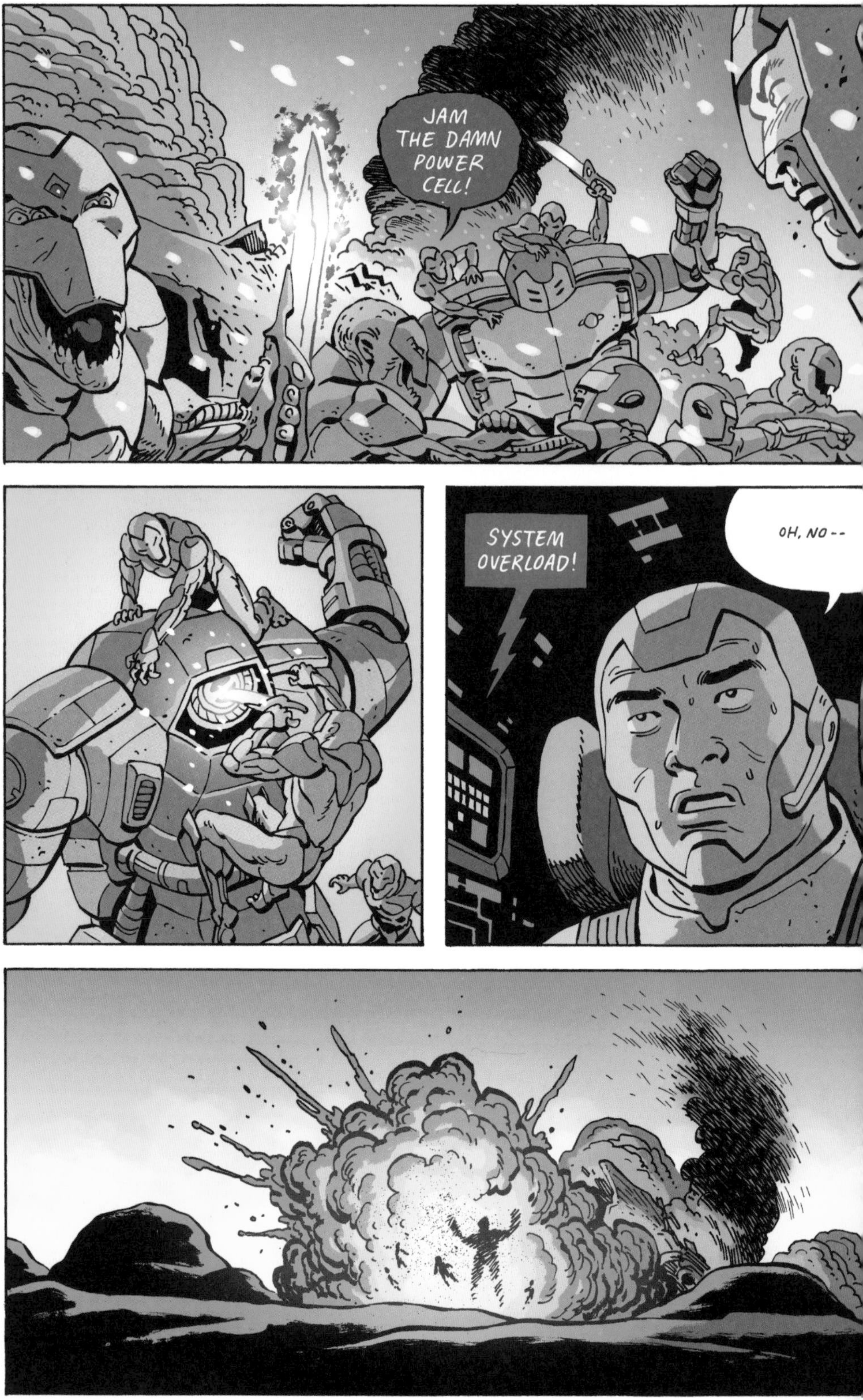
JAM THE DAMN POWER CELL!
SYSTEM OVERLOAD!
OH, NO--

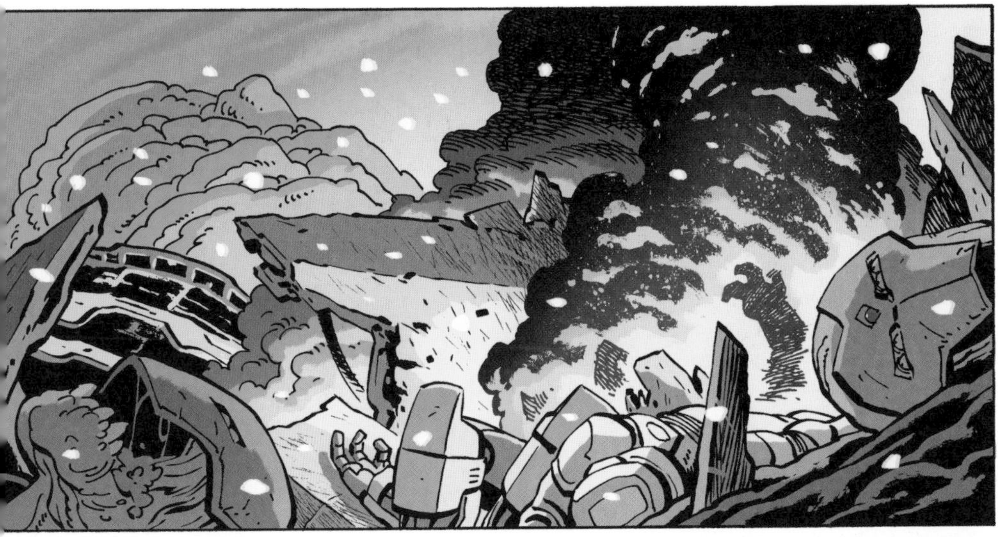

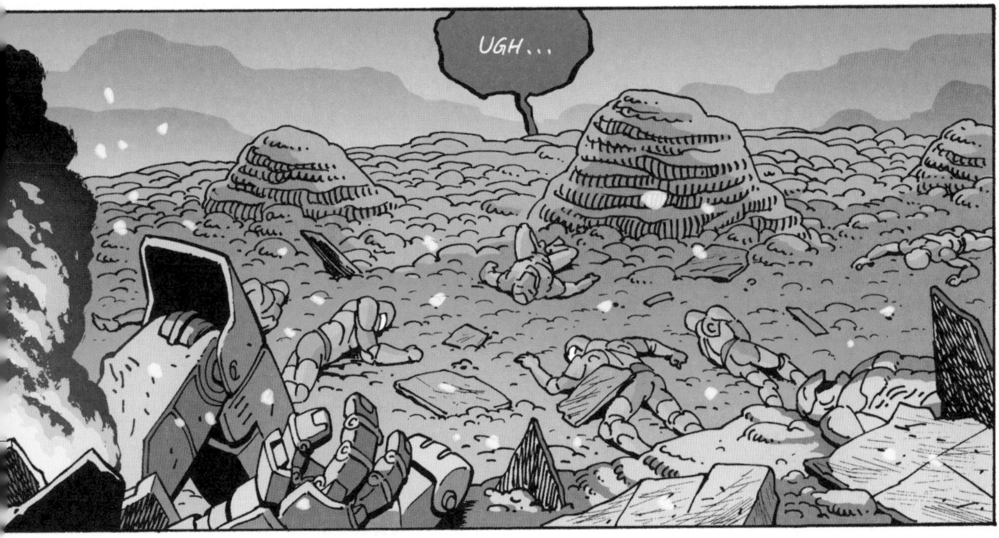
UGH...

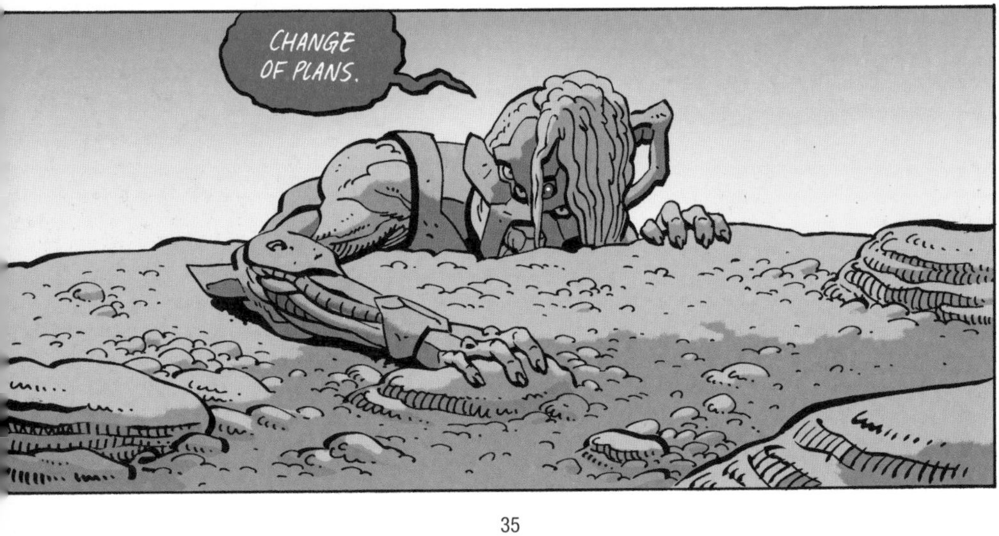
CHANGE OF PLANS.

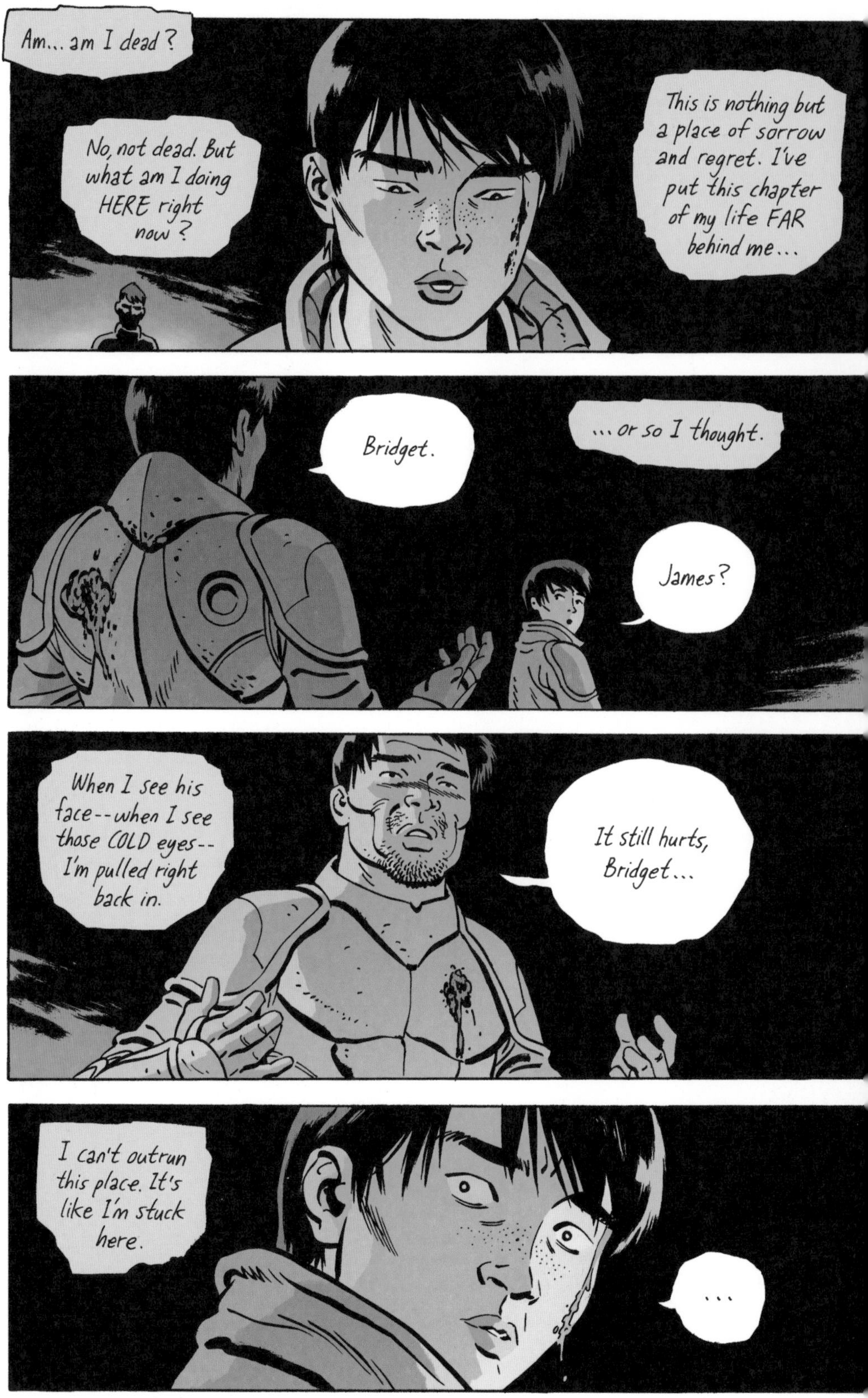
Am... am I dead?
No, not dead. But what am I doing HERE right now?
This is nothing but a place of sorrow and regret. I've put this chapter of my life FAR behind me...
Bridget.
...or so I thought.
James?
When I see his face--when I see those COLD eyes--I'm pulled right back in.
It still hurts, Bridget...
I can't outrun this place. It's like I'm stuck here.
...

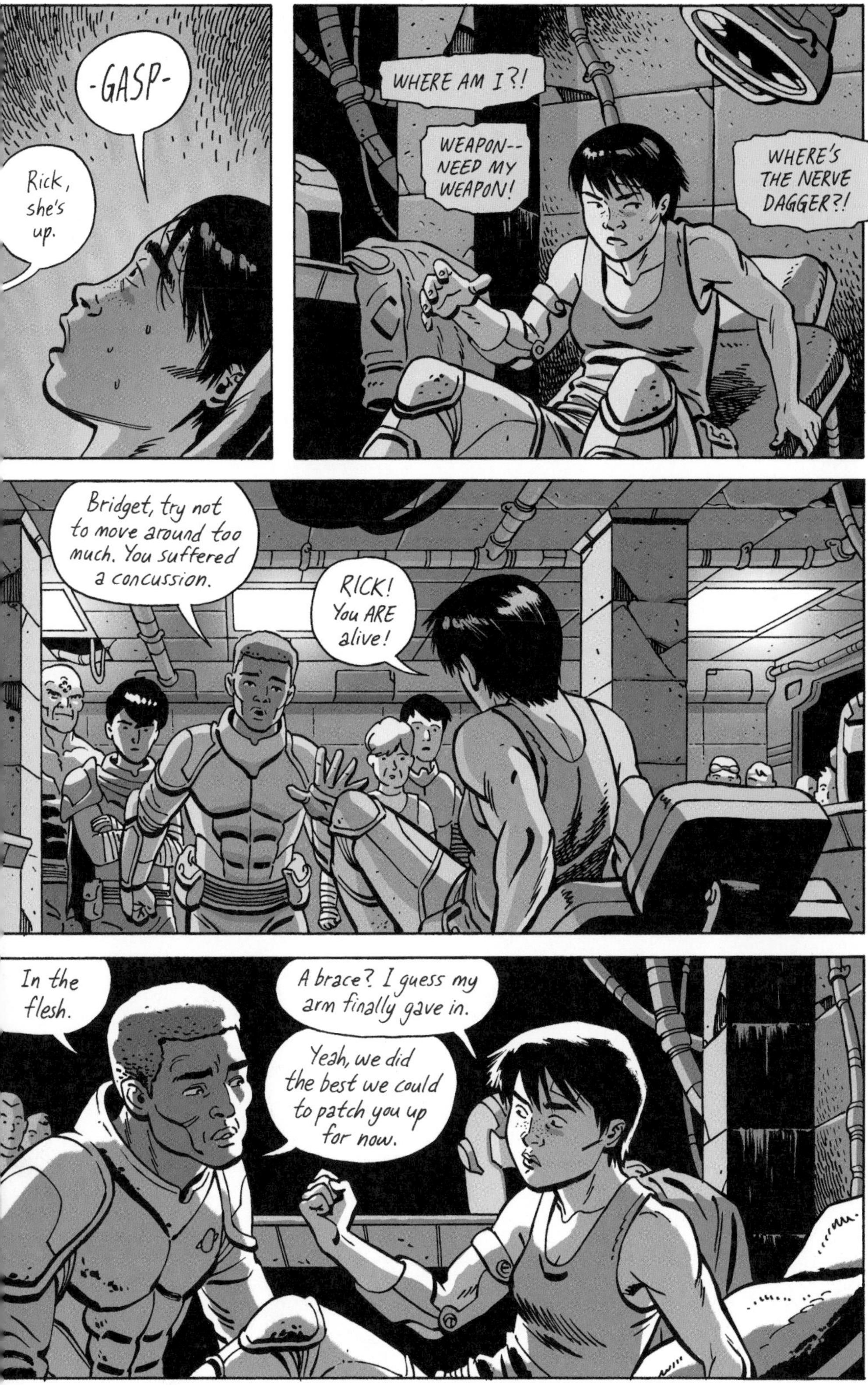
-GASP-
Rick, she's up.
WHERE AM I?!
WEAPON-- NEED MY WEAPON!
WHERE'S THE NERVE DAGGER?!
Bridget, try not to move around too much. You suffered a concussion.
RICK! You ARE alive!
In the flesh.
A brace? I guess my arm finally gave in.
Yeah, we did the best we could to patch you up for now.

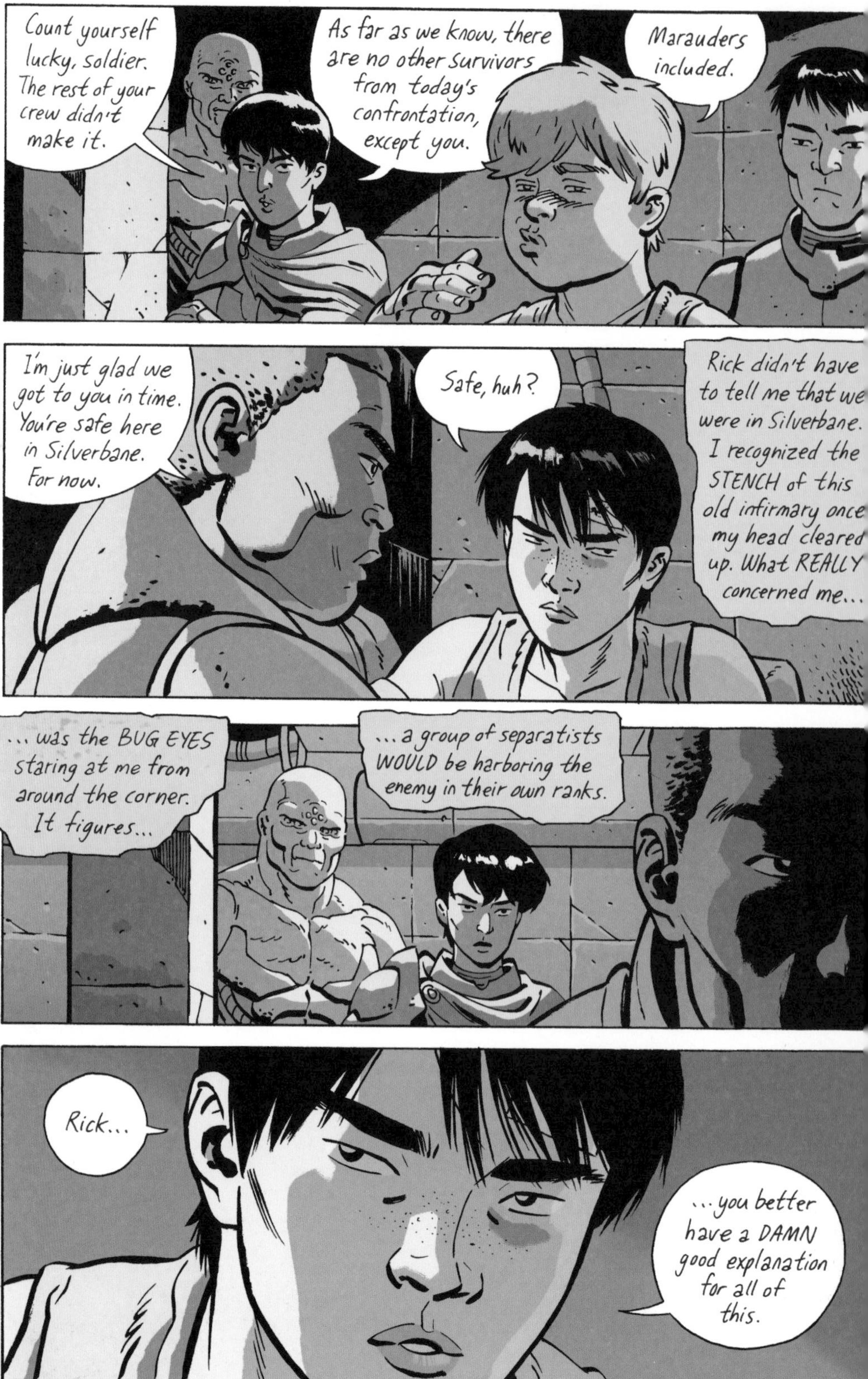
Count yourself lucky, soldier. The rest of your crew didn't make it.
As far as we know, there are no other survivors from today's confrontation, except you.
Marauders included.
I'm just glad we got to you in time. You're safe here in Silverbane. For now.
Safe, huh?
Rick didn't have to tell me that we were in Silverbane. I recognized the STENCH of this old infirmary once my head cleared up. What REALLY concerned me...
...was the BUG EYES staring at me from around the corner. It figures...
...a group of separatists WOULD be harboring the enemy in their own ranks.
Rick...
...you better have a DAMN good explanation for all of this.

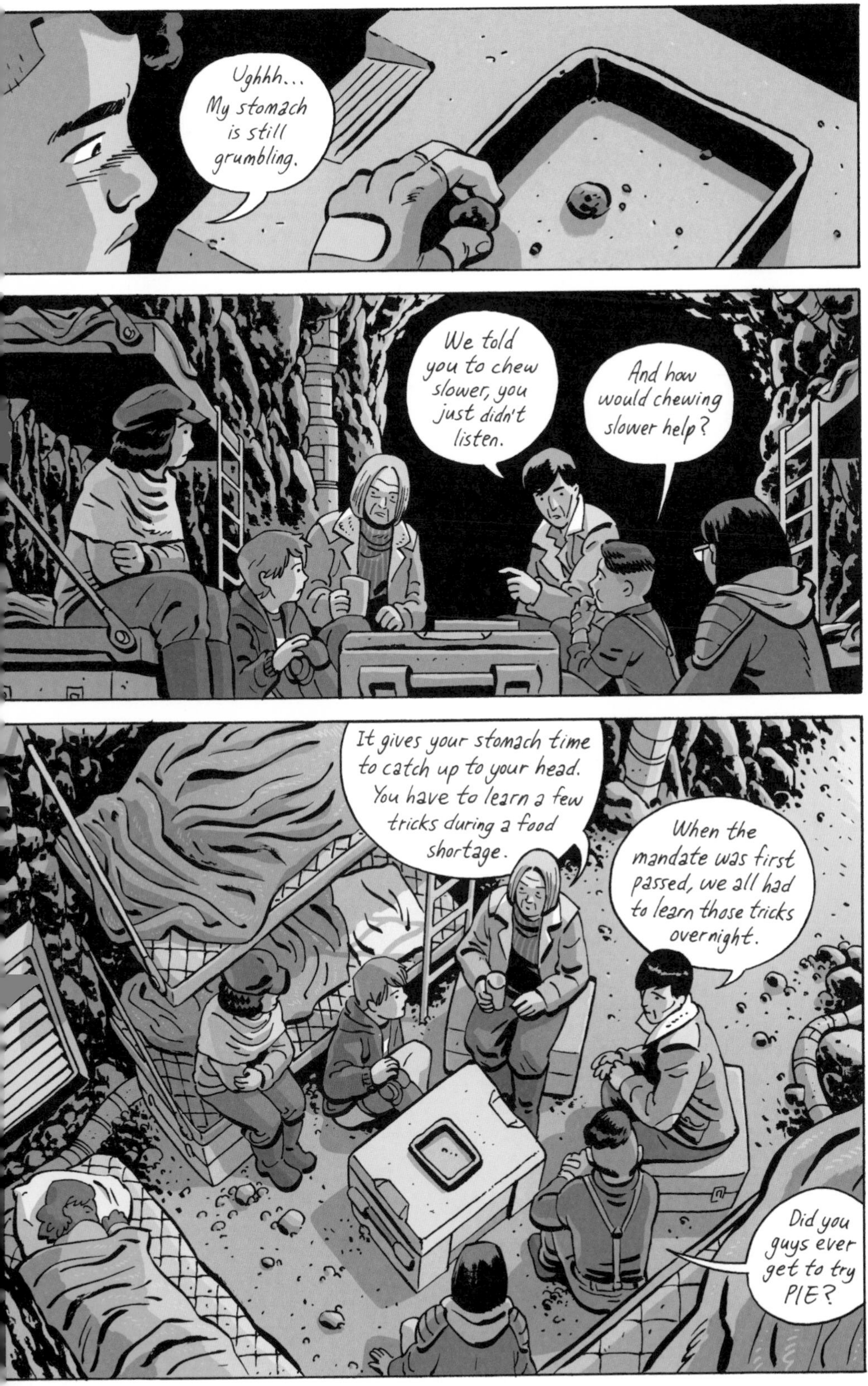
Ughhh... My stomach is still grumbling.
We told you to chew slower, you just didn't listen.
And how would chewing slower help?
It gives your stomach time to catch up to your head. You have to learn a few tricks during a food shortage.
When the mandate was first passed, we all had to learn those tricks overnight.
Did you guys ever get to try PIE?

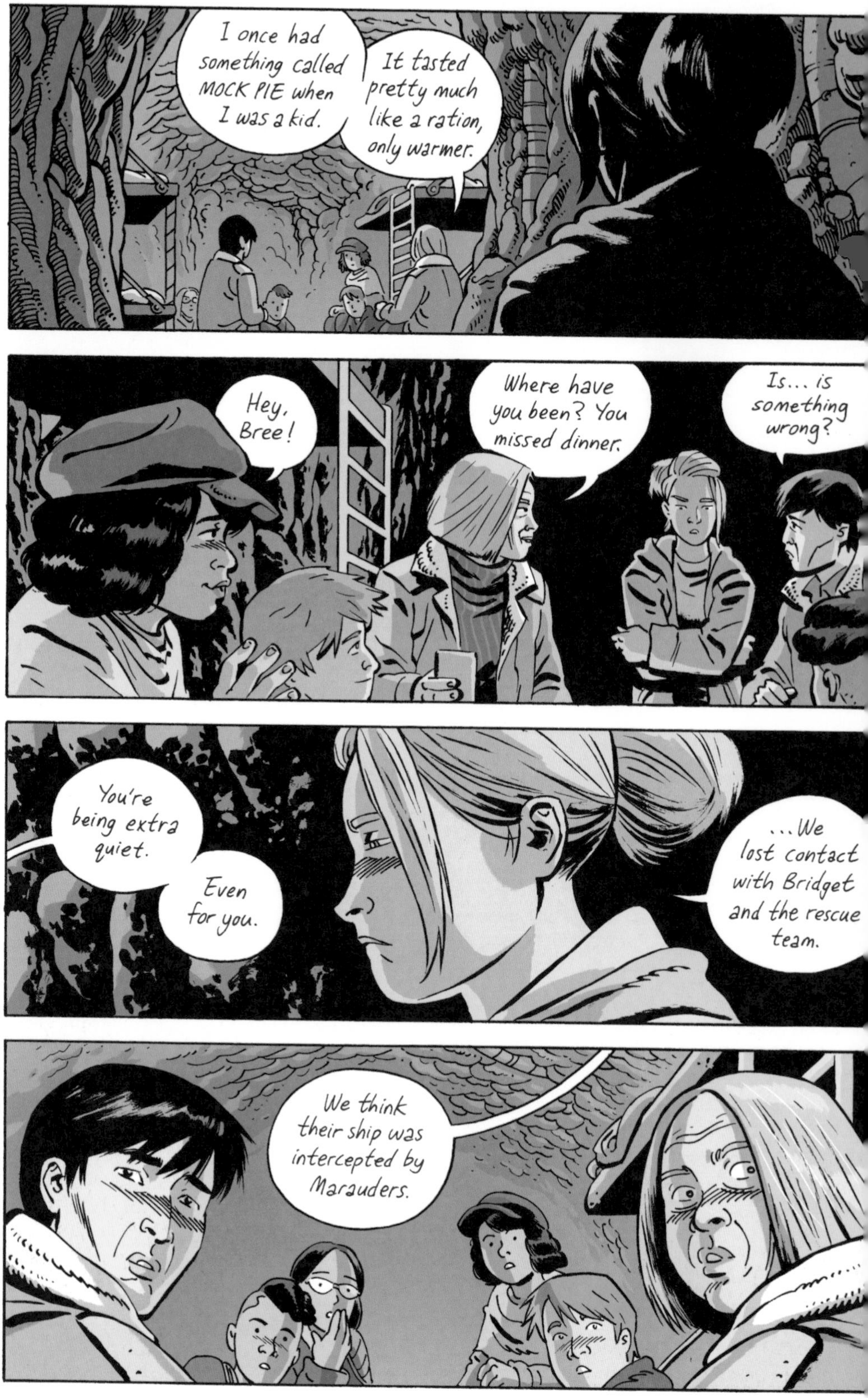
I once had something called MOCK PIE when I was a kid.
It tasted pretty much like a ration, only warmer.
Hey, Bree!
Where have you been? You missed dinner.
Is... is something wrong?
You're being extra quiet.
Even for you.
...We lost contact with Bridget and the rescue team.
We think their ship was intercepted by Marauders.

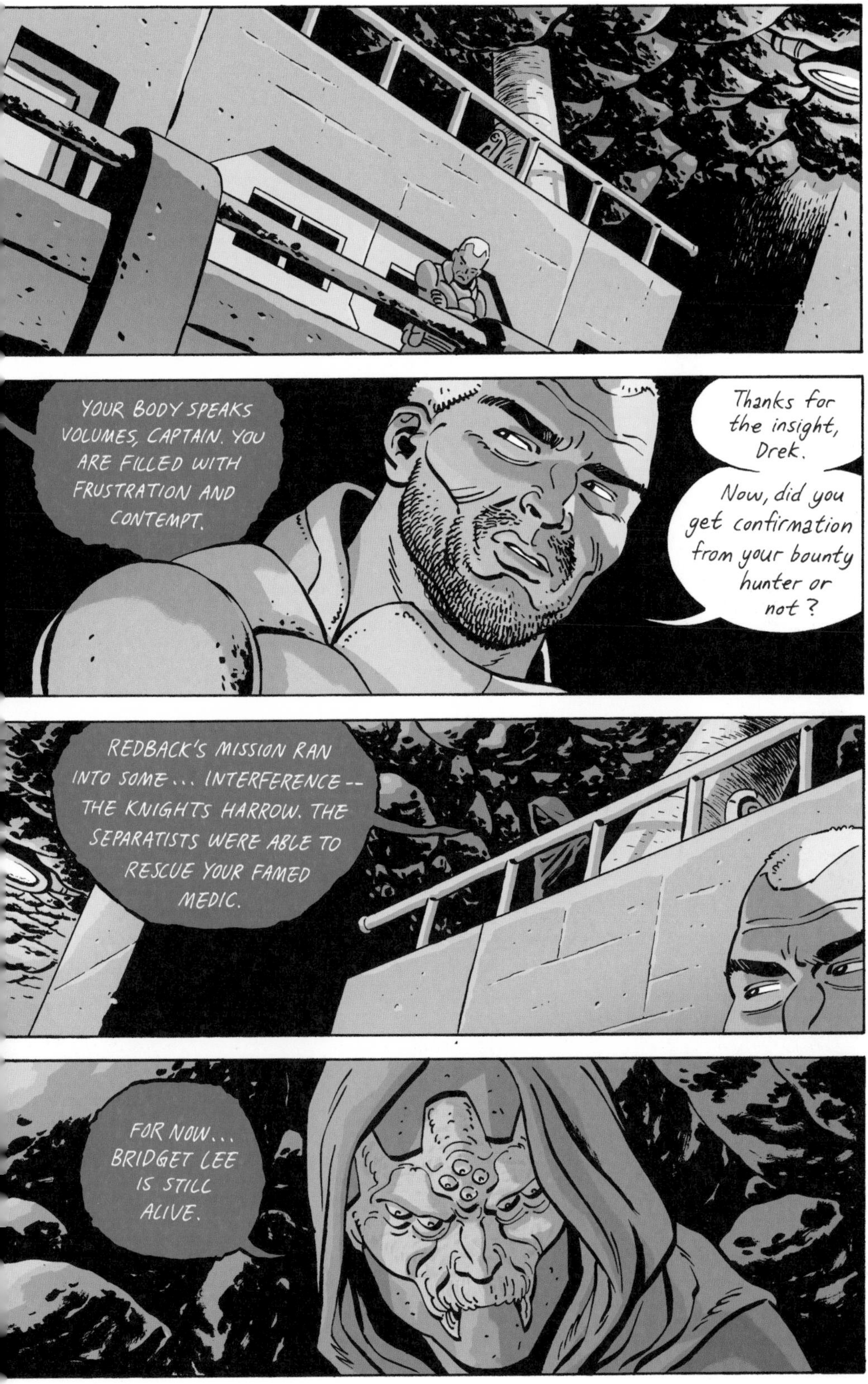
YOUR BODY SPEAKS VOLUMES, CAPTAIN. YOU ARE FILLED WITH FRUSTRATION AND CONTEMPT.
Thanks for the insight, Drek.
Now, did you get confirmation from your bounty hunter or not?
REDBACK'S MISSION RAN INTO SOME... INTERFERENCE -- THE KNIGHTS HARROW. THE SEPARATISTS WERE ABLE TO RESCUE YOUR FAMED MEDIC.
FOR NOW... BRIDGET LEE IS STILL ALIVE.

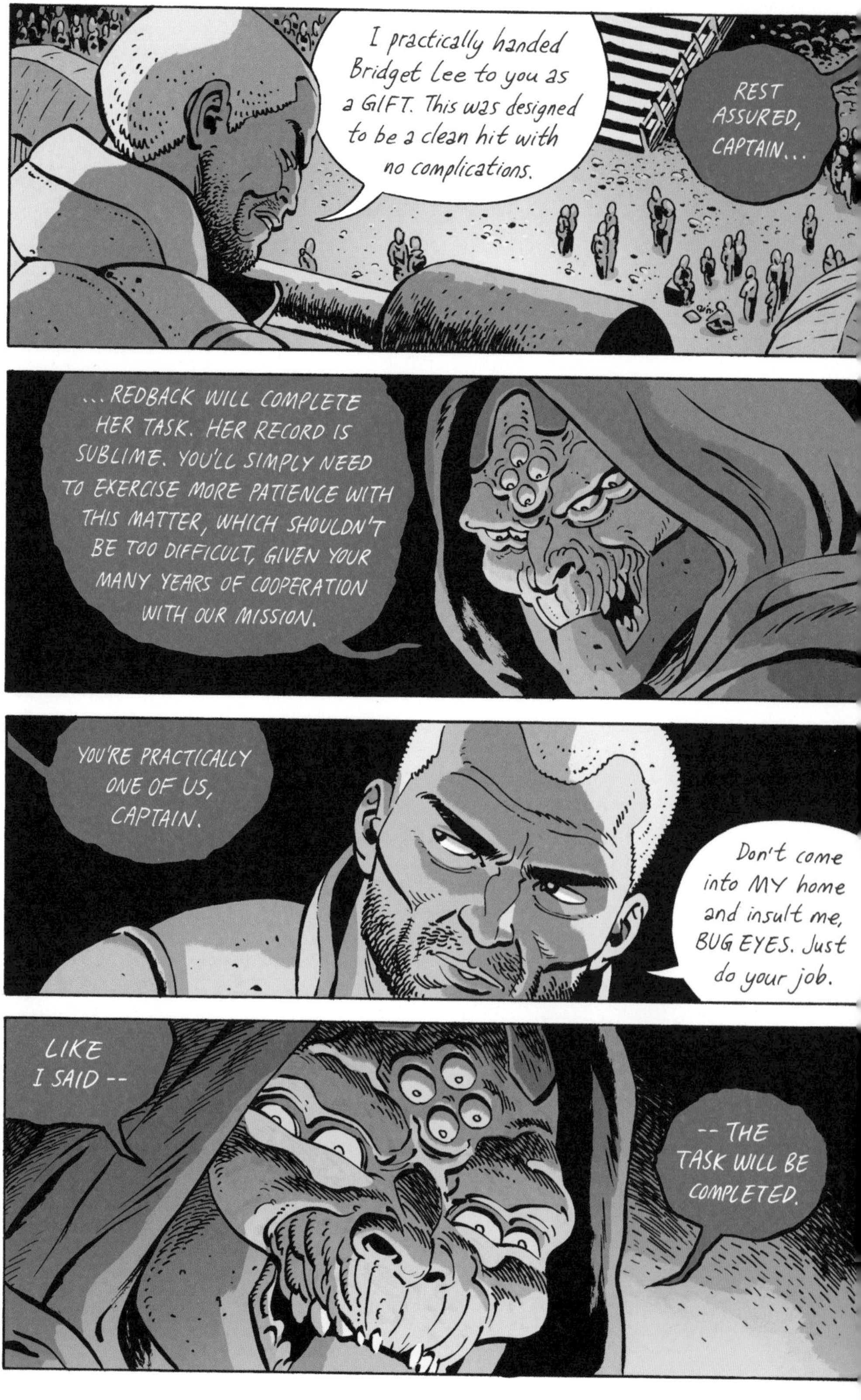
I practically handed Bridget Lee to you as a GIFT. This was designed to be a clean hit with no complications.
REST ASSURED, CAPTAIN...
...REDBACK WILL COMPLETE HER TASK. HER RECORD IS SUBLIME. YOU'LL SIMPLY NEED TO EXERCISE MORE PATIENCE WITH THIS MATTER, WHICH SHOULDN'T BE TOO DIFFICULT, GIVEN YOUR MANY YEARS OF COOPERATION WITH OUR MISSION.
YOU'RE PRACTICALLY ONE OF US, CAPTAIN.
Don't come into MY home and insult me, BUG EYES. Just do your job.
LIKE I SAID --
-- THE TASK WILL BE COMPLETED.

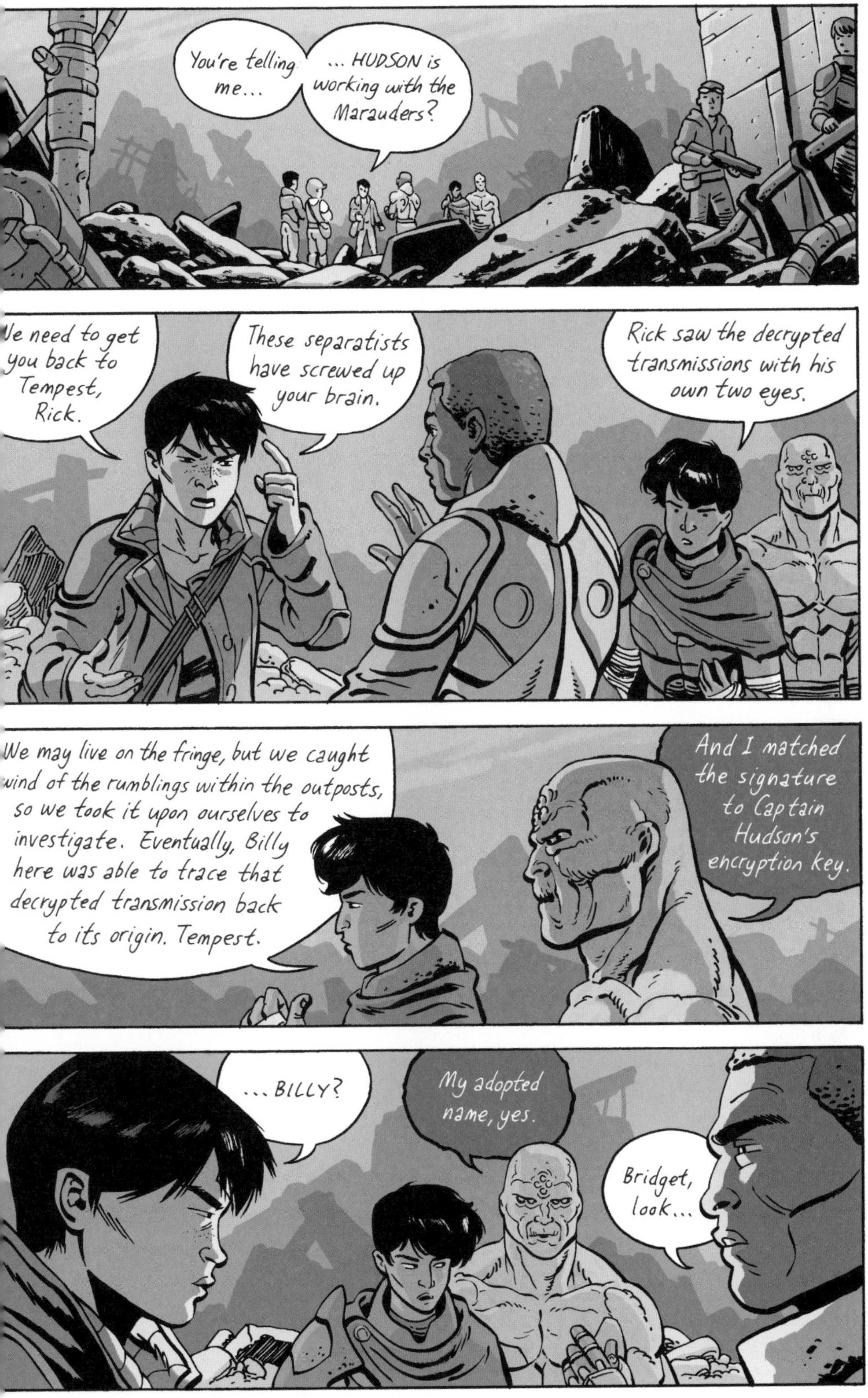
You're telling me...
... HUDSON is working with the Marauders?
We need to get you back to Tempest, Rick.
These separatists have screwed up your brain.
Rick saw the decrypted transmissions with his own two eyes.
We may live on the fringe, but we caught wind of the rumblings within the outposts, so we took it upon ourselves to investigate. Eventually, Billy here was able to trace that decrypted transmission back to its origin. Tempest.
And I matched the signature to Captain Hudson's encryption key.
...BILLY?
My adopted name, yes.
Bridget, look...

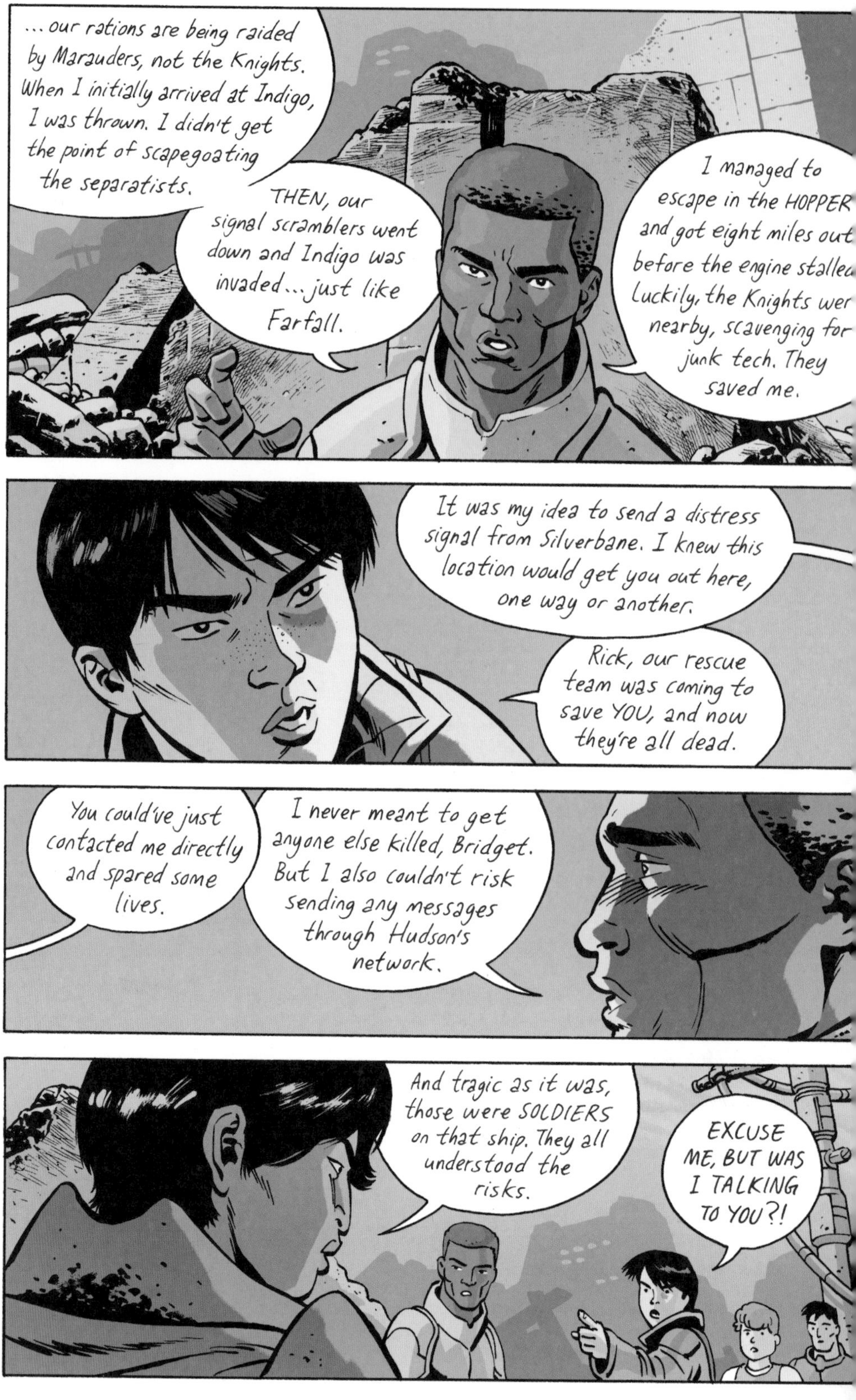
...our rations are being raided by Marauders, not the Knights. When I initially arrived at Indigo, I was thrown. I didn't get the point of scapegoating the separatists.
THEN, our signal scramblers went down and Indigo was invaded...just like Farfall.
I managed to escape in the HOPPER and got eight miles out before the engine stalle Luckily, the Knights wer nearby, scavenging for junk tech. They saved me.
It was my idea to send a distress signal from Silverbane. I knew this location would get you out here, one way or another.
Rick, our rescue team was coming to save YOU, and now they're all dead.
You could've just contacted me directly and spared some lives.
I never meant to get anyone else killed, Bridget. But I also couldn't risk sending any messages through Hudson's network.
And tragic as it was, those were SOLDIERS on that ship. They all understood the risks.
EXCUSE ME, BUT WAS I TALKING TO YOU?!

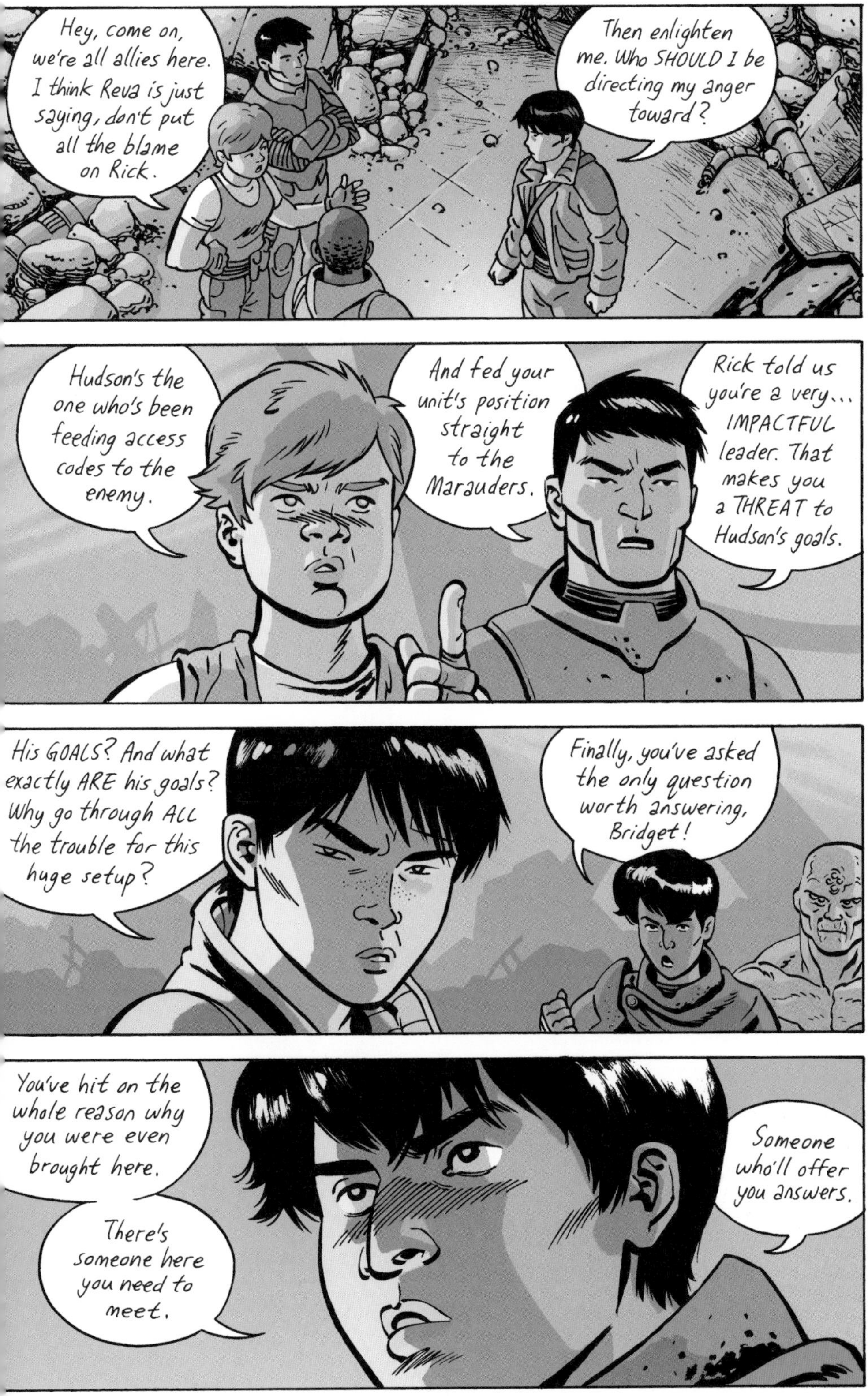
Hey, come on, we're all allies here. I think Reva is just saying, don't put all the blame on Rick.
Then enlighten me. Who SHOULD I be directing my anger toward?
Hudson's the one who's been feeding access codes to the enemy.
And fed your unit's position straight to the Marauders.
Rick told us you're a very... IMPACTFUL leader. That makes you a THREAT to Hudson's goals.
His GOALS? And what exactly ARE his goals? Why go through ALL the trouble for this huge setup?
Finally, you've asked the only question worth answering, Bridget!
You've hit on the whole reason why you were even brought here.
There's someone here you need to meet.
Someone who'll offer you answers.

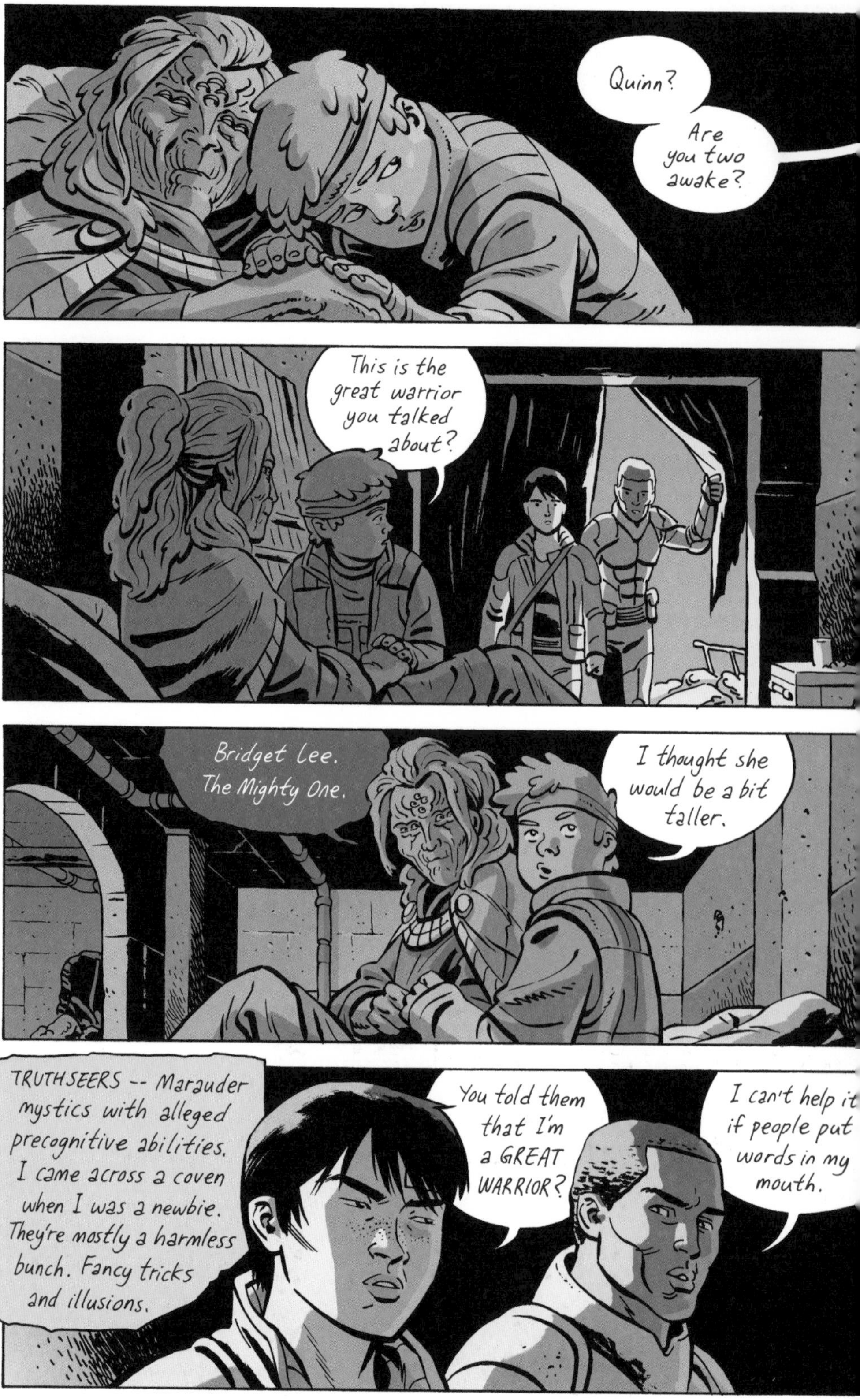
Quinn?
Are you two awake?
This is the great warrior you talked about?
Bridget Lee. The Mighty One.
I thought she would be a bit taller.
TRUTHSEERS -- Marauder mystics with alleged precognitive abilities. I came across a coven when I was a newbie. They're mostly a harmless bunch. Fancy tricks and illusions.
You told them that I'm a GREAT WARRIOR?
I can't help it if people put words in my mouth.

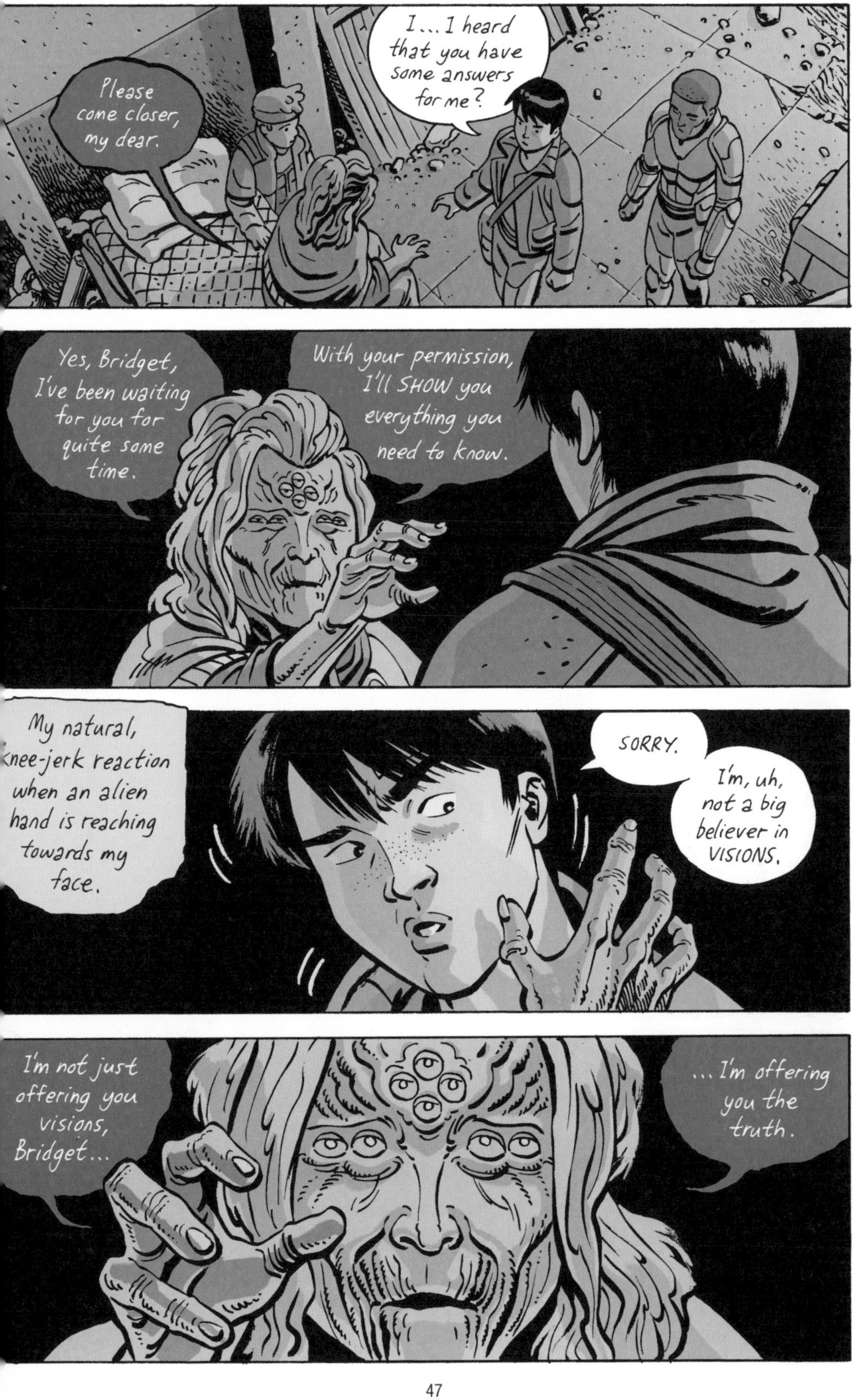
Please come closer, my dear.
I... I heard that you have some answers for me?
Yes, Bridget, I've been waiting for you for quite some time.
With your permission, I'll SHOW you everything you need to know.
My natural, knee-jerk reaction when an alien hand is reaching towards my face.
SORRY.
I'm, uh, not a big believer in VISIONS.
I'm not just offering you visions, Bridget...
...I'm offering you the truth.

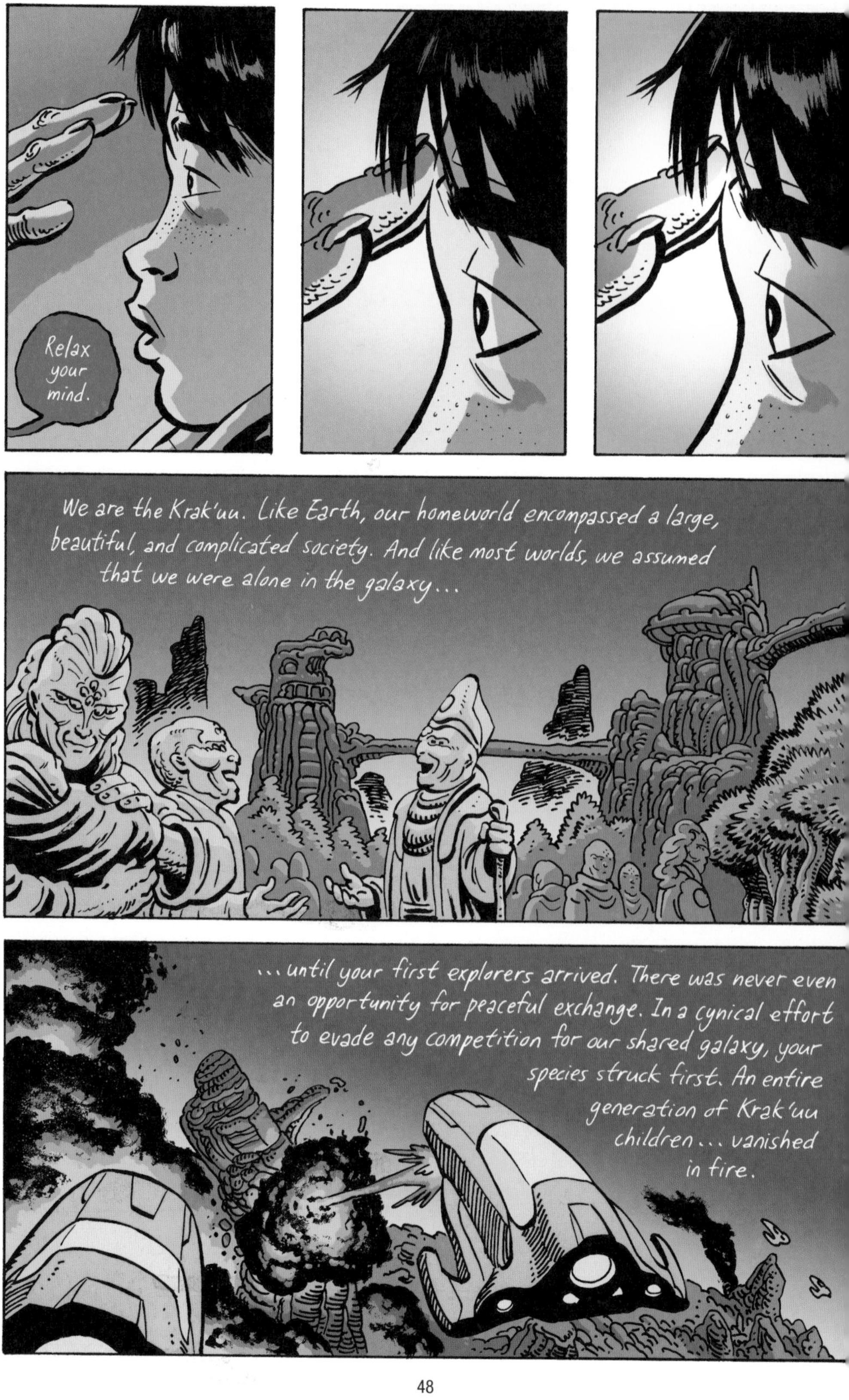
Relax your mind.
We are the Krak'uu. Like Earth, our homeworld encompassed a large, beautiful, and complicated society. And like most worlds, we assumed that we were alone in the galaxy...
...until your first explorers arrived. There was never even an opportunity for peaceful exchange. In a cynical effort to evade any competition for our shared galaxy, your species struck first. An entire generation of Krak'uu children... vanished in fire.

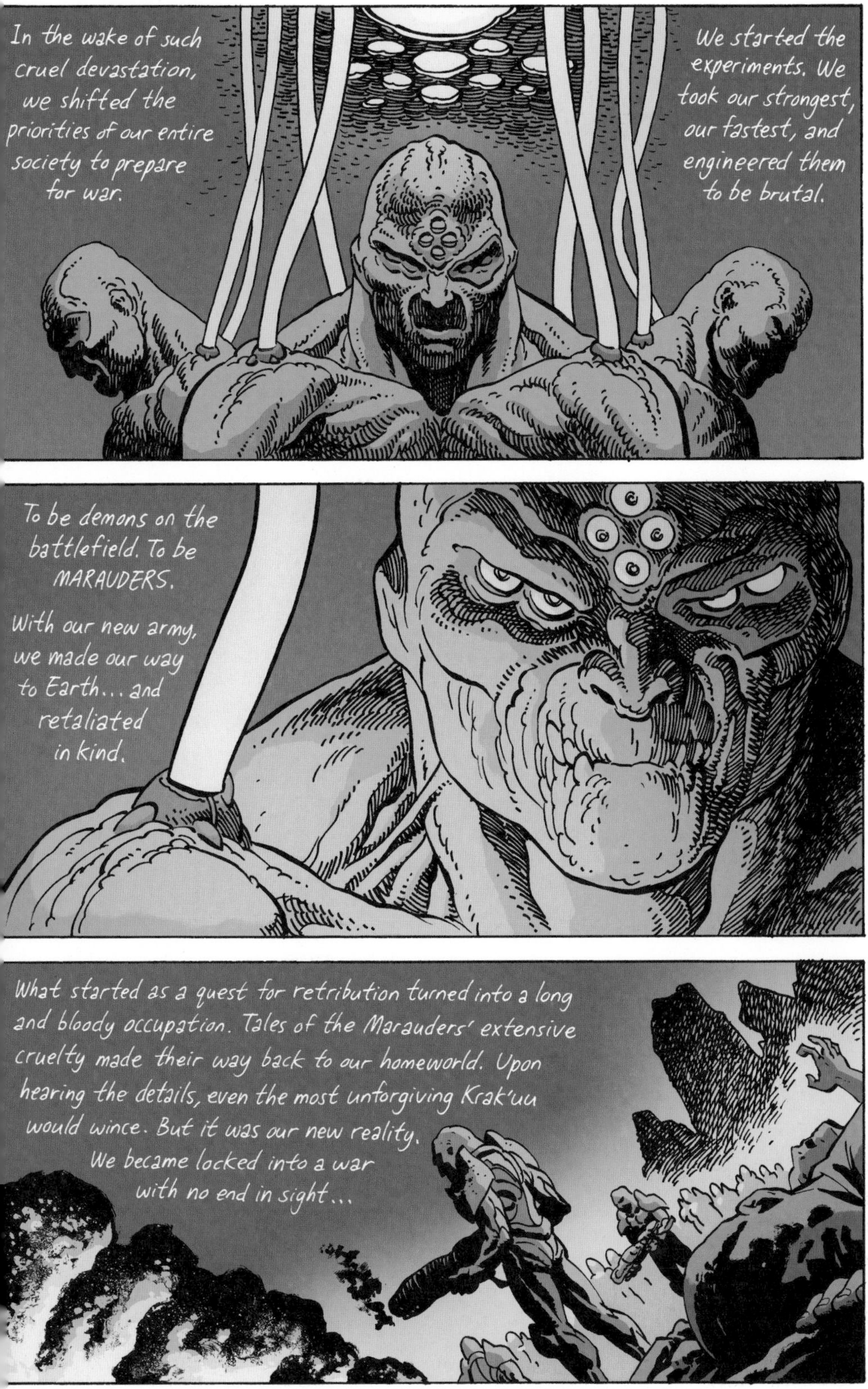
In the wake of such cruel devastation, we shifted the priorities of our entire society to prepare for war.
We started the experiments. We took our strongest, our fastest, and engineered them to be brutal.
To be demons on the battlefield. To be MARAUDERS.
With our new army, we made our way to Earth... and retaliated in kind.
What started as a quest for retribution turned into a long and bloody occupation. Tales of the Marauders' extensive cruelty made their way back to our homeworld. Upon hearing the details, even the most unforgiving Krak'uu would wince. But it was our new reality.
We became locked into a war with no end in sight...

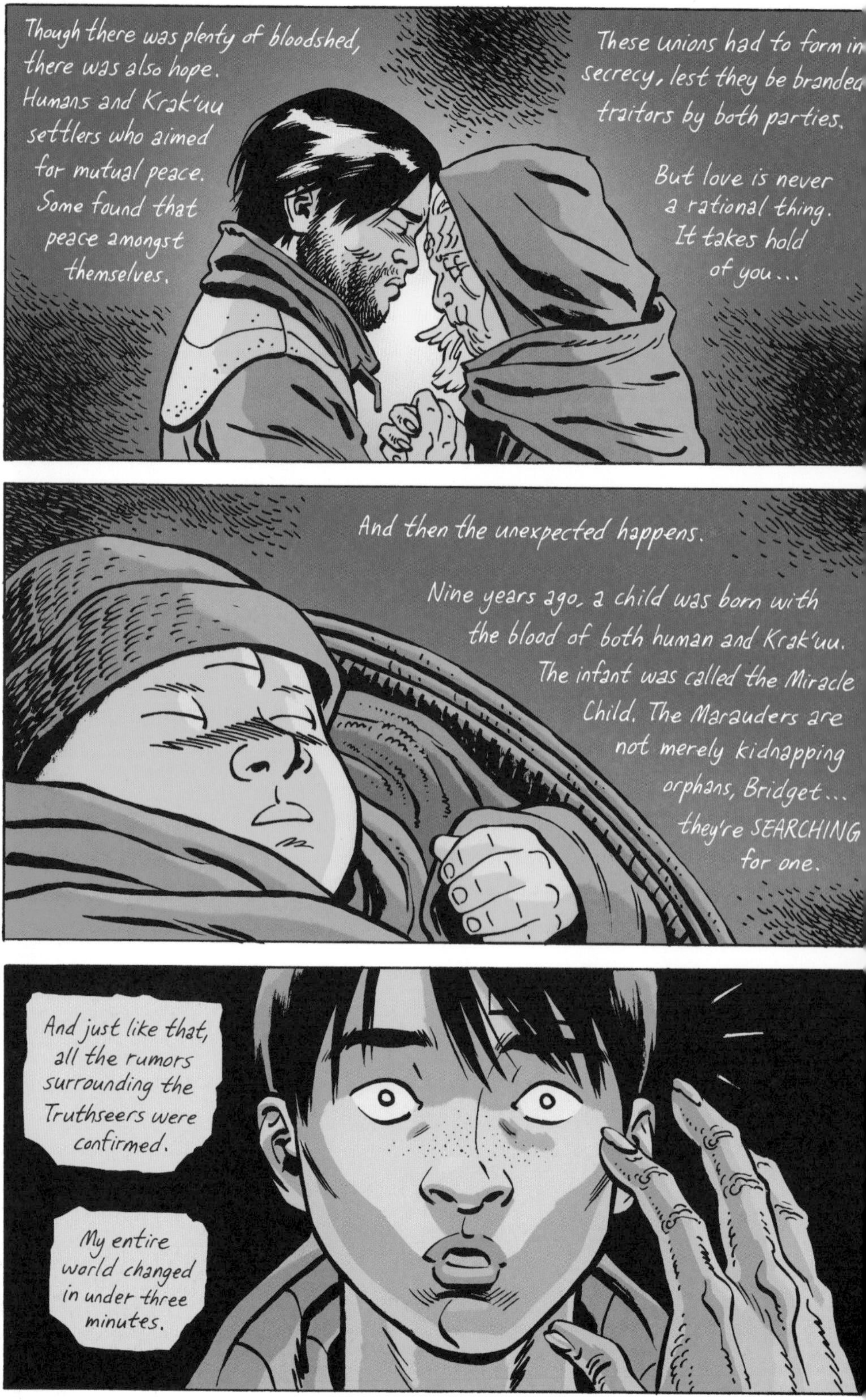
Though there was plenty of bloodshed, there was also hope. Humans and Krak'uu settlers who aimed for mutual peace. Some found that peace amongst themselves.
These unions had to form in secrecy, lest they be branded traitors by both parties.
But love is never a rational thing. It takes hold of you...
And then the unexpected happens.
Nine years ago, a child was born with the blood of both human and Krak'uu. The infant was called the Miracle Child. The Marauders are not merely kidnapping orphans, Bridget... they're SEARCHING for one.
And just like that, all the rumors surrounding the Truthseers were confirmed.
My entire world changed in under three minutes.

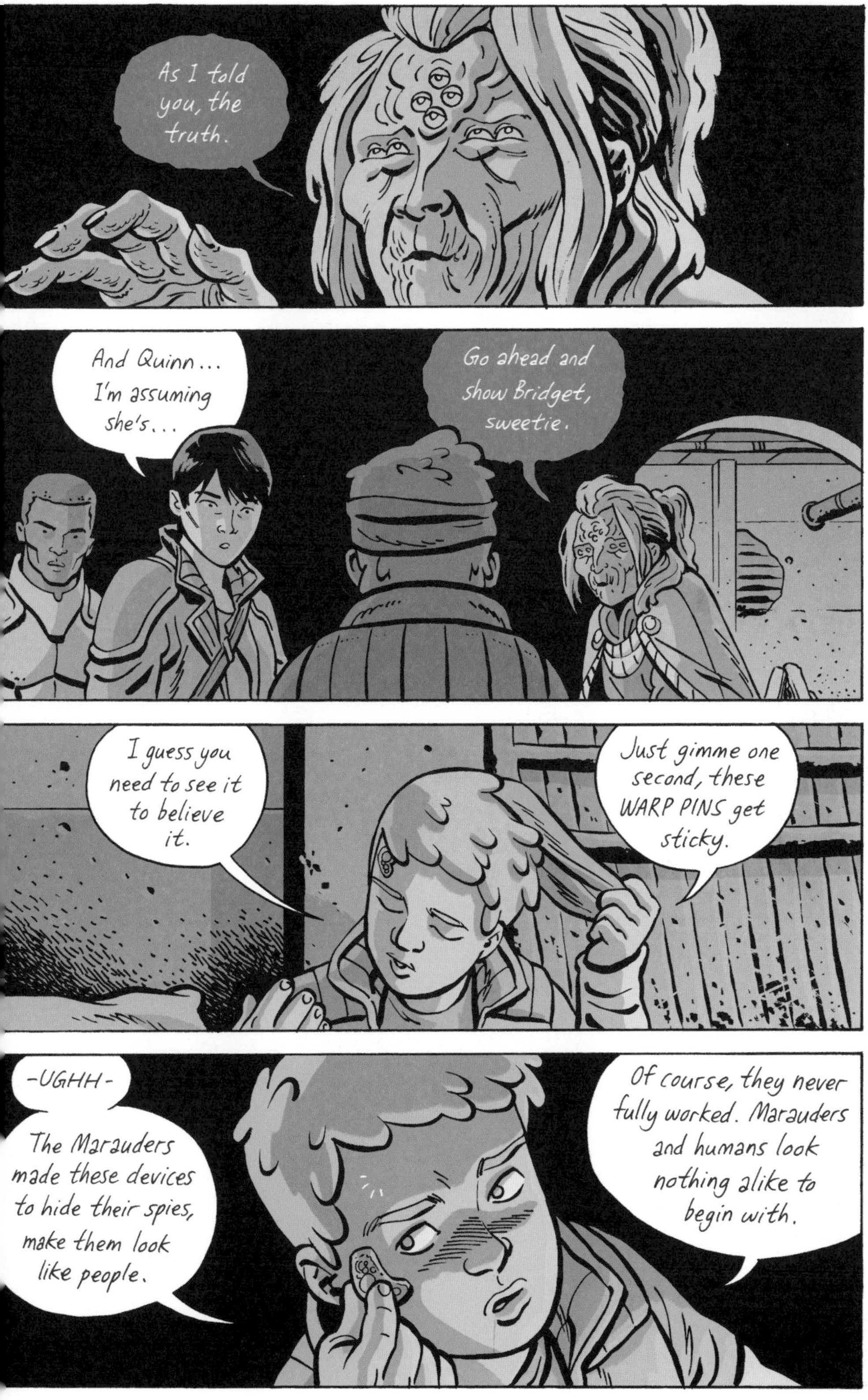
As I told you, the truth.
And Quinn... I'm assuming she's...
Go ahead and show Bridget, sweetie.
I guess you need to see it to believe it.
Just gimme one second, these WARP PINS get sticky.
-UGHH-
The Marauders made these devices to hide their spies, make them look like people.
Of course, they never fully worked. Marauders and humans look nothing alike to begin with.

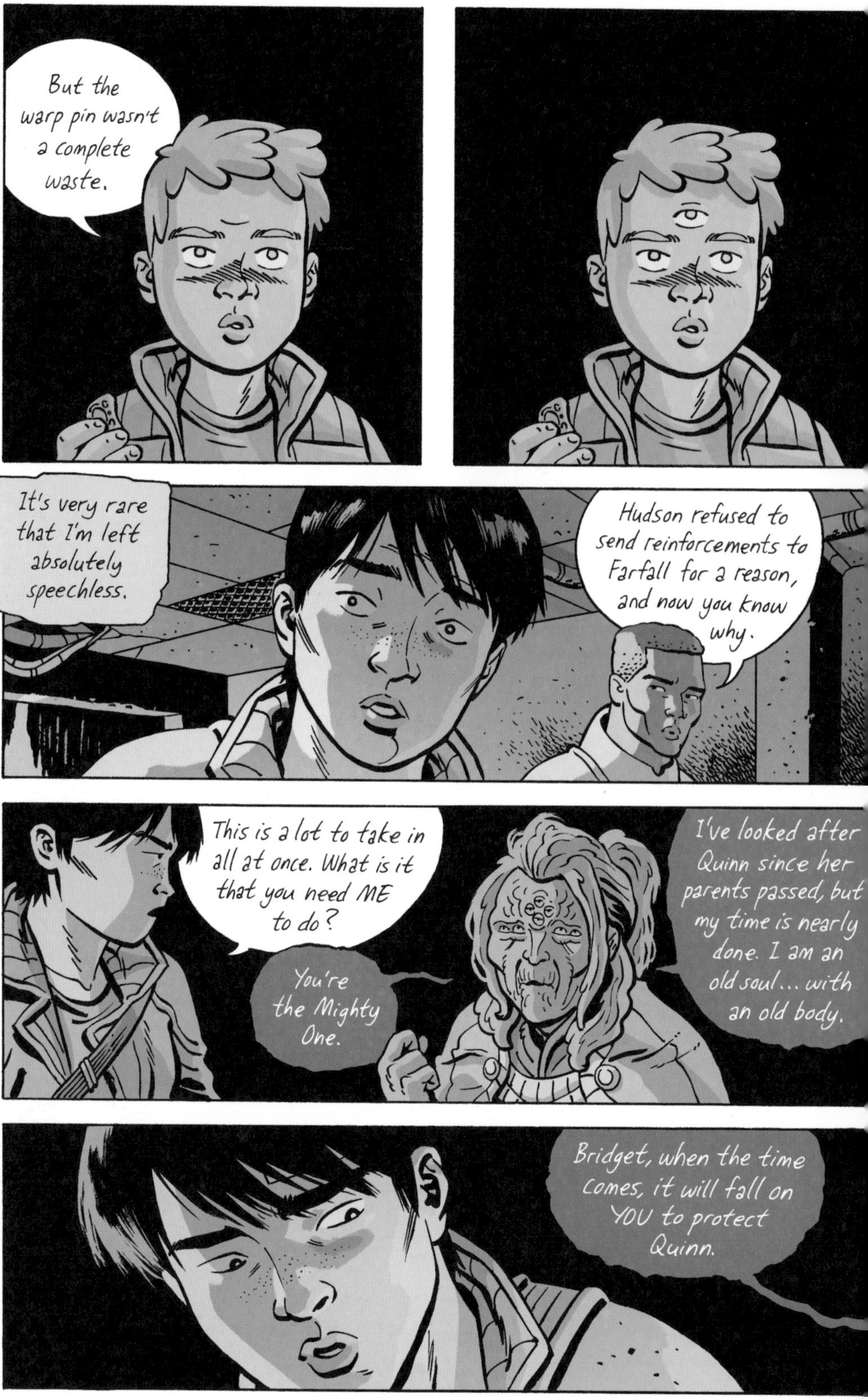
But the warp pin wasn't a complete waste.
It's very rare that I'm left absolutely speechless.
Hudson refused to send reinforcements to Farfall for a reason, and now you know why.
This is a lot to take in all at once. What is it that you need ME to do?
I've looked after Quinn since her parents passed, but my time is nearly done. I am an old soul... with an old body.
You're the Mighty One.
Bridget, when the time comes, it will fall on YOU to protect Quinn.

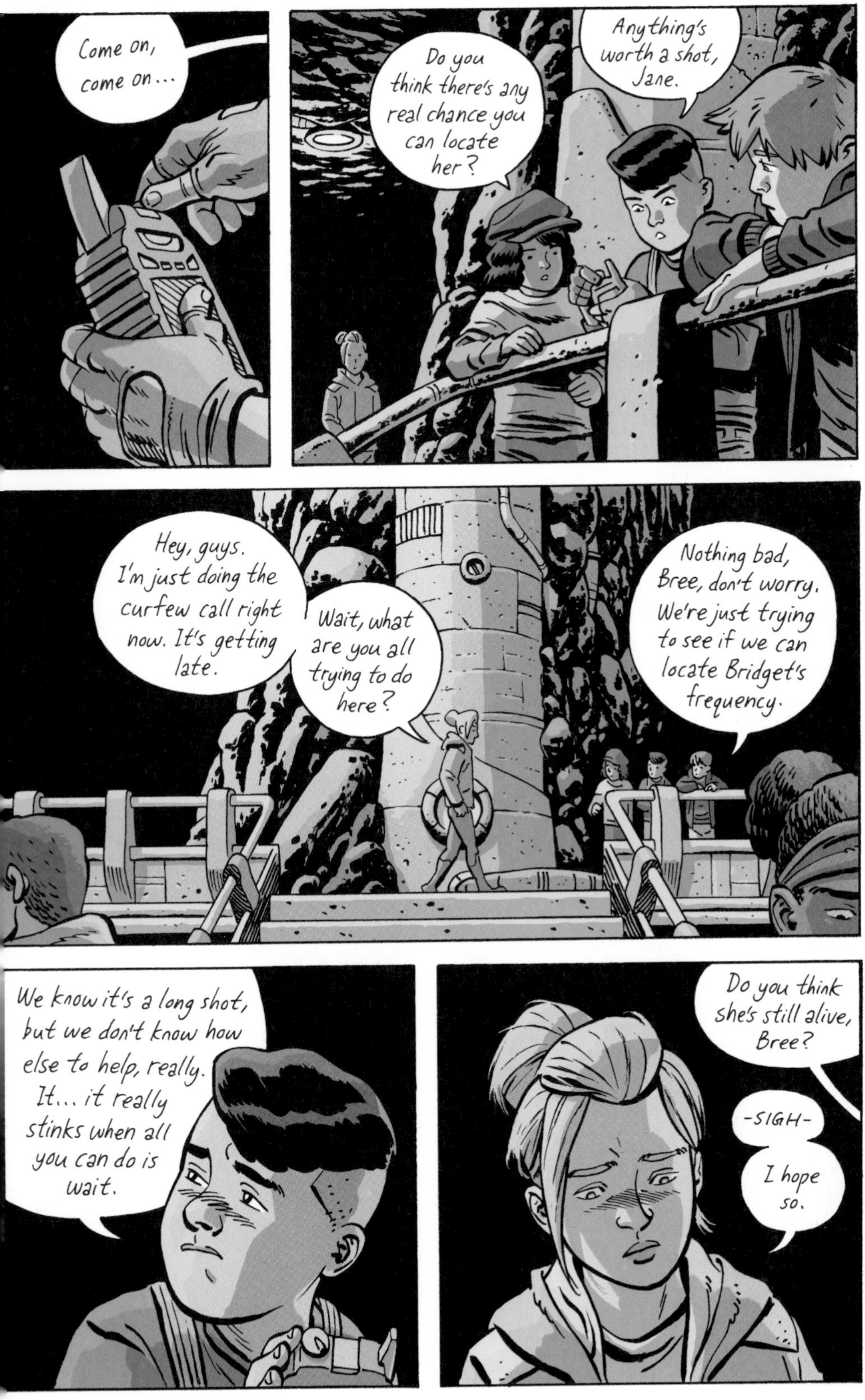
Come on, come on...
Do you think there's any real chance you can locate her?
Anything's worth a shot, Jane.
Hey, guys. I'm just doing the curfew call right now. It's getting late.
Wait, what are you all trying to do here?
Nothing bad, Bree, don't worry. We're just trying to see if we can locate Bridget's frequency.
We know it's a long shot, but we don't know how else to help, really. It... it really stinks when all you can do is wait.
Do you think she's still alive, Bree?
-SIGH-
I hope so.

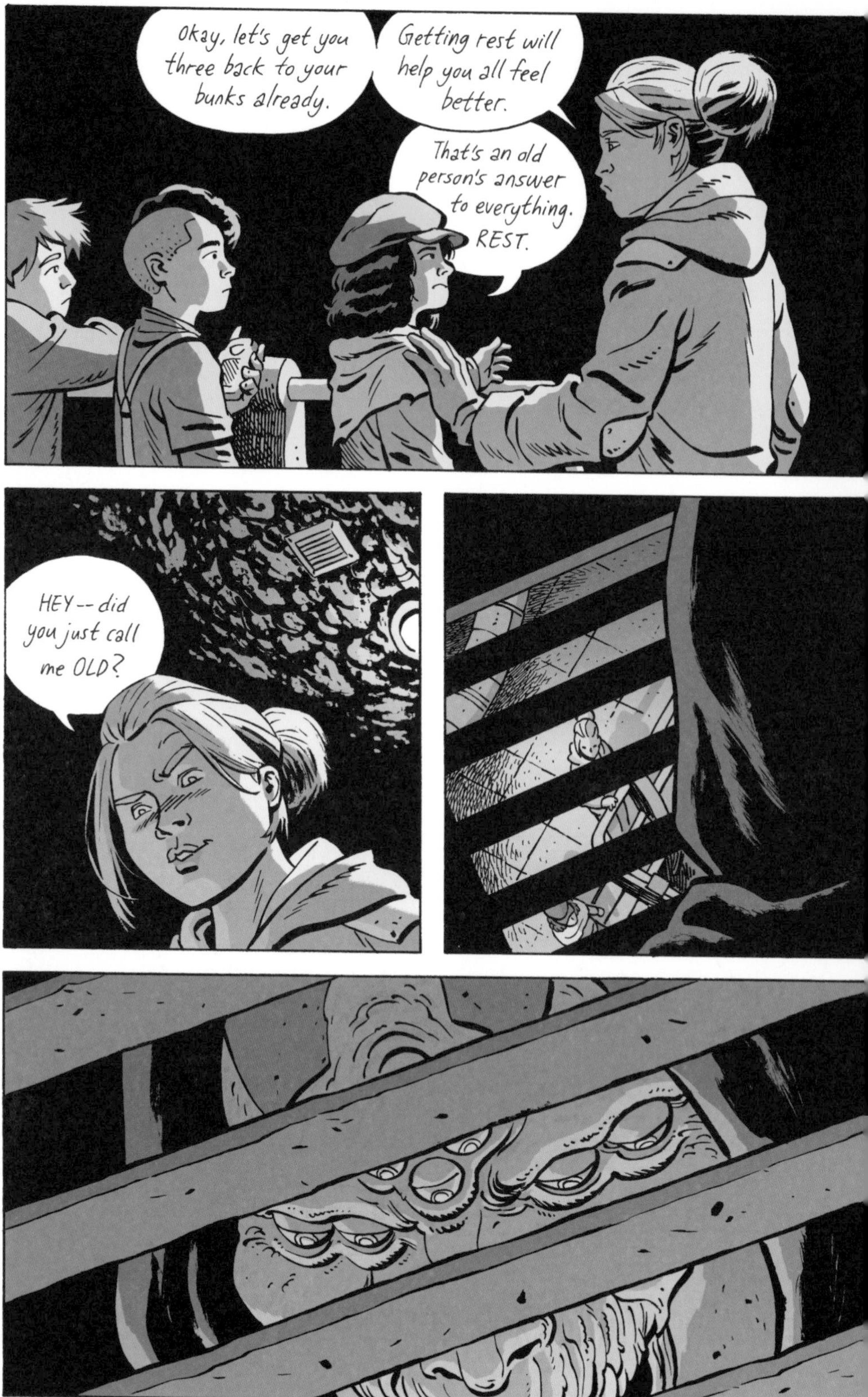
Okay, let's get you three back to your bunks already.
Getting rest will help you all feel better.
That's an old person's answer to everything. REST.
HEY -- did you just call me OLD?

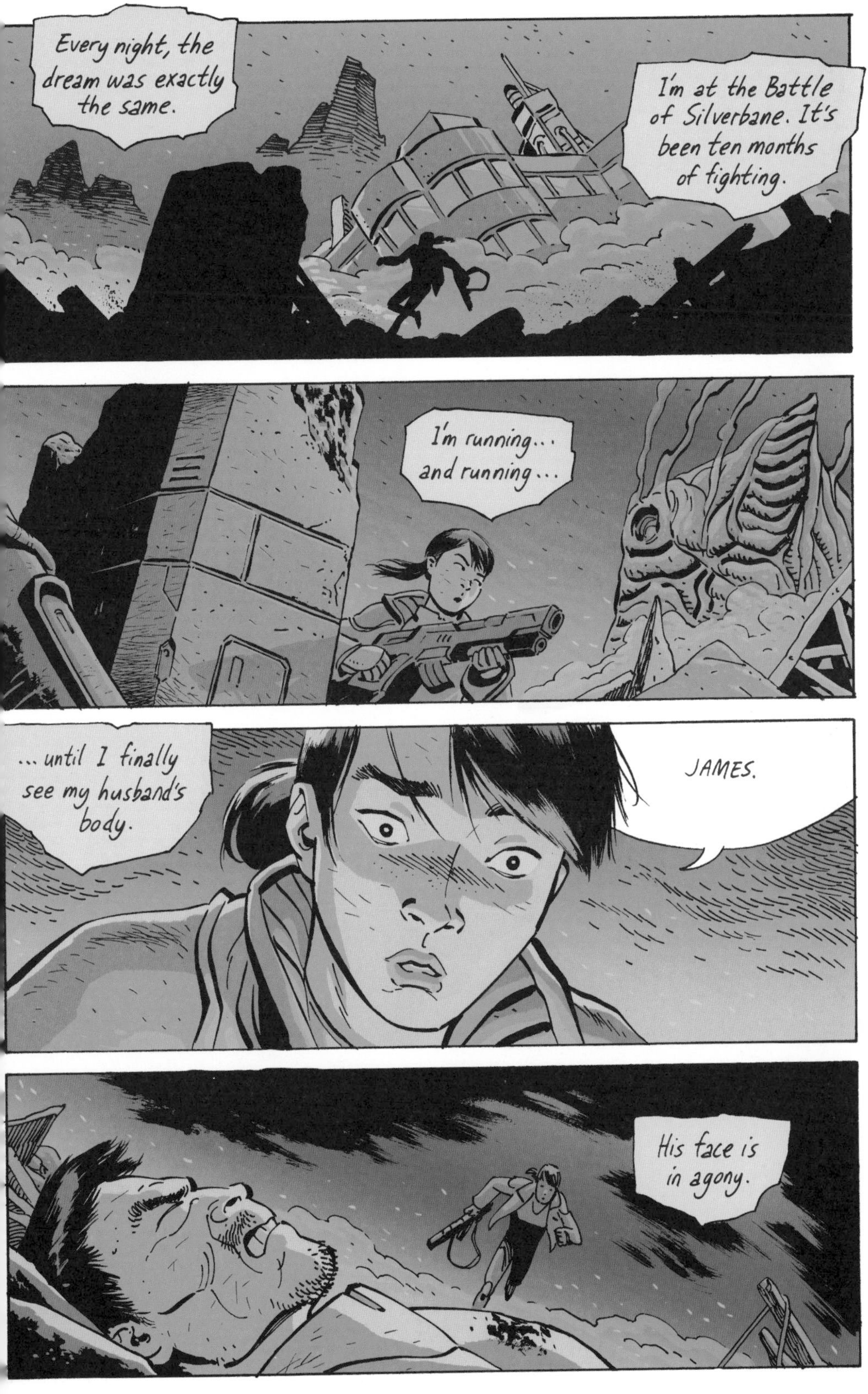
Every night, the dream was exactly the same.
I'm at the Battle of Silverbane. It's been ten months of fighting.
I'm running... and running...
...until I finally see my husband's body.
JAMES.
His face is in agony.

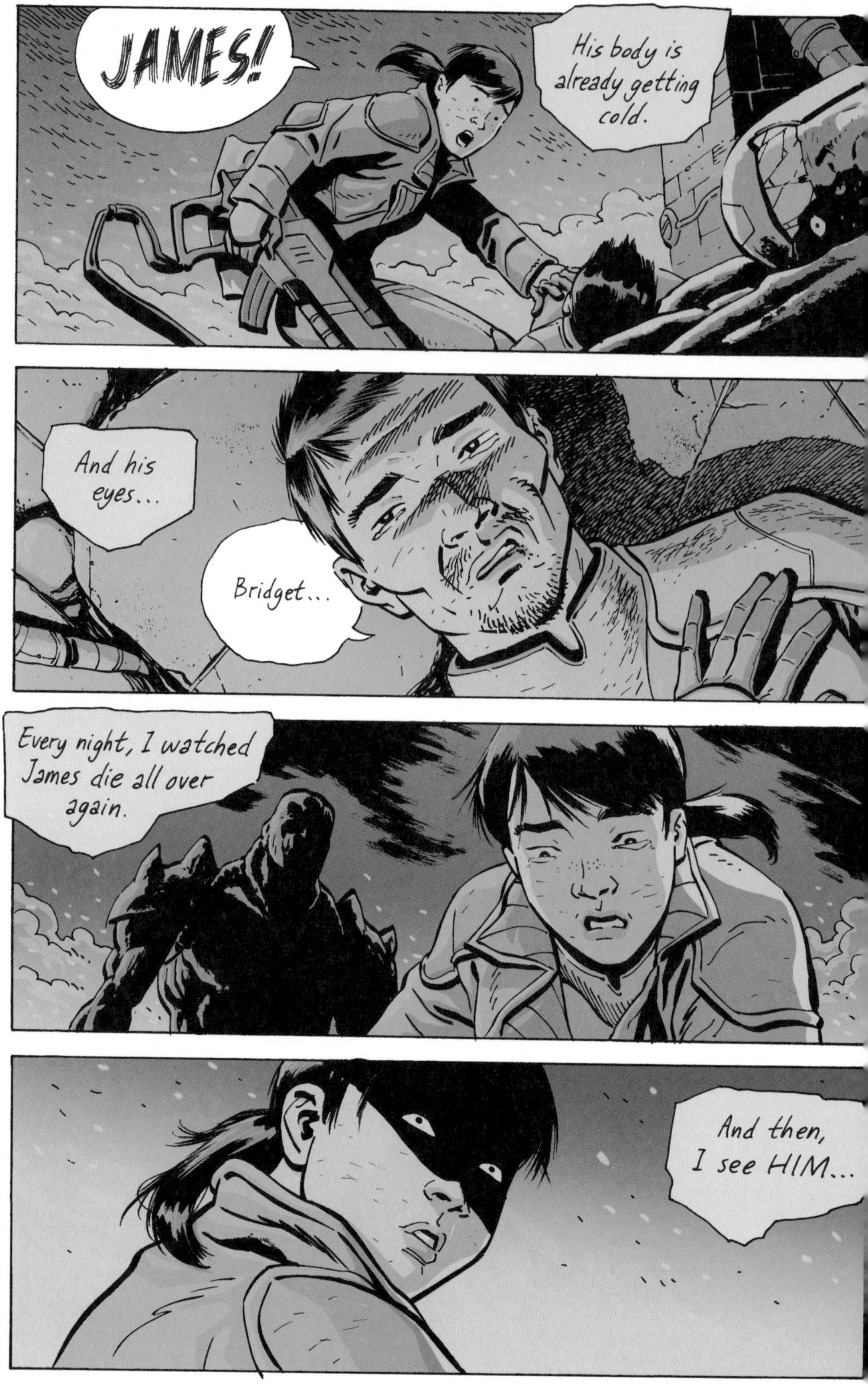
JAMES!
His body is already getting cold.
And his eyes...
Bridget...
Every night, I watched James die all over again.
And then, I see HIM...

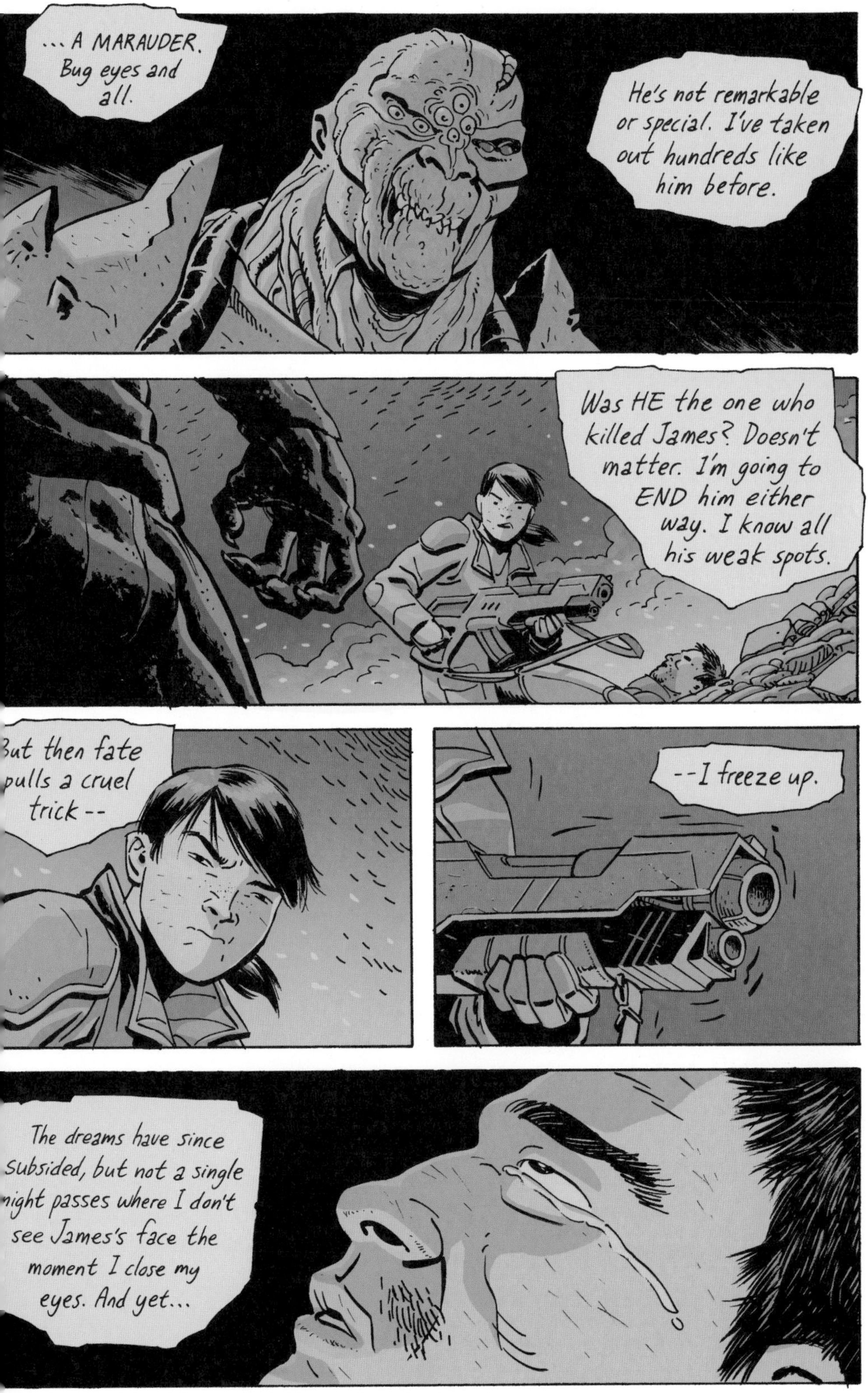

... A MARAUDER. Bug eyes and all.
He's not remarkable or special. I've taken out hundreds like him before.
Was HE the one who killed James? Doesn't matter. I'm going to END him either way. I know all his weak spots.
But then fate pulls a cruel trick --
--I freeze up.
The dreams have since subsided, but not a single night passes where I don't see James's face the moment I close my eyes. And yet...

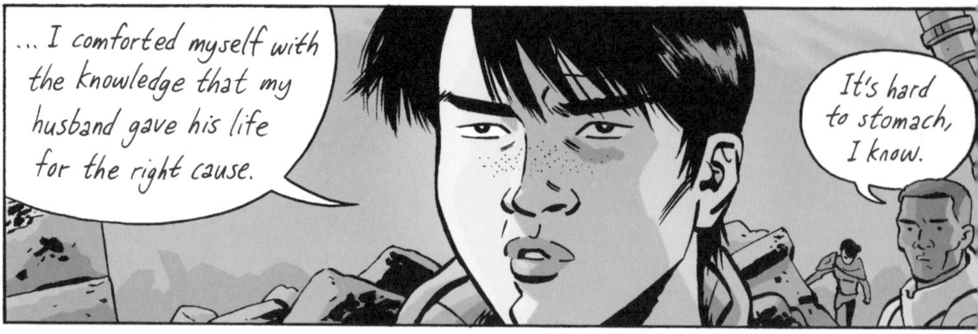
... I comforted myself with the knowledge that my husband gave his life for the right cause.
It's hard to stomach, I know.

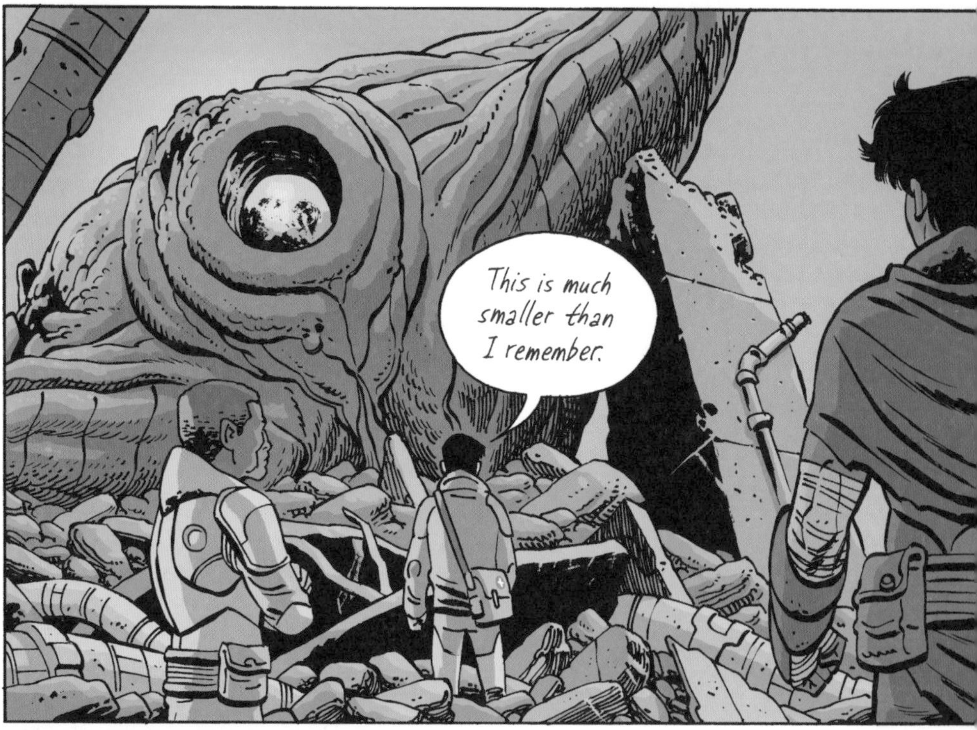
This is much smaller than I remember.

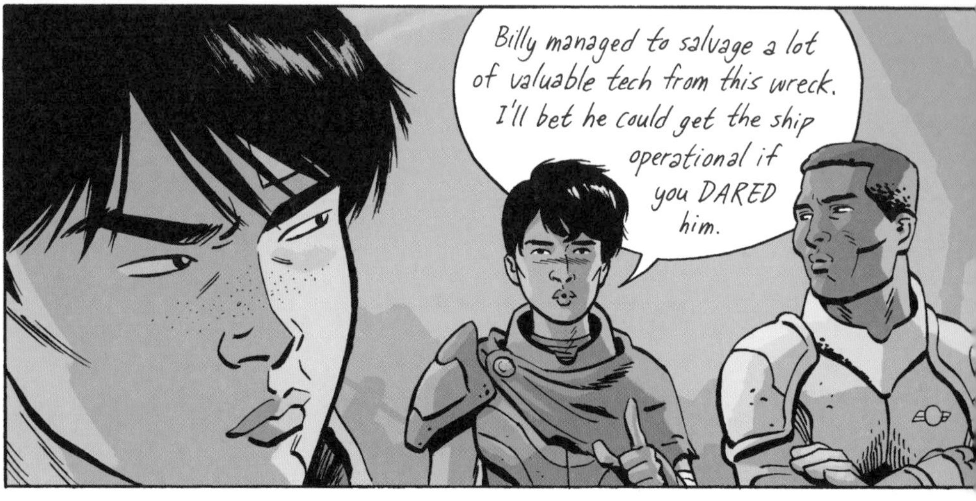
Billy managed to salvage a lot of valuable tech from this wreck. I'll bet he could get the ship operational if you DARED him.

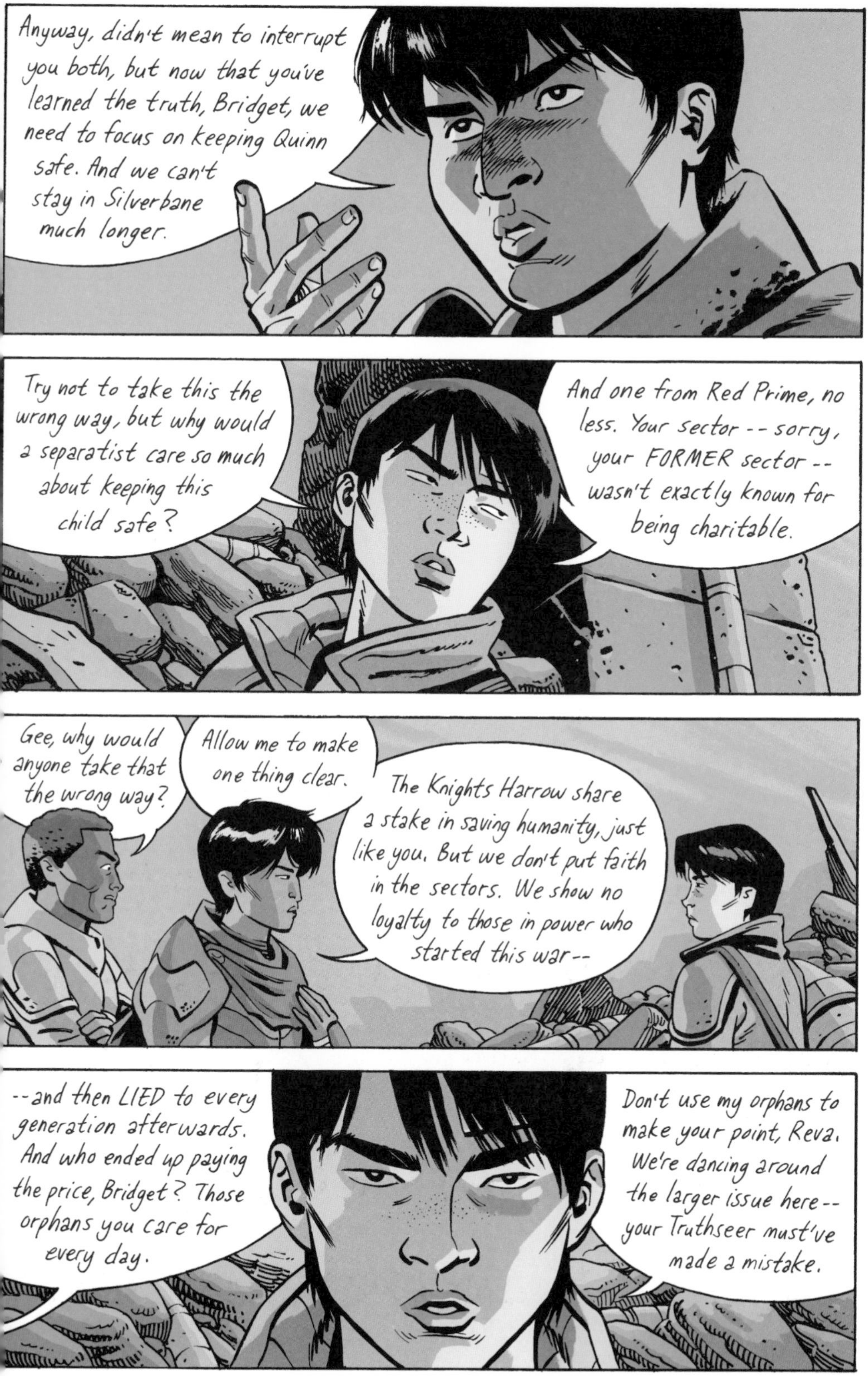

Anyway, didn't mean to interrupt you both, but now that you've learned the truth, Bridget, we need to focus on keeping Quinn safe. And we can't stay in Silverbane much longer.
Try not to take this the wrong way, but why would a separatist care so much about keeping this child safe?
And one from Red Prime, no less. Your sector -- sorry, your FORMER sector -- wasn't exactly known for being charitable.
Gee, why would anyone take that the wrong way?
Allow me to make one thing clear.
The Knights Harrow share a stake in saving humanity, just like you. But we don't put faith in the sectors. We show no loyalty to those in power who started this war--
--and then LIED to every generation afterwards. And who ended up paying the price, Bridget? Those orphans you care for every day.
Don't use my orphans to make your point, Reva. We're dancing around the larger issue here -- your Truthseer must've made a mistake.

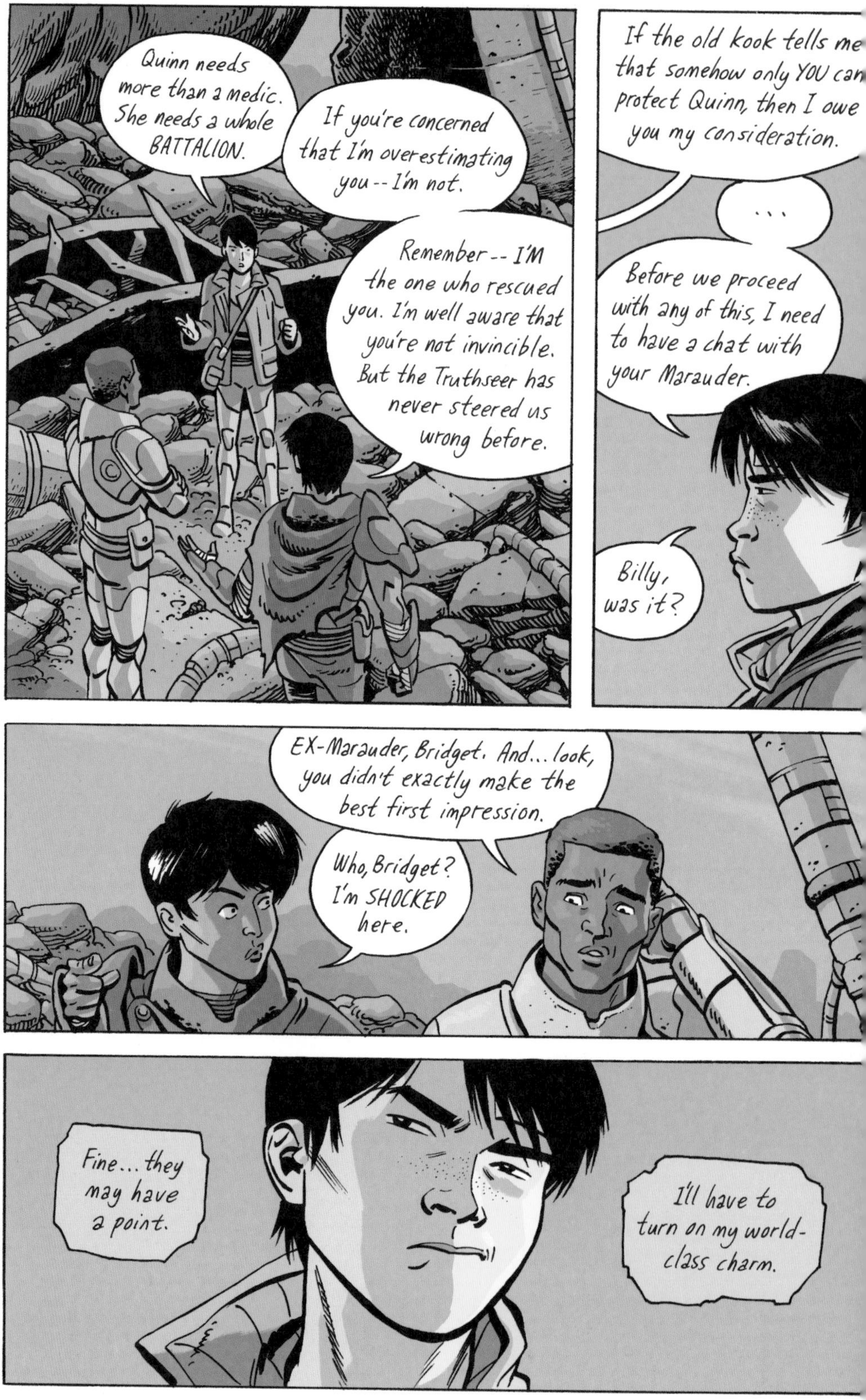
Quinn needs more than a medic. She needs a whole BATTALION.
If you're concerned that I'm overestimating you -- I'm not.
Remember -- I'M the one who rescued you. I'm well aware that you're not invincible. But the Truthseer has never steered us wrong before.
If the old kook tells me that somehow only YOU can protect Quinn, then I owe you my consideration.
...
Before we proceed with any of this, I need to have a chat with your Marauder.
Billy, was it?
EX-Marauder, Bridget. And... look, you didn't exactly make the best first impression.
Who, Bridget? I'm SHOCKED here.
Fine... they may have a point.
I'll have to turn on my world-class charm.

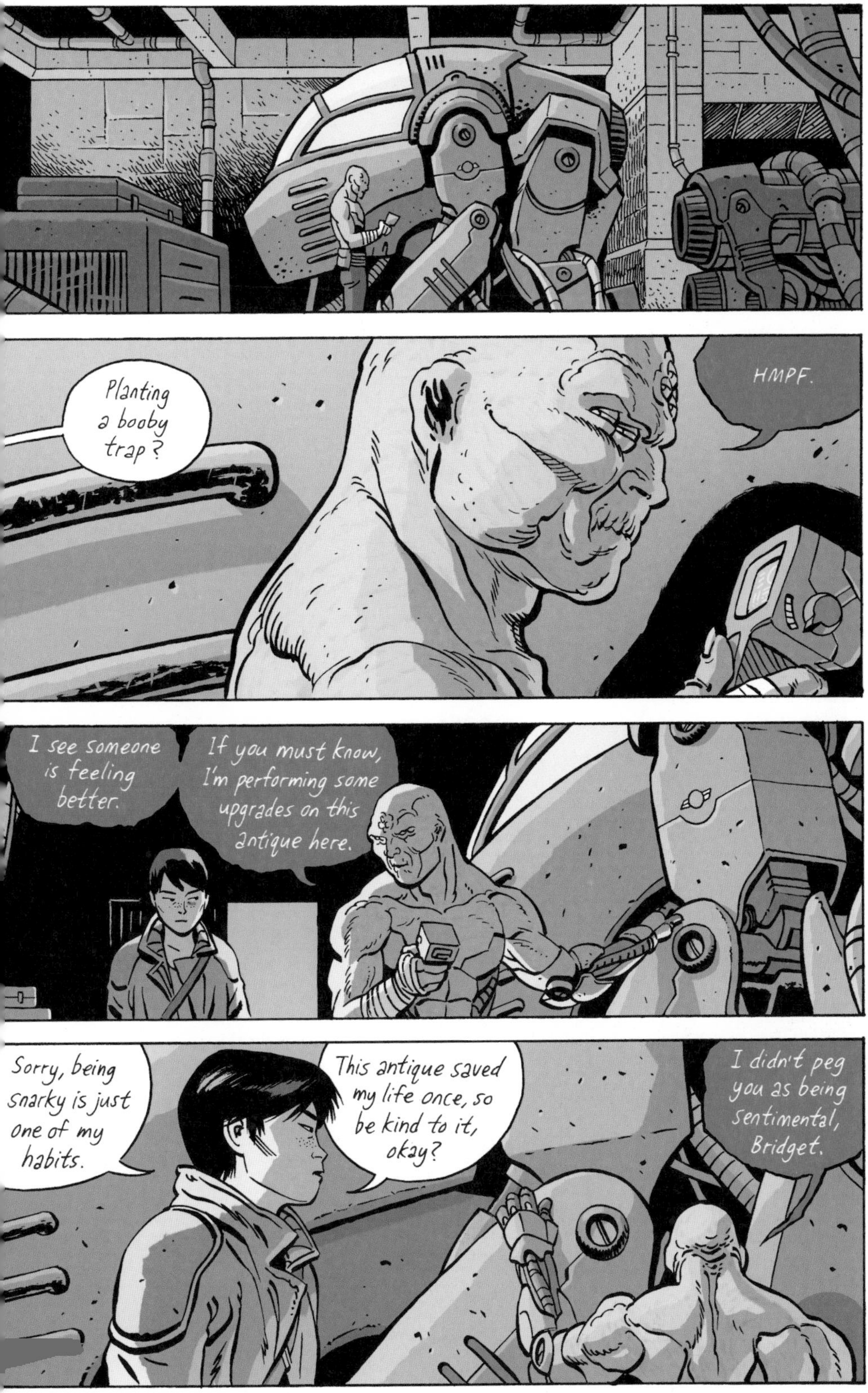
Planting a booby trap?
HMPF.
I see someone is feeling better.
If you must know, I'm performing some upgrades on this antique here.
Sorry, being snarky is just one of my habits.
This antique saved my life once, so be kind to it, okay?
I didn't peg you as being sentimental, Bridget.

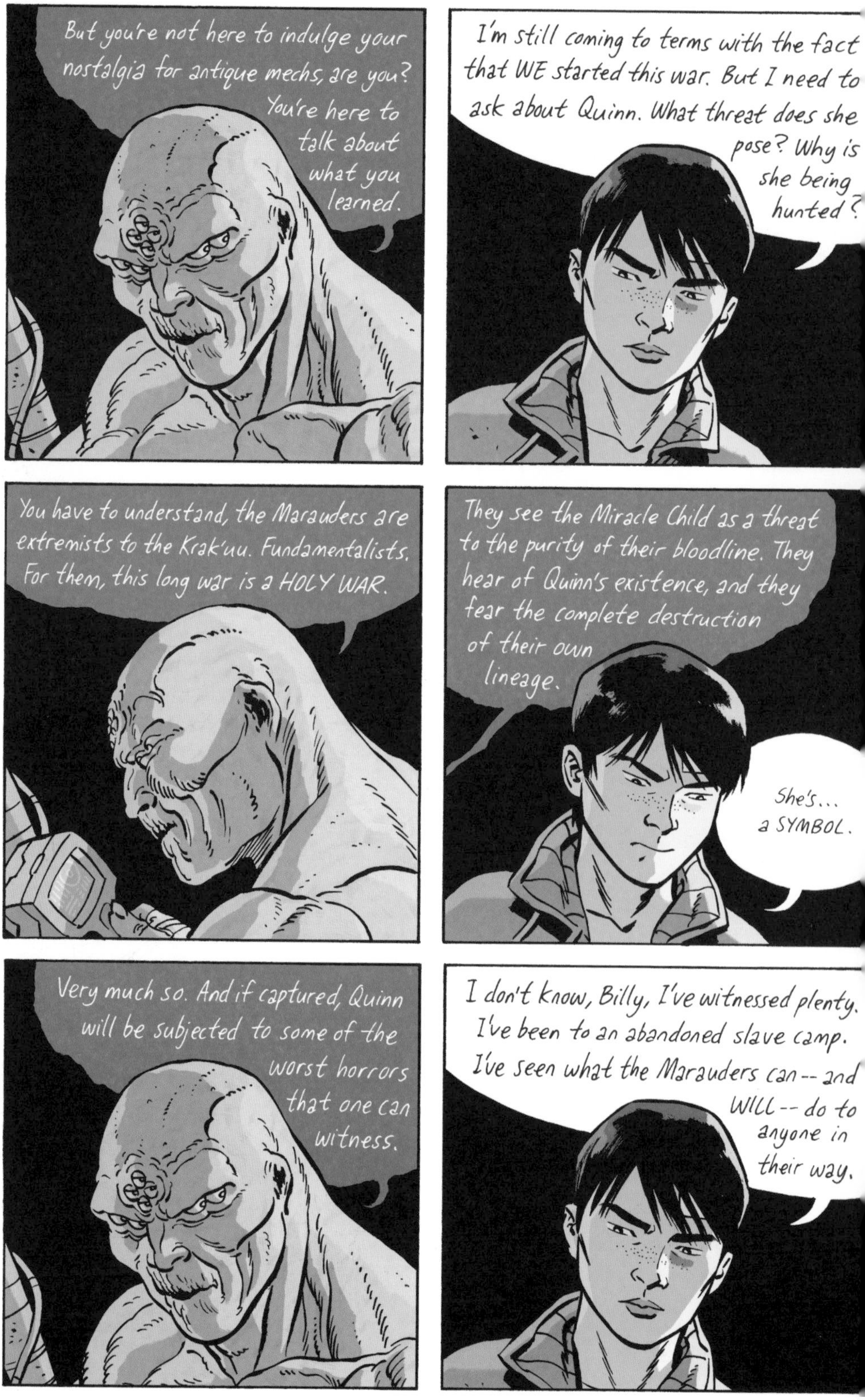
But you're not here to indulge your nostalgia for antique mechs, are you? You're here to talk about what you learned.
I'm still coming to terms with the fact that WE started this war. But I need to ask about Quinn. What threat does she pose? Why is she being hunted?
You have to understand, the Marauders are extremists to the Krak'uu. Fundamentalists. For them, this long war is a HOLY WAR.
They see the Miracle Child as a threat to the purity of their bloodline. They hear of Quinn's existence, and they fear the complete destruction of their own lineage.
She's... a SYMBOL.
Very much so. And if captured, Quinn will be subjected to some of the worst horrors that one can witness.
I don't know, Billy, I've witnessed plenty. I've been to an abandoned slave camp. I've seen what the Marauders can -- and WILL -- do to anyone in their way.

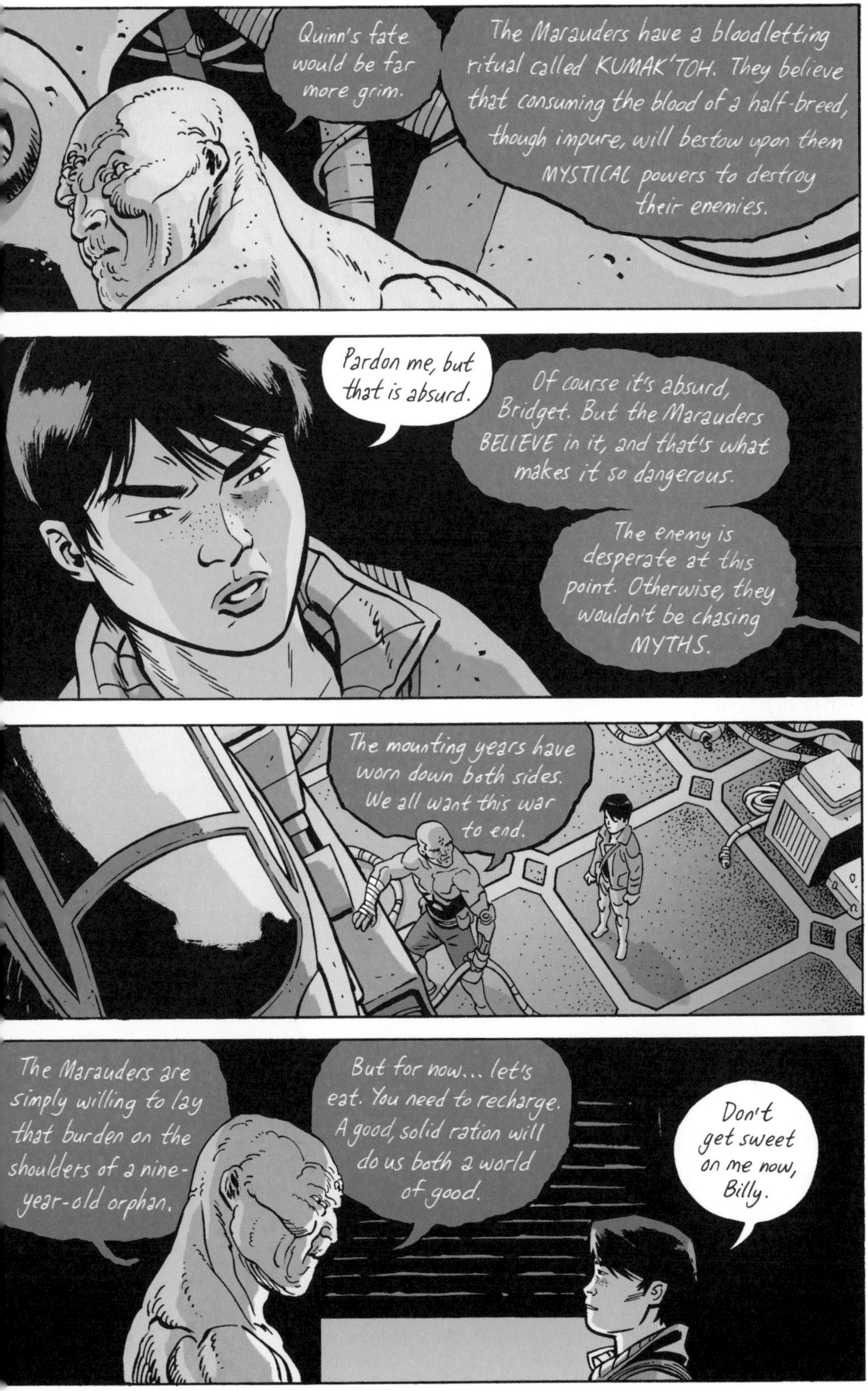
Quinn's fate would be far more grim.
The Marauders have a bloodletting ritual called KUMAK'TOH. They believe that consuming the blood of a half-breed, though impure, will bestow upon them MYSTICAL powers to destroy their enemies.
Pardon me, but that is absurd.
Of course it's absurd, Bridget. But the Marauders BELIEVE in it, and that's what makes it so dangerous.
The enemy is desperate at this point. Otherwise, they wouldn't be chasing MYTHS.
The mounting years have worn down both sides. We all want this war to end.
The Marauders are simply willing to lay that burden on the shoulders of a nine-year-old orphan.
But for now... let's eat. You need to recharge. A good, solid ration will do us both a world of good.
Don't get sweet on me now, Billy.

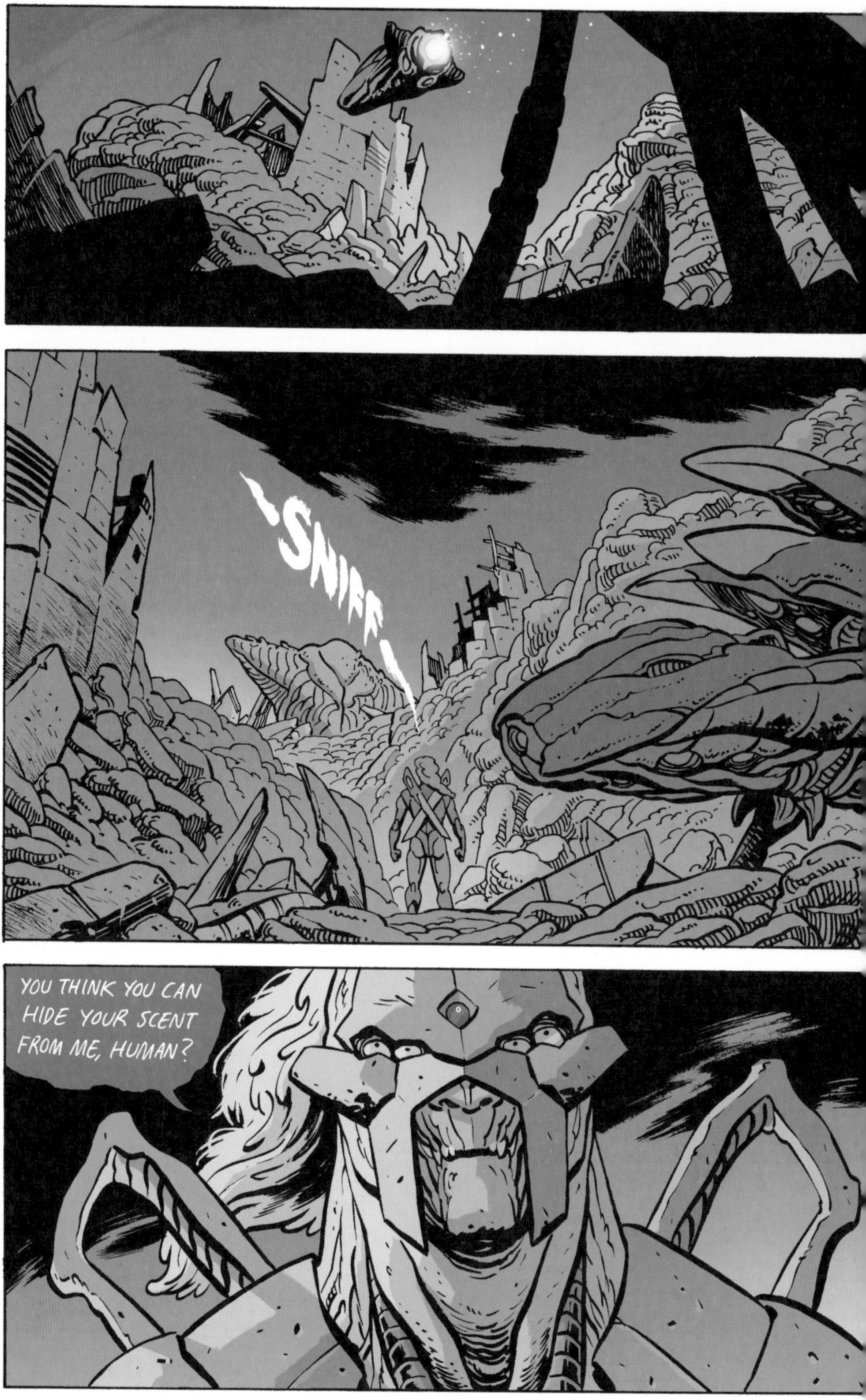
SNIFF
YOU THINK YOU CAN HIDE YOUR SCENT FROM ME, HUMAN?

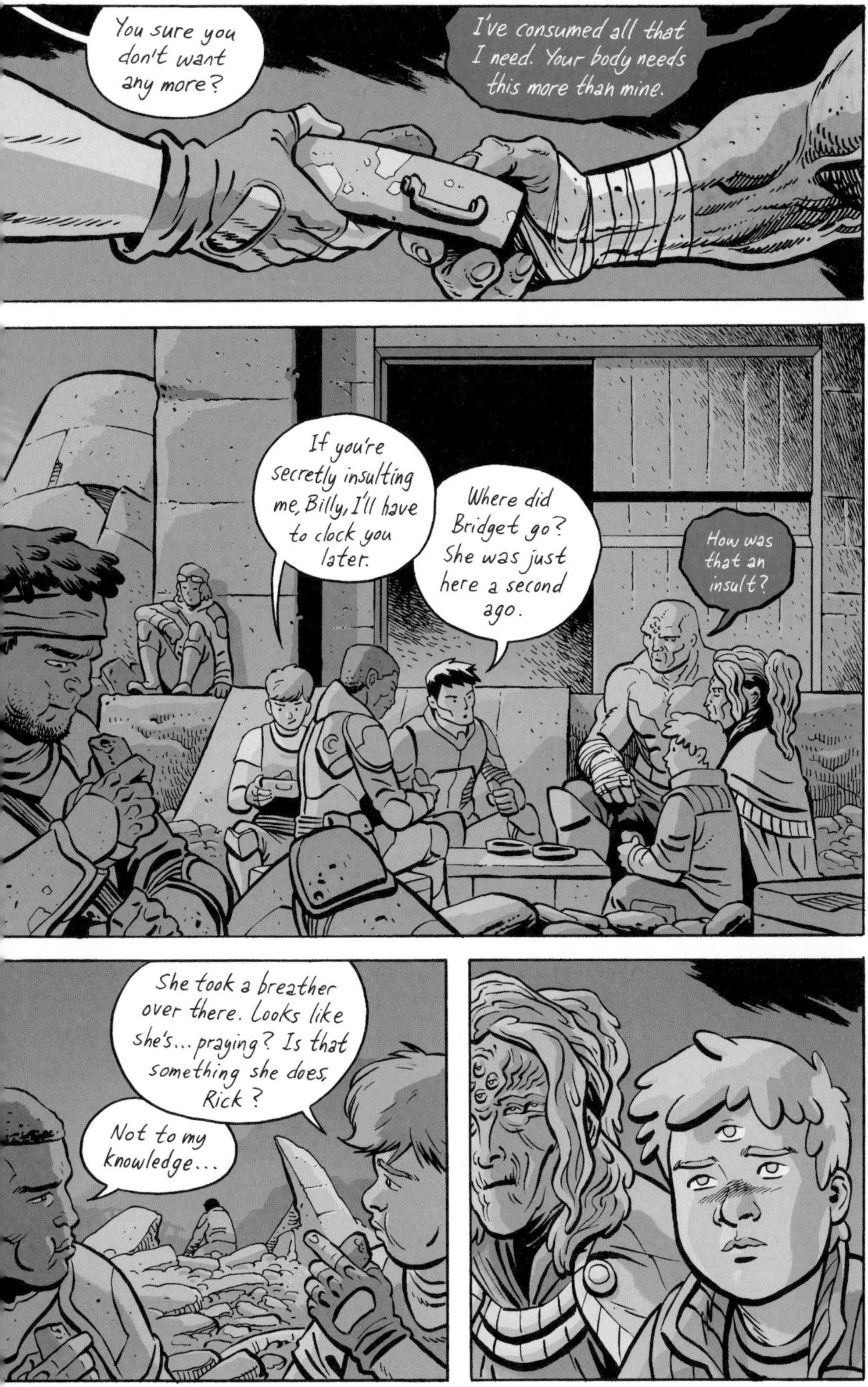
You sure you don't want any more?
I've consumed all that I need. Your body needs this more than mine.
If you're secretly insulting me, Billy, I'll have to clock you later.
Where did Bridget go? She was just here a second ago.
How was that an insult?
She took a breather over there. Looks like she's... praying? Is that something she does, Rick?
Not to my knowledge...

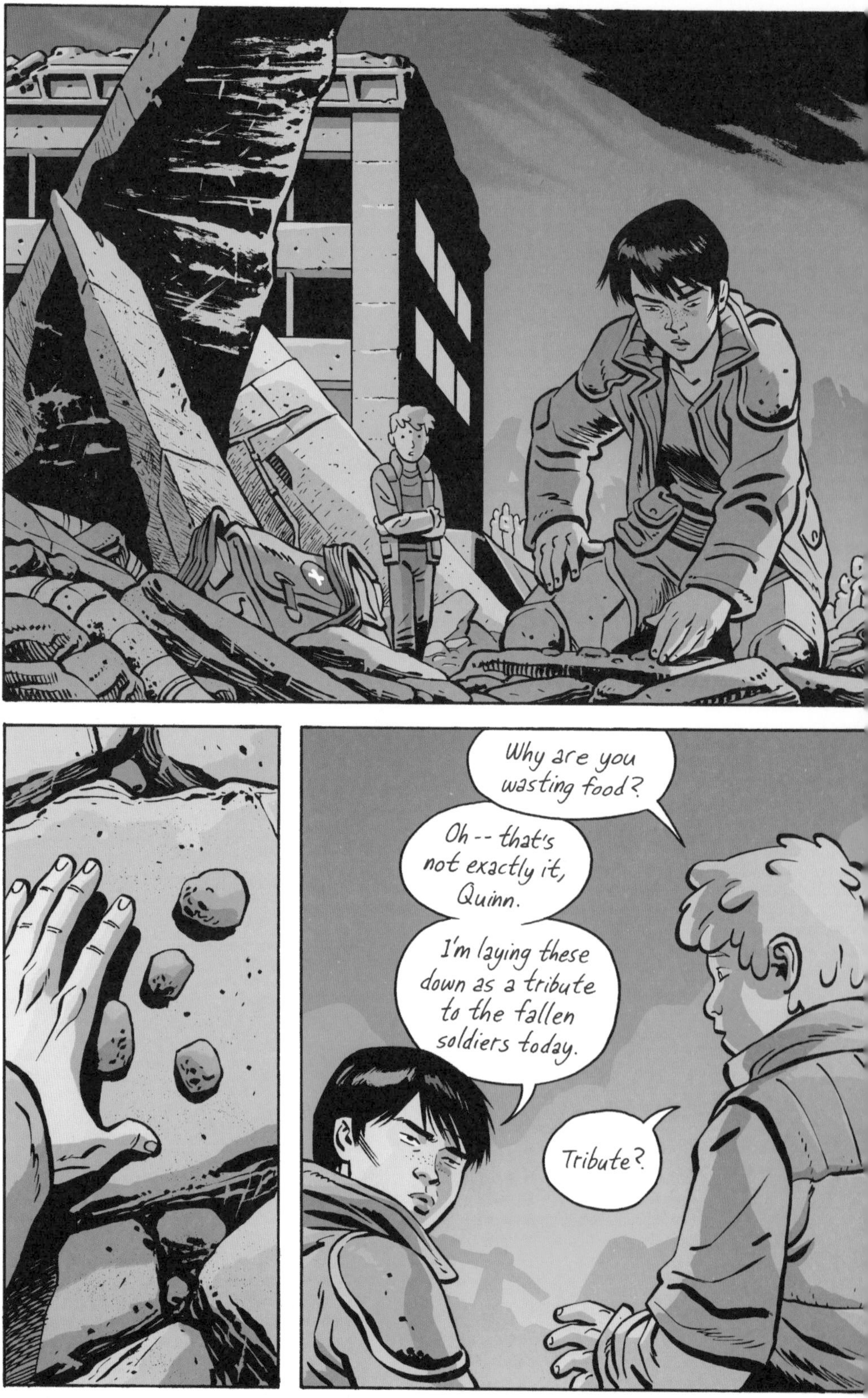
Why are you wasting food?
Oh -- that's not exactly it, Quinn.
I'm laying these down as a tribute to the fallen soldiers today.
Tribute?

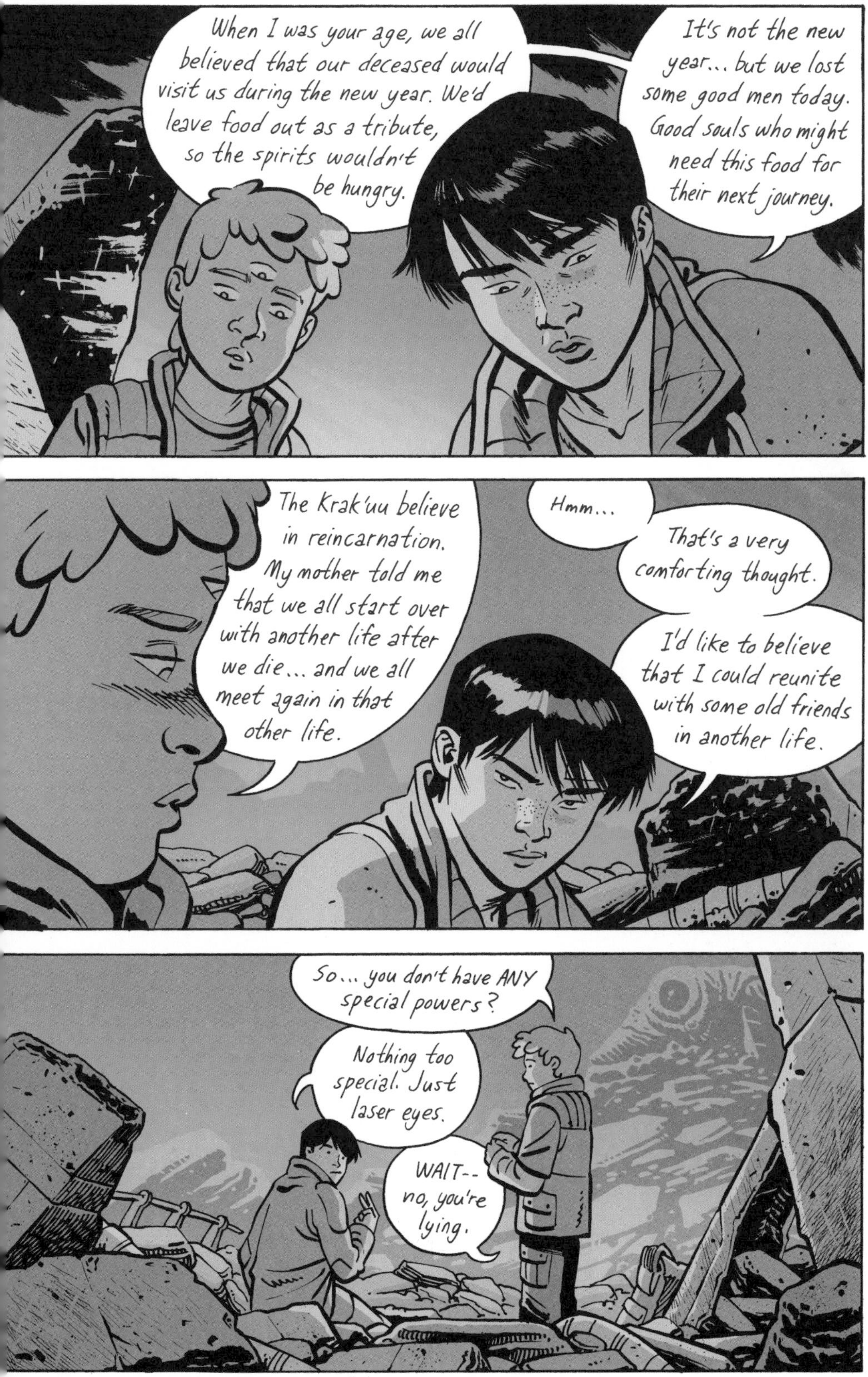
When I was your age, we all believed that our deceased would visit us during the new year. We'd leave food out as a tribute, so the spirits wouldn't be hungry.
It's not the new year... but we lost some good men today. Good souls who might need this food for their next journey.
The Krak'uu believe in reincarnation. My mother told me that we all start over with another life after we die... and we all meet again in that other life.
Hmm...
That's a very comforting thought.
I'd like to believe that I could reunite with some old friends in another life.
So... you don't have ANY special powers?
Nothing too special. Just laser eyes.
WAIT-- no, you're lying.

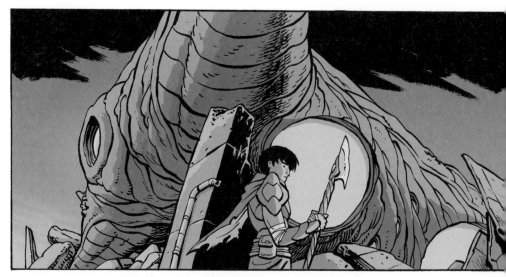

You can't go the entire night without a meal.

You're supposed to be resting, you old fool.

There will be plenty of time to rest later. You need to eat. I brought you a ration.

I can see that. Not hungry, though.

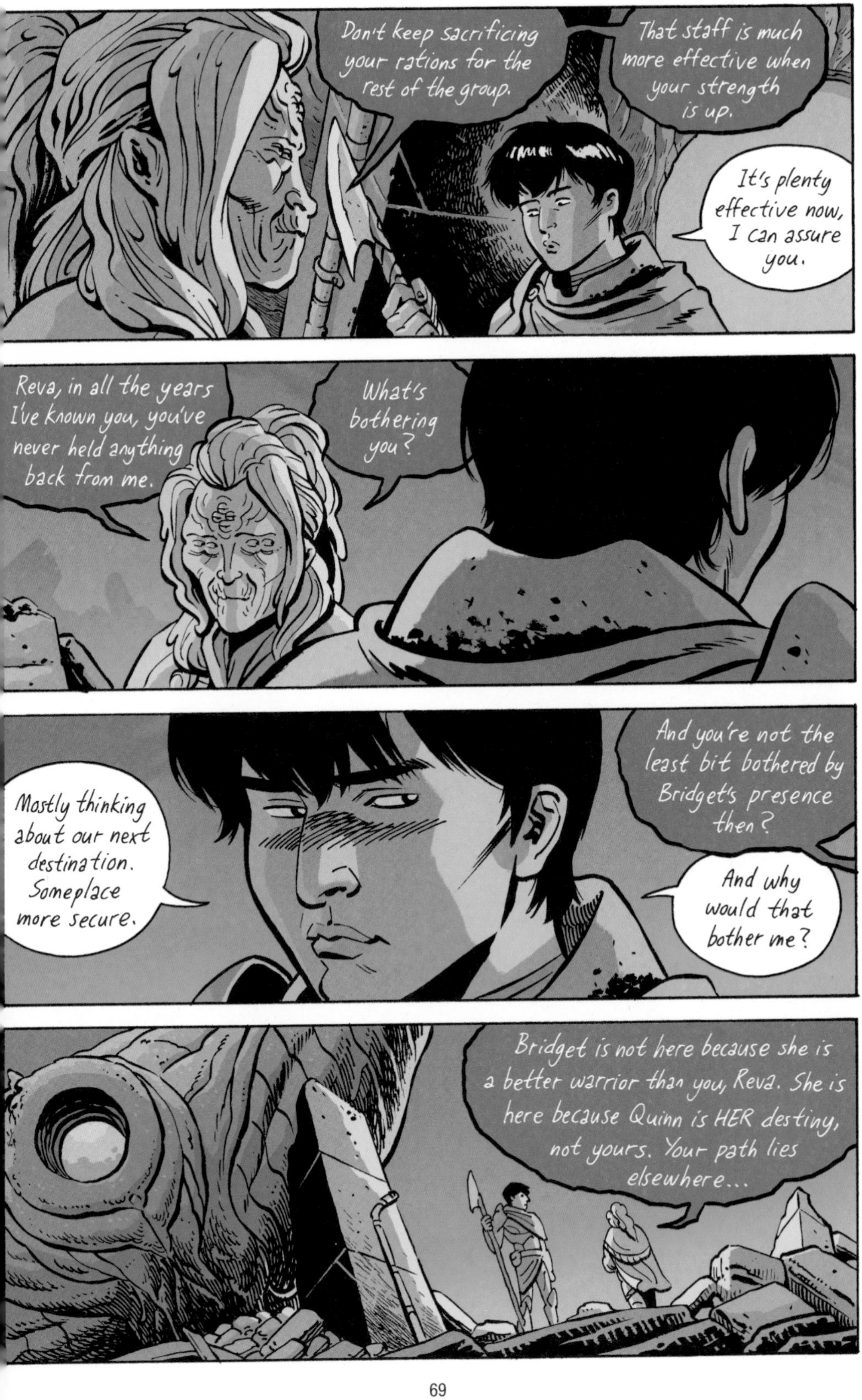

Don't keep sacrificing your rations for the rest of the group.
That staff is much more effective when your strength is up.
It's plenty effective now, I can assure you.
Reva, in all the years I've known you, you've never held anything back from me.
What's bothering you?
Mostly thinking about our next destination. Someplace more secure.
And you're not the least bit bothered by Bridget's presence then?
And why would that bother me?
Bridget is not here because she is a better warrior than you, Reva. She is here because Quinn is HER destiny, not yours. Your path lies elsewhere...

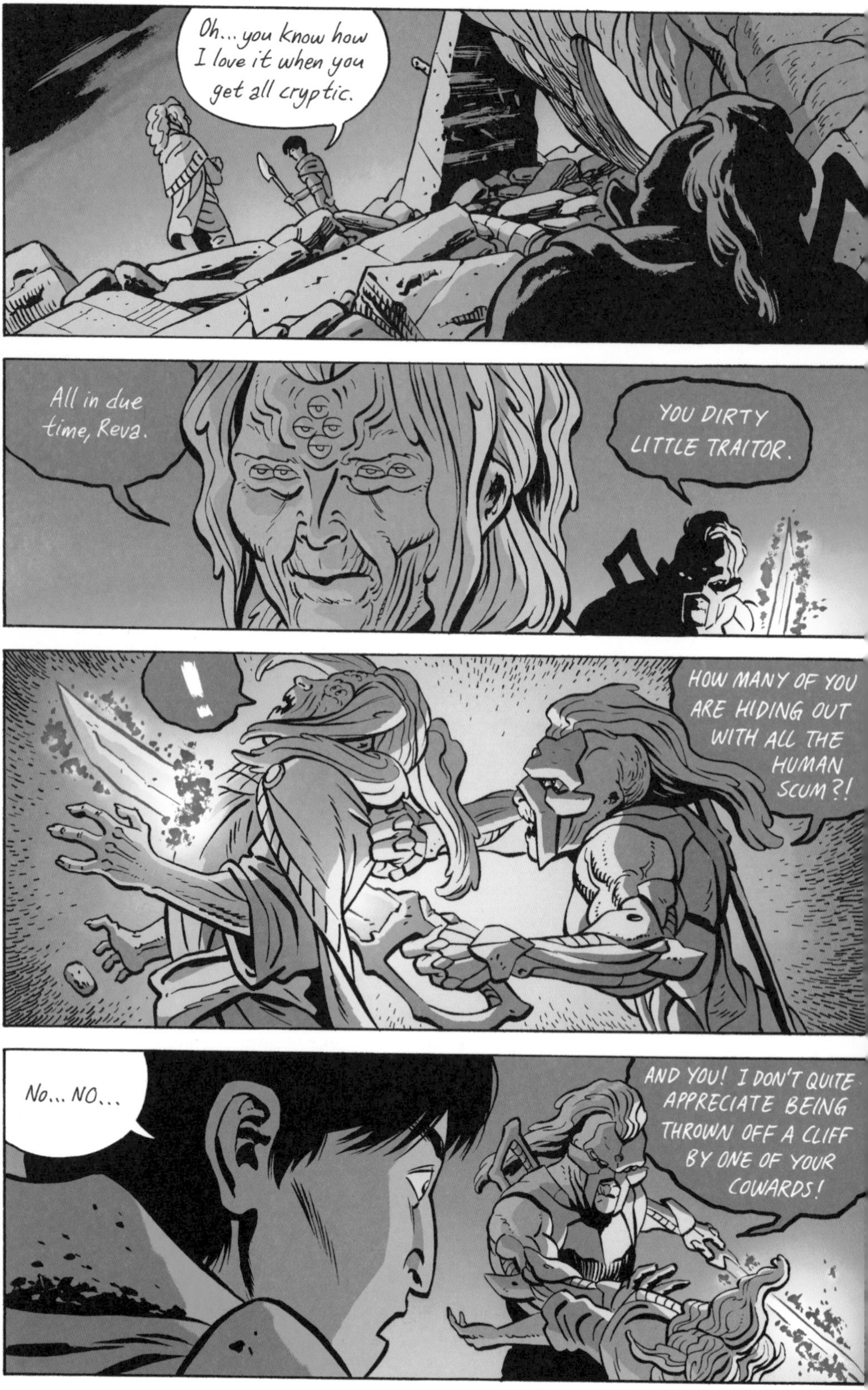
Oh... you know how I love it when you get all cryptic.
All in due time, Reva.
YOU DIRTY LITTLE TRAITOR.
!
HOW MANY OF YOU ARE HIDING OUT WITH ALL THE HUMAN SCUM?!
No... NO...
AND YOU! I DON'T QUITE APPRECIATE BEING THROWN OFF A CLIFF BY ONE OF YOUR COWARDS!

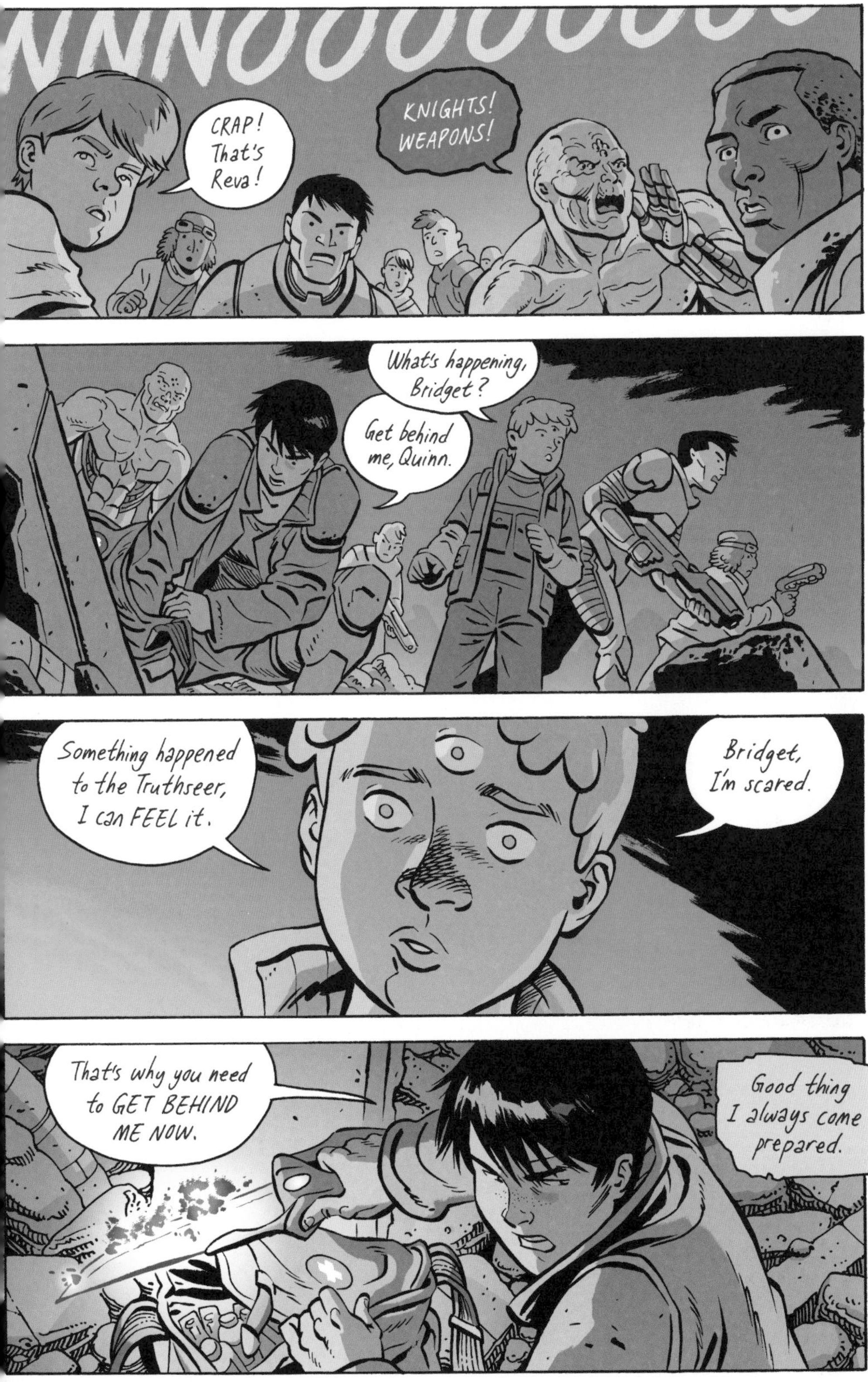
NNNOOOOOOOO
CRAP! That's Reva!
KNIGHTS! WEAPONS!
What's happening, Bridget?
Get behind me, Quinn.
Something happened to the Truthseer, I can FEEL it.
Bridget, I'm scared.
That's why you need to GET BEHIND ME NOW.
Good thing I always come prepared.

I'LL MAKE QUICK WORK OF YOU BEFORE I SLICE UP THAT MEDIC!

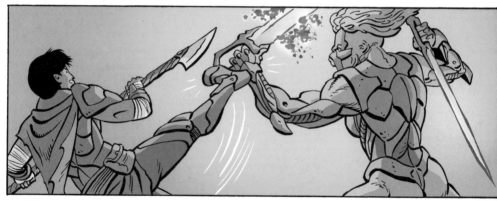

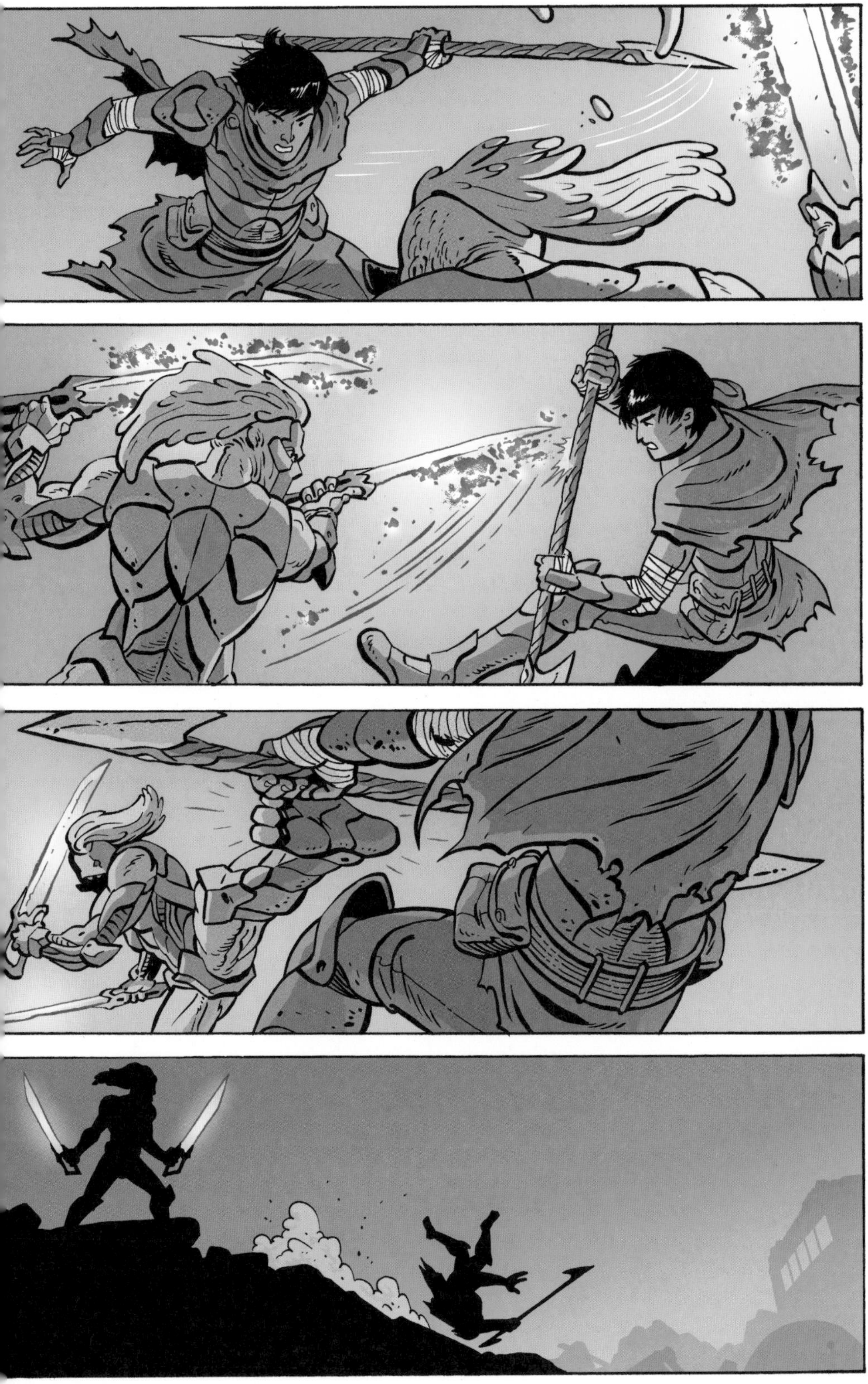

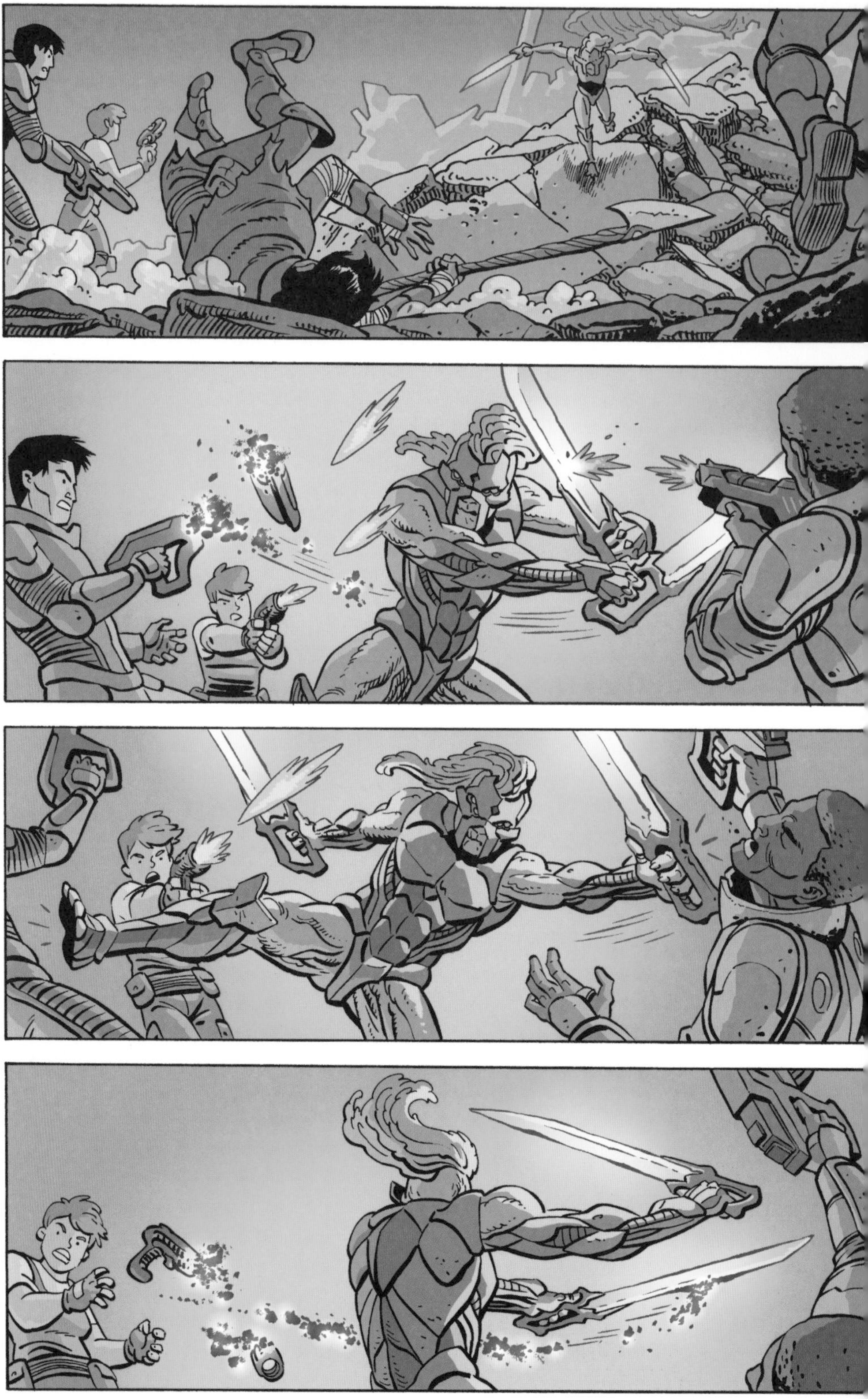

THAT'S ENOUGH!

AH--

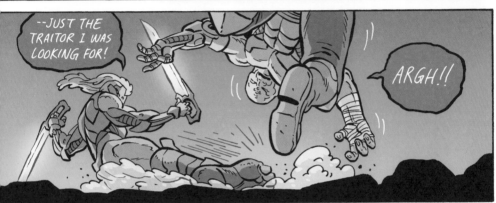

--JUST THE TRAITOR I WAS LOOKING FOR!

ARGH!!

I OWE YOU A WORLD OF PAIN...

...AND I KNOW JUST WHERE TO START!

So do I.

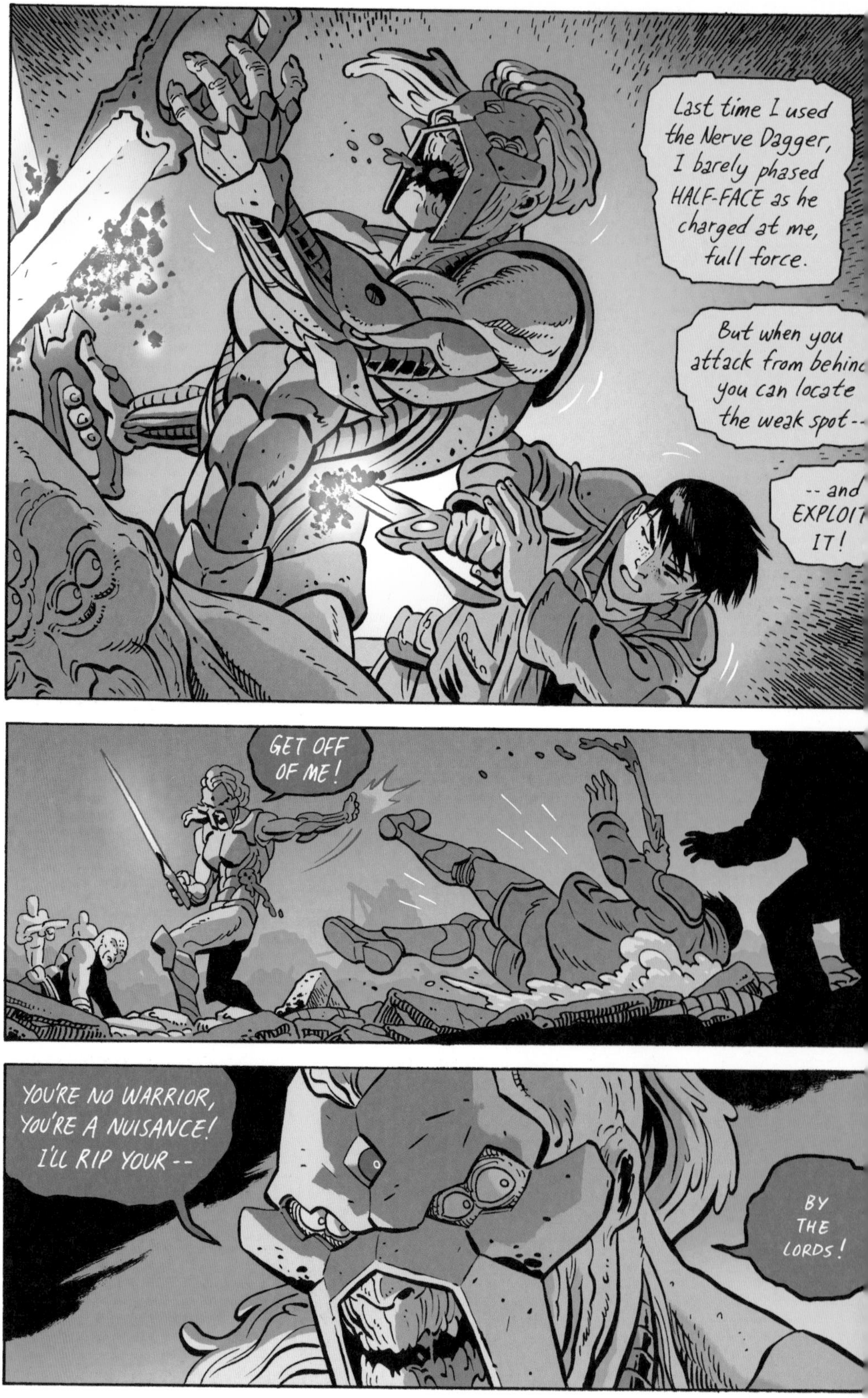
Last time I used the Nerve Dagger, I barely phased HALF-FACE as he charged at me, full force.
But when you attack from behin
you can locate the weak spot --
-- and EXPLOIT IT!
GET OFF OF ME!
YOU'RE NO WARRIOR, YOU'RE A NUISANCE! I'LL RIP YOUR --
BY THE LORDS!

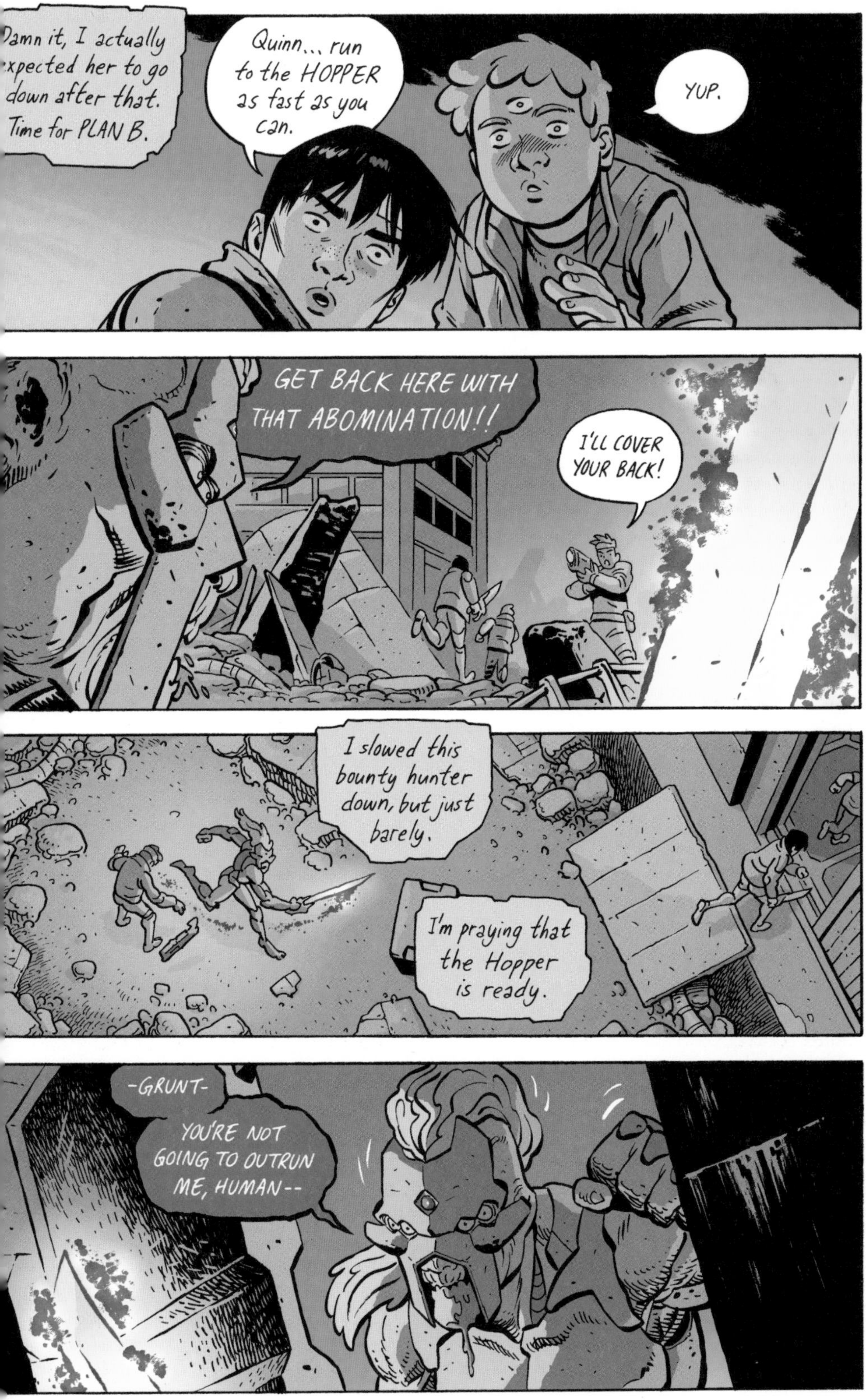
Damn it, I actually expected her to go down after that. Time for PLAN B.
Quinn... run to the HOPPER as fast as you can.
YUP.
GET BACK HERE WITH THAT ABOMINATION!!
I'LL COVER YOUR BACK!
I slowed this bounty hunter down, but just barely.
I'm praying that the Hopper is ready.
-GRUNT-
YOU'RE NOT GOING TO OUTRUN ME, HUMAN--

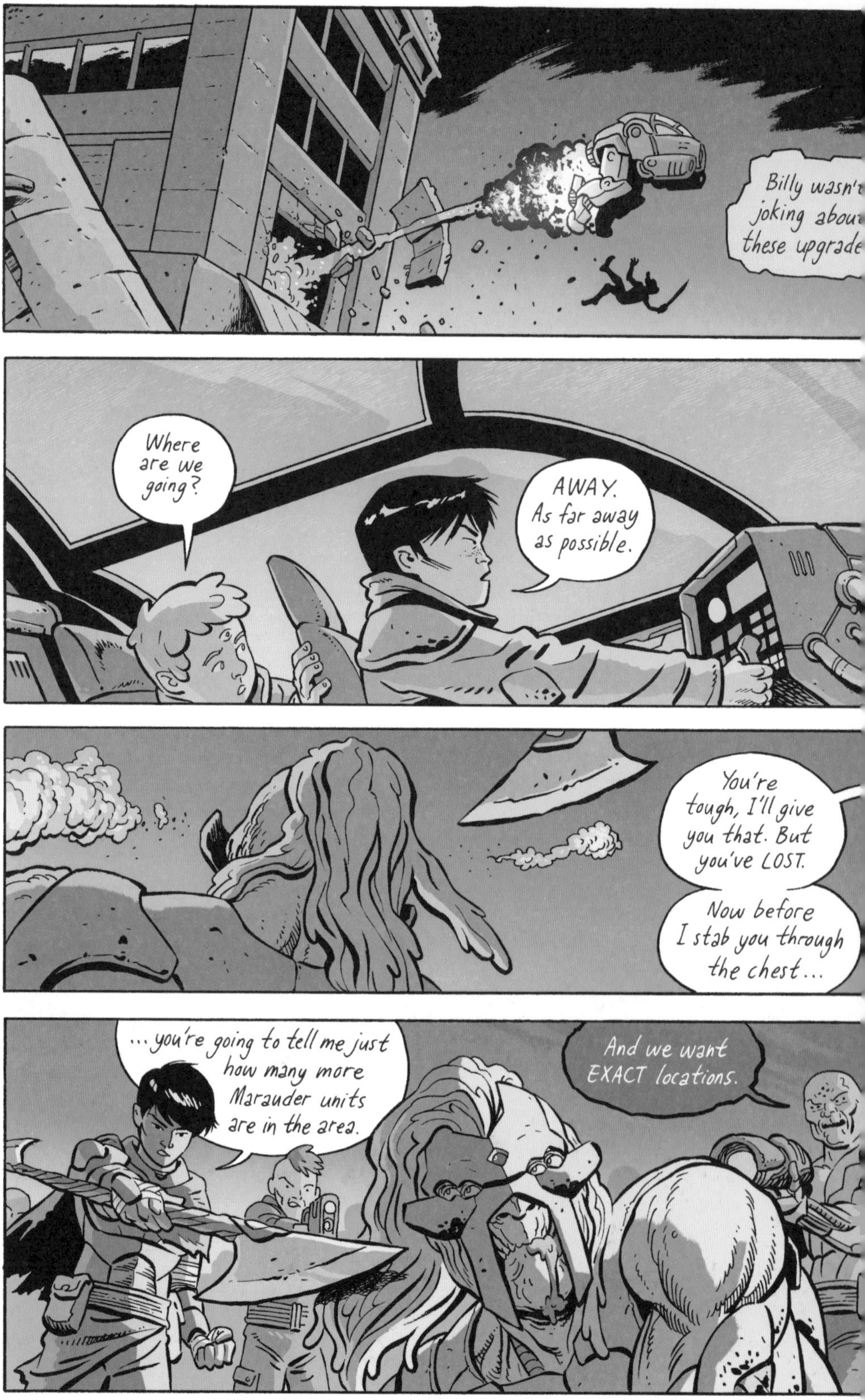
Billy wasn't joking about these upgrade
Where are we going?
AWAY. As far away as possible.
You're tough, I'll give you that. But you've LOST.
Now before I stab you through the chest...
...you're going to tell me just how many more Marauder units are in the area.
And we want EXACT locations.

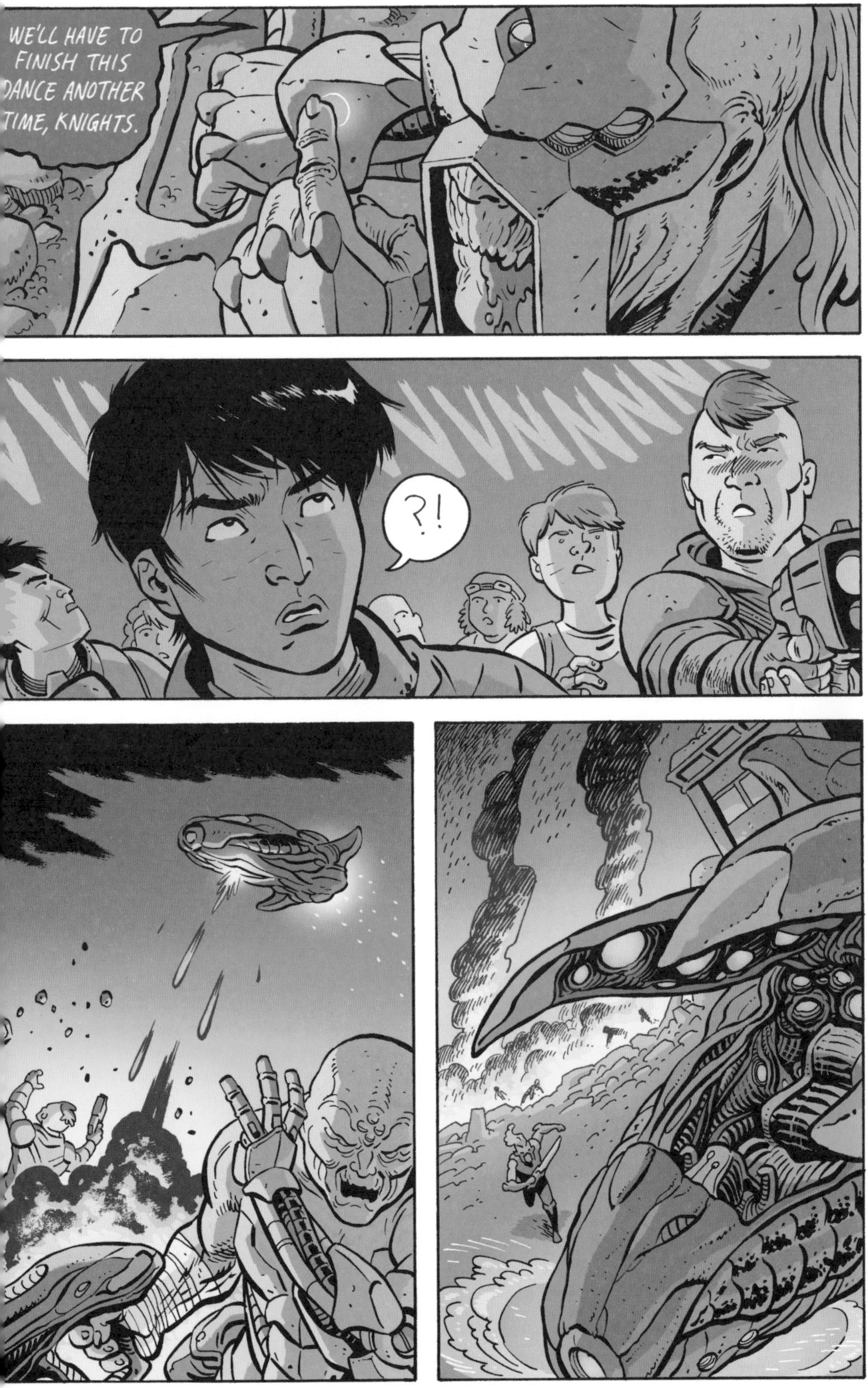
WE'LL HAVE TO FINISH THIS DANCE ANOTHER TIME, KNIGHTS.
VVNNNN
?!

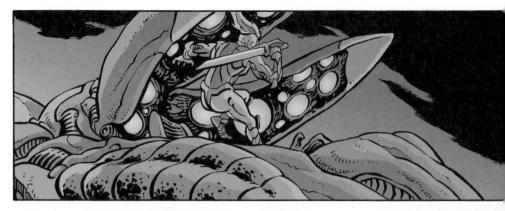

DREK, YOU WON'T BELIEVE WHO I'VE LOCATED...

Bridget... don't you dare give up on Quinn.

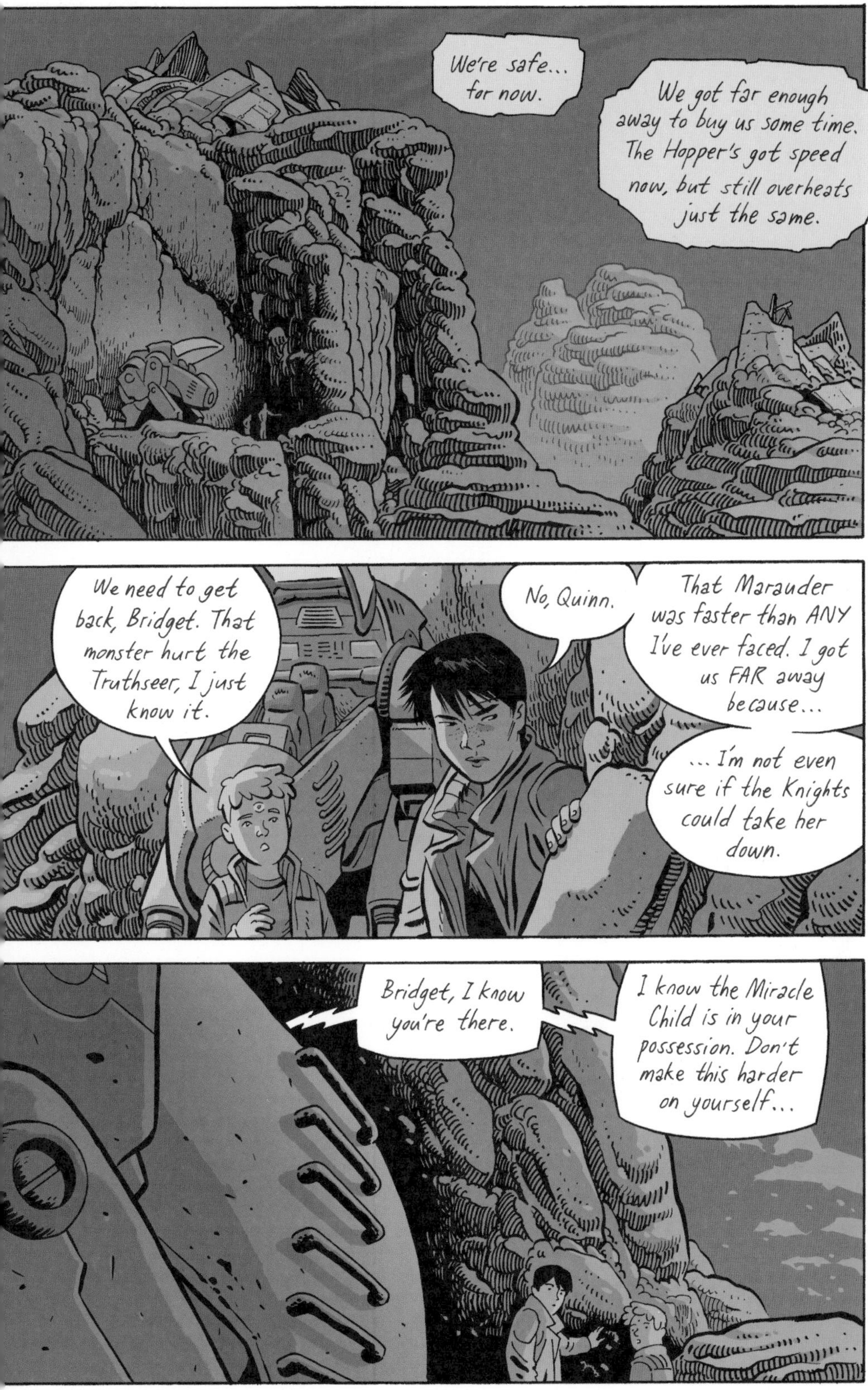
We're safe... for now.
We got far enough away to buy us some time. The Hopper's got speed now, but still overheats just the same.
We need to get back, Bridget. That monster hurt the Truthseer, I just know it.
No, Quinn.
That Marauder was faster than ANY I've ever faced. I got us FAR away because...
...I'm not even sure if the Knights could take her down.
Bridget, I know you're there.
I know the Miracle Child is in your possession. Don't make this harder on yourself...

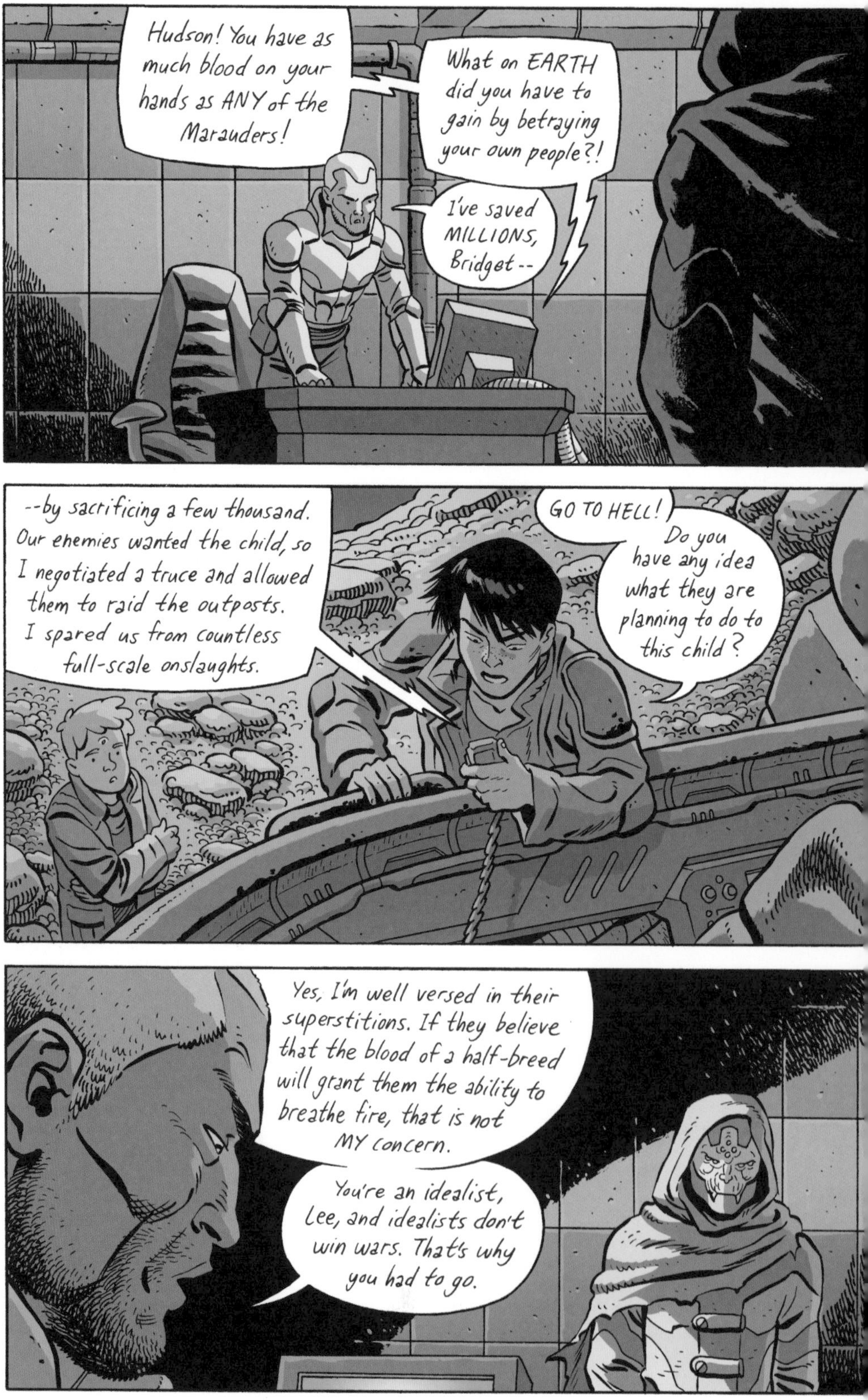
Hudson! You have as much blood on your hands as ANY of the Marauders!
What on EARTH did you have to gain by betraying your own people?!
I've saved MILLIONS, Bridget --
--by sacrificing a few thousand. Our enemies wanted the child, so I negotiated a truce and allowed them to raid the outposts. I spared us from countless full-scale onslaughts.
GO TO HELL!
Do you have any idea what they are planning to do to this child?
Yes, I'm well versed in their superstitions. If they believe that the blood of a half-breed will grant them the ability to breathe fire, that is not MY concern.
You're an idealist, Lee, and idealists don't win wars. That's why you had to go.

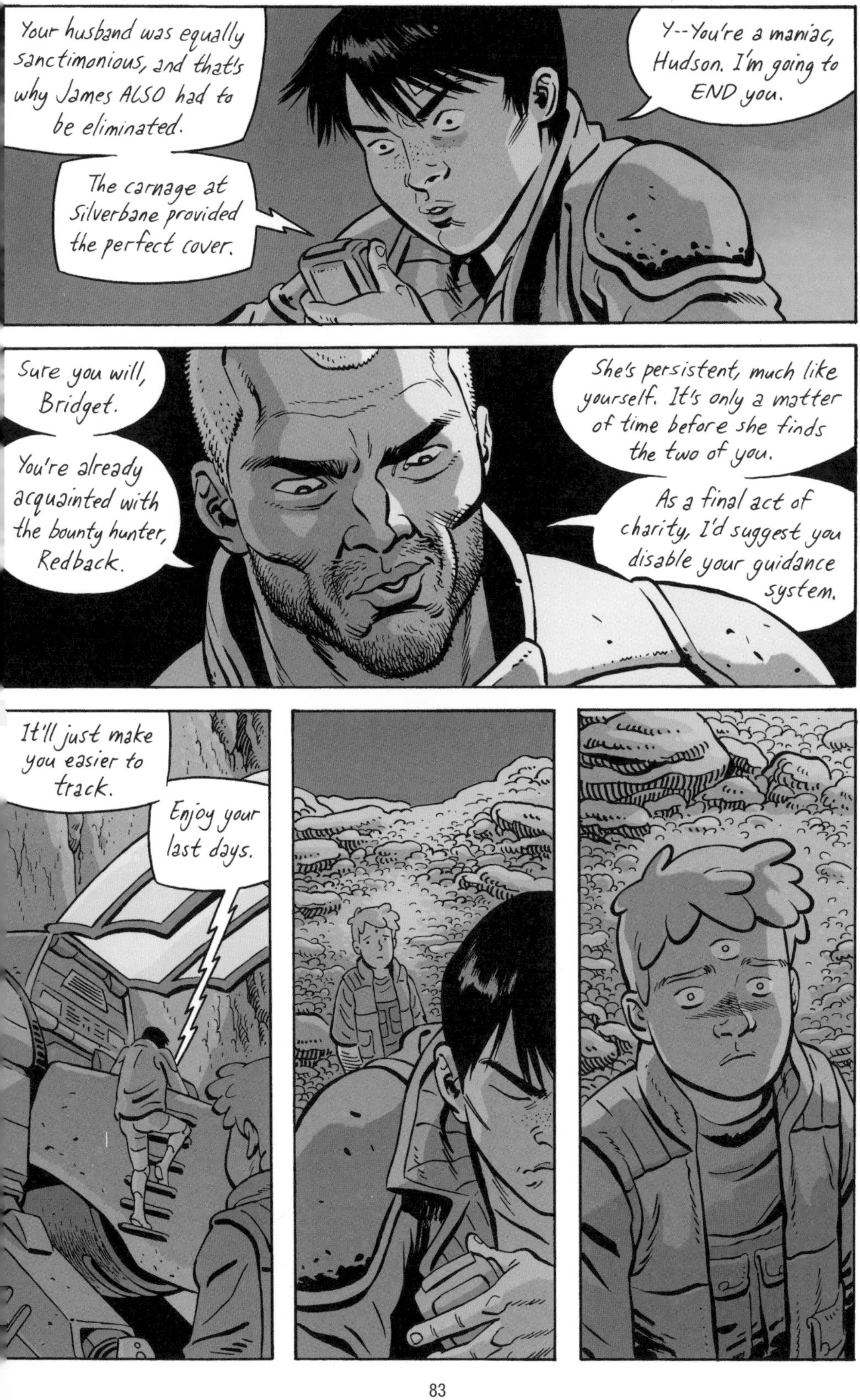
Your husband was equally sanctimonious, and that's why James ALSO had to be eliminated.
The carnage at Silverbane provided the perfect cover.
Y--You're a maniac, Hudson. I'm going to END you.
Sure you will, Bridget.
You're already acquainted with the bounty hunter, Redback.
She's persistent, much like yourself. It's only a matter of time before she finds the two of you.
As a final act of charity, I'd suggest you disable your guidance system.
It'll just make you easier to track.
Enjoy your last days.

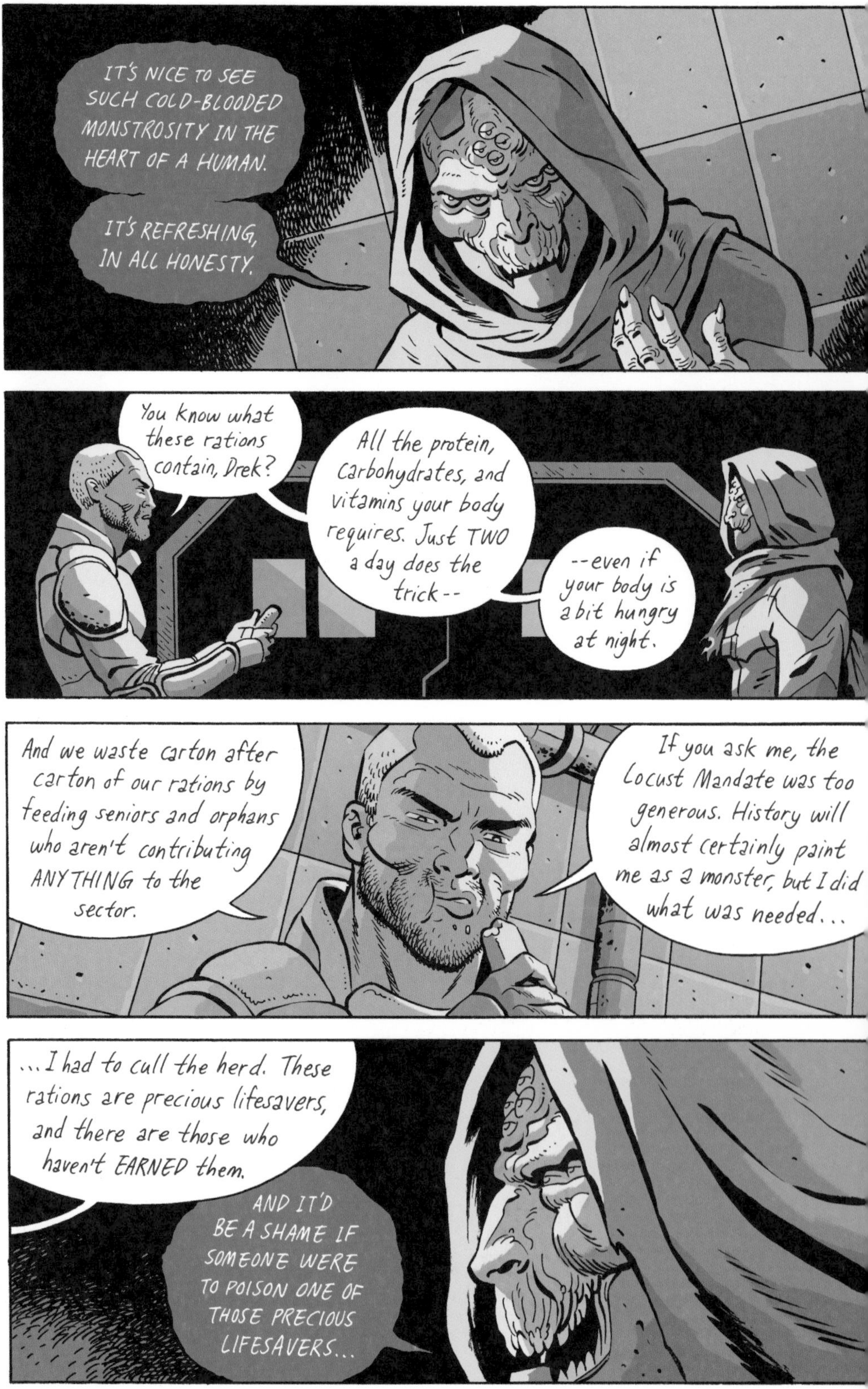
IT'S NICE TO SEE SUCH COLD-BLOODED MONSTROSITY IN THE HEART OF A HUMAN.
IT'S REFRESHING, IN ALL HONESTY.
You know what these rations contain, Drek?
All the protein, carbohydrates, and vitamins your body requires. Just TWO a day does the trick--
--even if your body is a bit hungry at night.
And we waste carton after carton of our rations by feeding seniors and orphans who aren't contributing ANYTHING to the sector.
If you ask me, the Locust Mandate was too generous. History will almost certainly paint me as a monster, but I did what was needed...
...I had to cull the herd. These rations are precious lifesavers, and there are those who haven't EARNED them.
AND IT'D BE A SHAME IF SOMEONE WERE TO POISON ONE OF THOSE PRECIOUS LIFESAVERS...

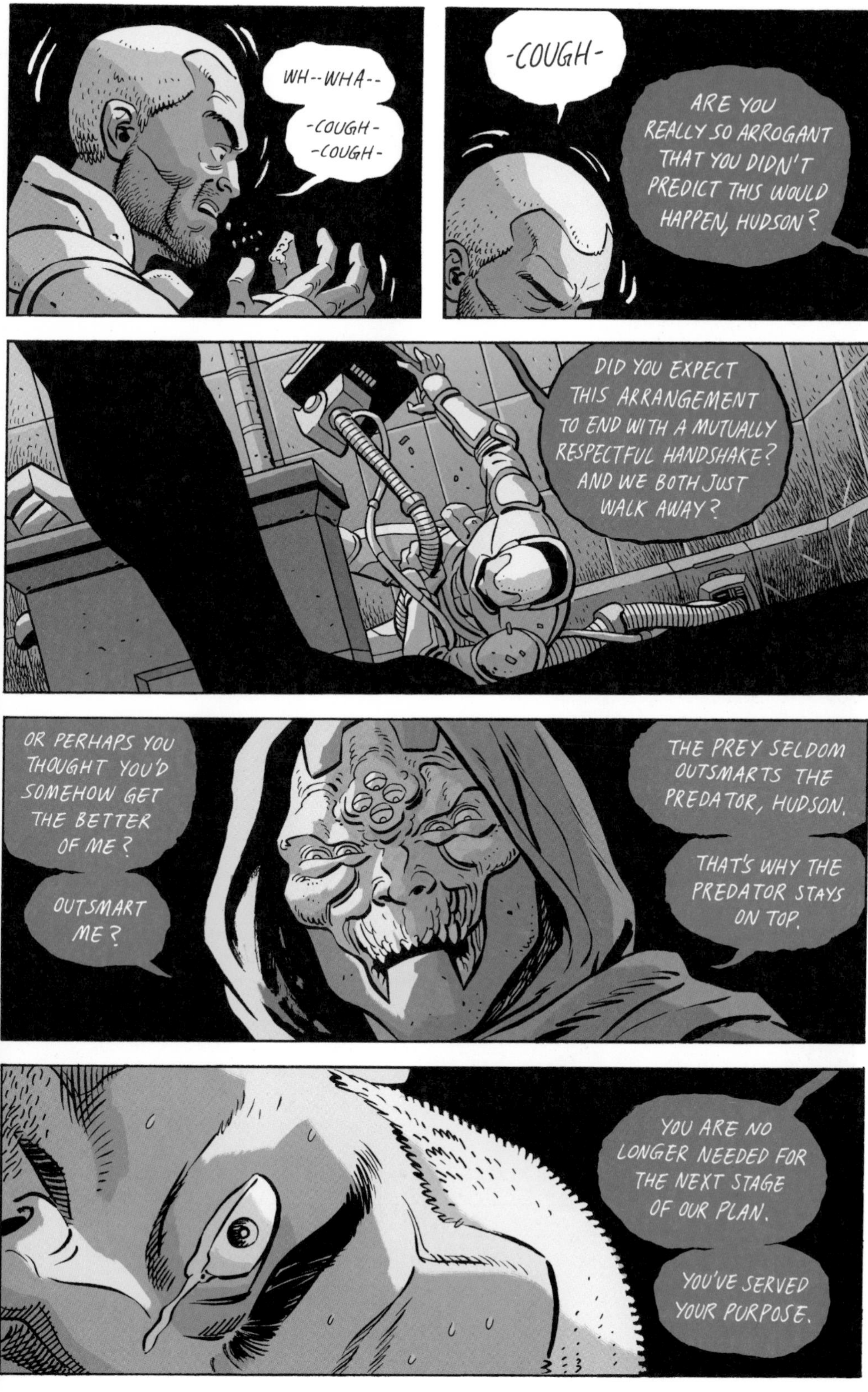
WH--WHA--
-COUGH-
-COUGH-
-COUGH-
ARE YOU REALLY SO ARROGANT THAT YOU DIDN'T PREDICT THIS WOULD HAPPEN, HUDSON?
DID YOU EXPECT THIS ARRANGEMENT TO END WITH A MUTUALLY RESPECTFUL HANDSHAKE? AND WE BOTH JUST WALK AWAY?
OR PERHAPS YOU THOUGHT YOU'D SOMEHOW GET THE BETTER OF ME?
OUTSMART ME?
THE PREY SELDOM OUTSMARTS THE PREDATOR, HUDSON.
THAT'S WHY THE PREDATOR STAYS ON TOP.
YOU ARE NO LONGER NEEDED FOR THE NEXT STAGE OF OUR PLAN.
YOU'VE SERVED YOUR PURPOSE.

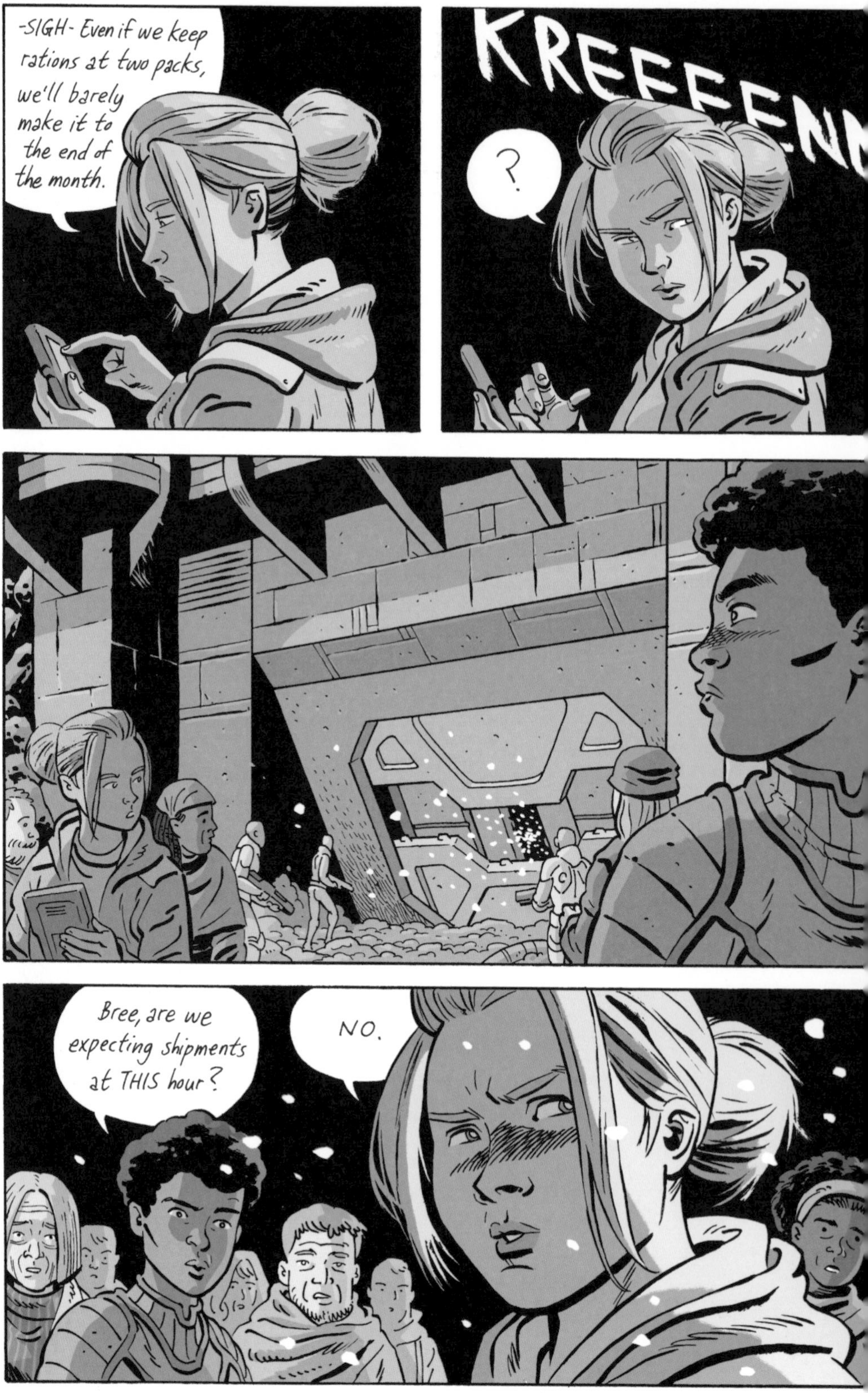
-SIGH- Even if we keep rations at two packs, we'll barely make it to the end of the month.
KREEEENN
?
Bree, are we expecting shipments at THIS hour?
NO.

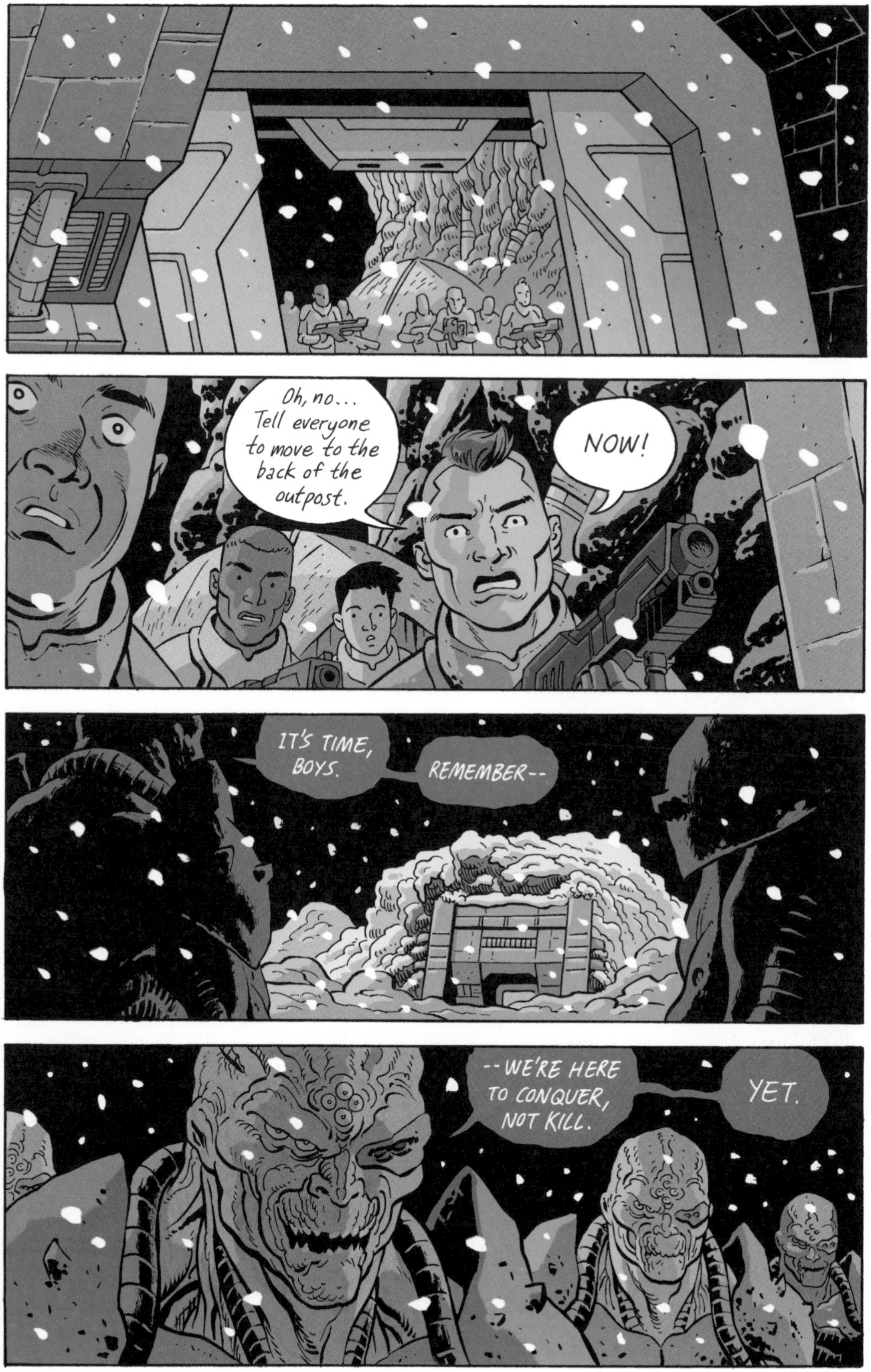
Oh, no... Tell everyone to move to the back of the outpost.
NOW!
IT'S TIME, BOYS.
REMEMBER--
--WE'RE HERE TO CONQUER, NOT KILL.
YET.

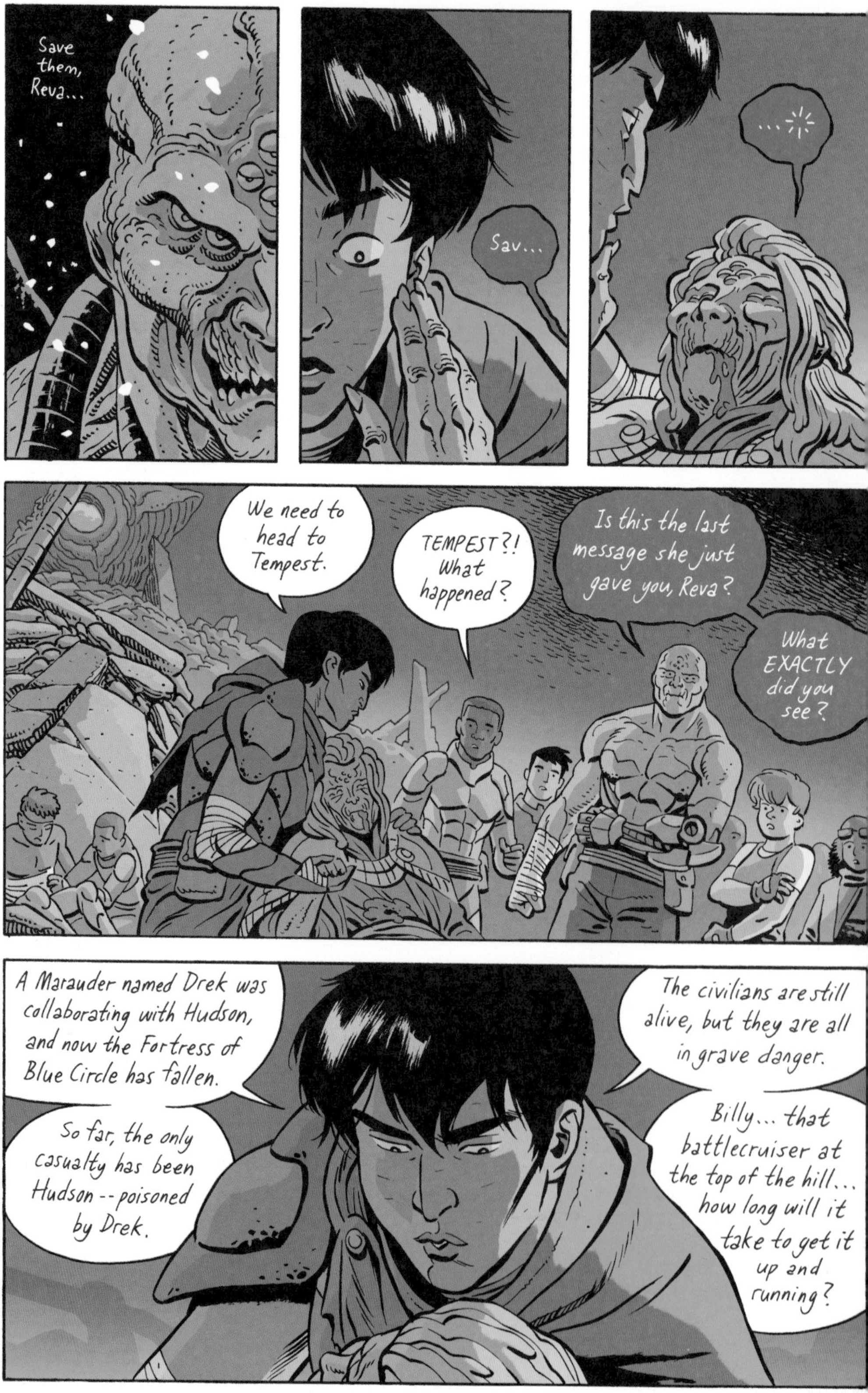
Save them, Reva...
Sav...
...!
We need to head to Tempest.
TEMPEST?! What happened?
Is this the last message she just gave you, Reva?
What EXACTLY did you see?
A Marauder named Drek was collaborating with Hudson, and now the Fortress of Blue Circle has fallen.
So far, the only casualty has been Hudson -- poisoned by Drek.
The civilians are still alive, but they are all in grave danger.
Billy... that battlecruiser at the top of the hill... how long will it take to get it up and running?

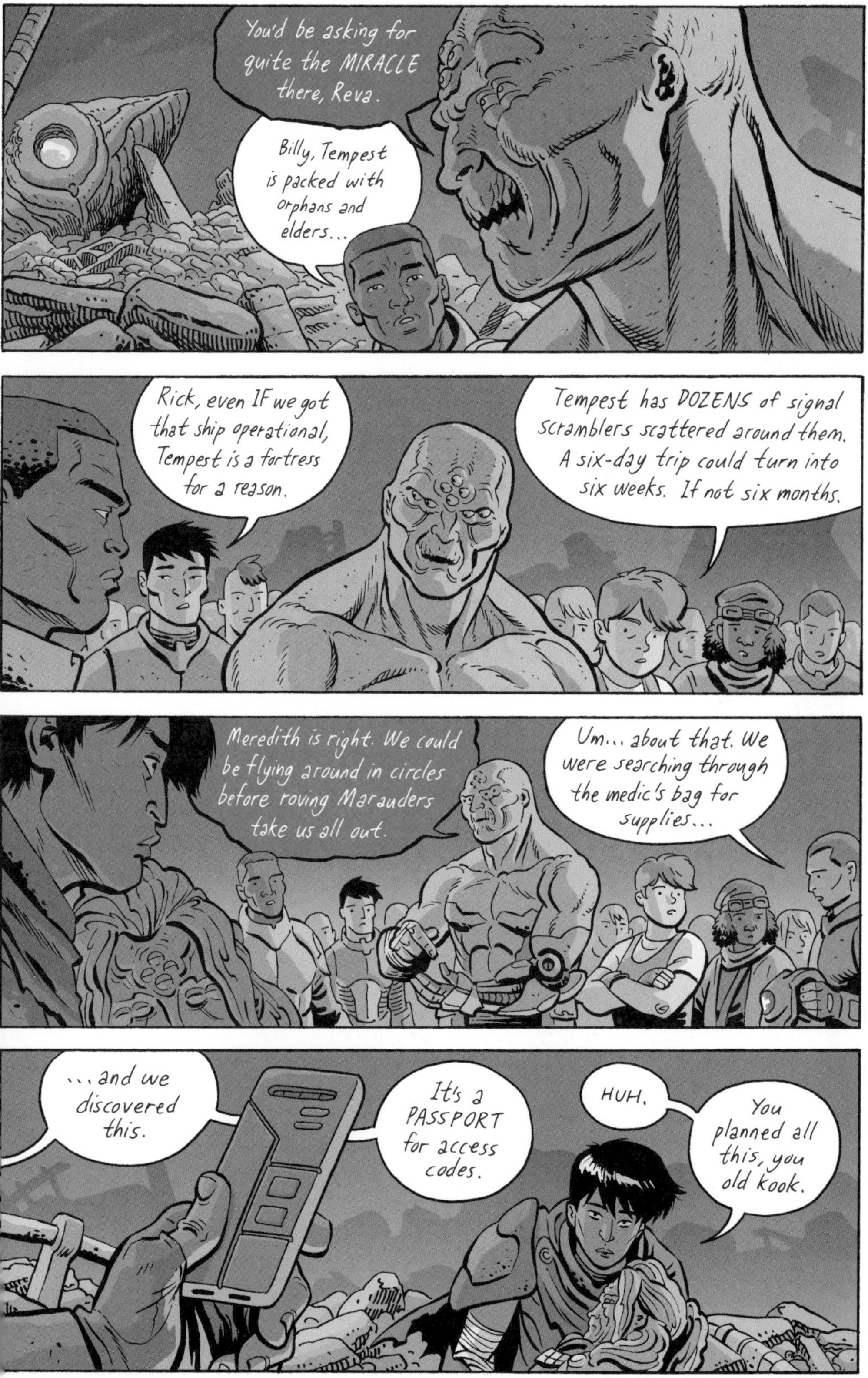
You'd be asking for quite the MIRACLE there, Reva.
Billy, Tempest is packed with orphans and elders...
Rick, even IF we got that ship operational, Tempest is a fortress for a reason.
Tempest has DOZENS of signal scramblers scattered around them. A six-day trip could turn into six weeks. If not six months.
Meredith is right. We could be flying around in circles before roving Marauders take us all out.
Um... about that. We were searching through the medic's bag for supplies...
...and we discovered this.
It's a PASSPORT for access codes.
HUH.
You planned all this, you old kook.

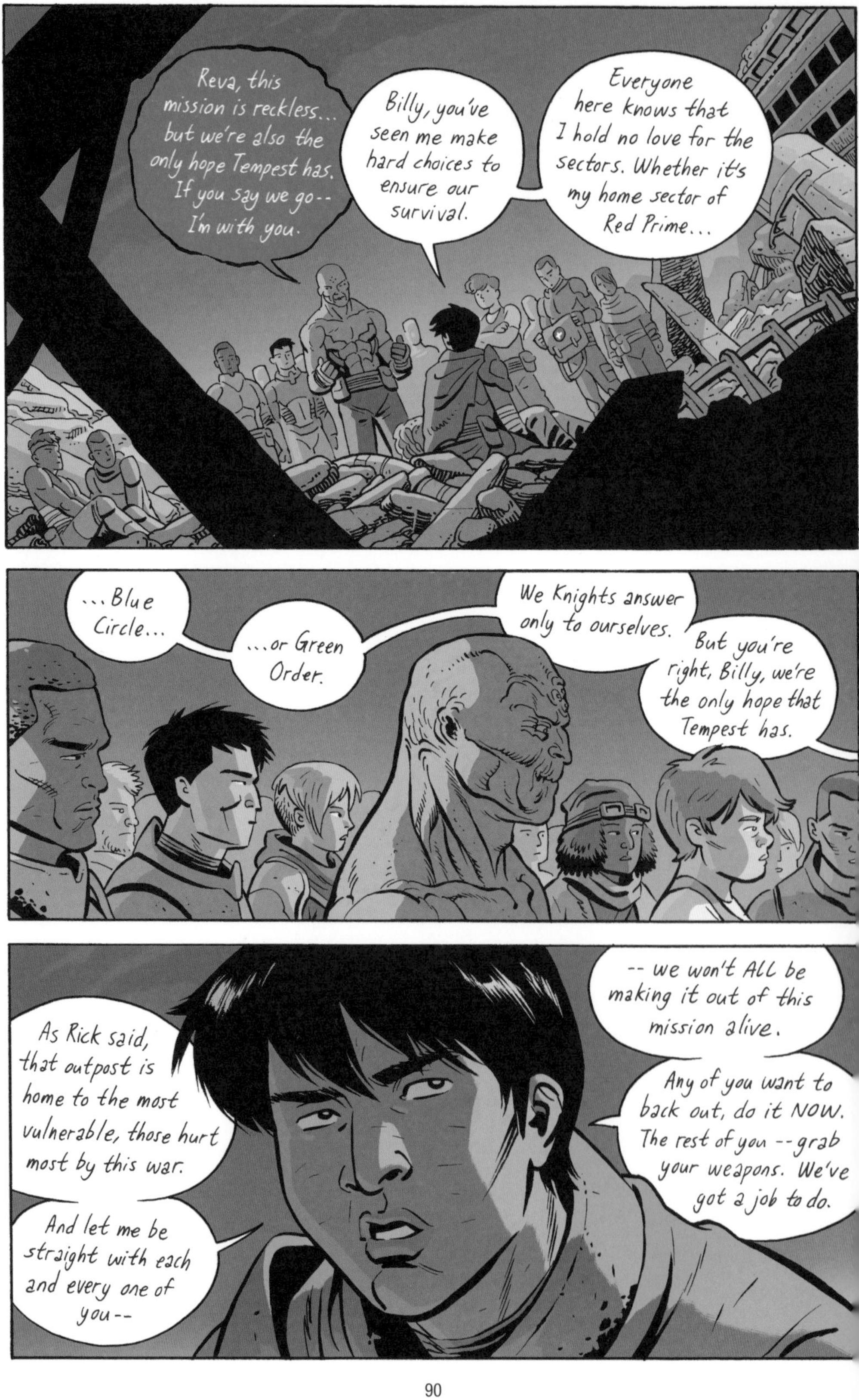
Reva, this mission is reckless... but we're also the only hope Tempest has. If you say we go-- I'm with you.
Billy, you've seen me make hard choices to ensure our survival.
Everyone here knows that I hold no love for the sectors. Whether it's my home sector of Red Prime...
...Blue Circle...
...or Green Order.
We Knights answer only to ourselves.
But you're right, Billy, we're the only hope that Tempest has.
As Rick said, that outpost is home to the most vulnerable, those hurt most by this war.
And let me be straight with each and every one of you--
-- we won't ALL be making it out of this mission alive.
Any of you want to back out, do it NOW. The rest of you --grab your weapons. We've got a job to do.

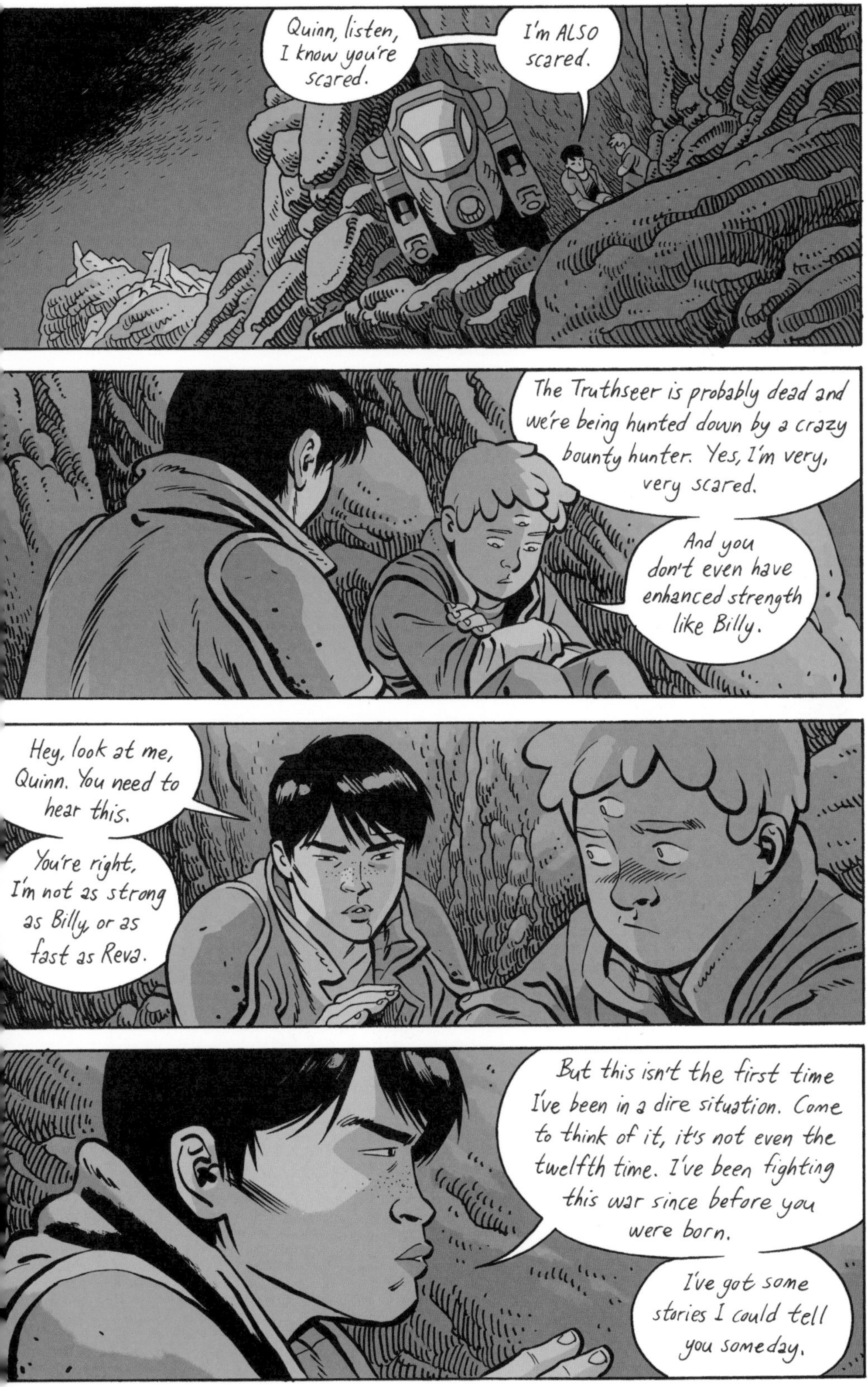
Quinn, listen, I know you're scared.
I'm ALSO scared.
The Truthseer is probably dead and we're being hunted down by a crazy bounty hunter. Yes, I'm very, very scared.
And you don't even have enhanced strength like Billy.
Hey, look at me, Quinn. You need to hear this.
You're right, I'm not as strong as Billy, or as fast as Reva.
But this isn't the first time I've been in a dire situation. Come to think of it, it's not even the twelfth time. I've been fighting this war since before you were born.
I've got some stories I could tell you someday.

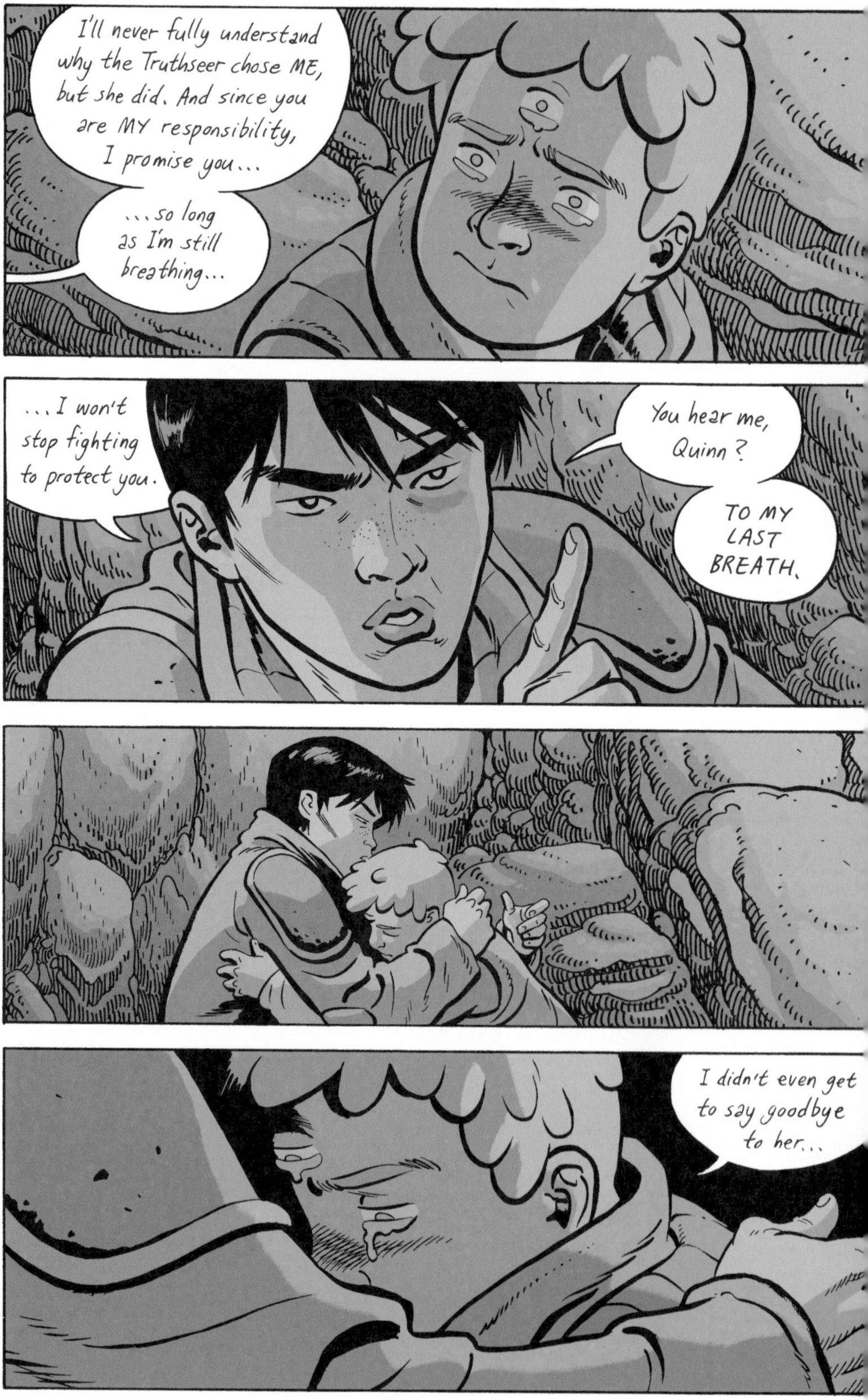

I'll never fully understand why the Truthseer chose ME, but she did. And since you are MY responsibility, I promise you...
...so long as I'm still breathing...
...I won't stop fighting to protect you.
You hear me, Quinn?
TO MY LAST BREATH.
I didn't even get to say goodbye to her...

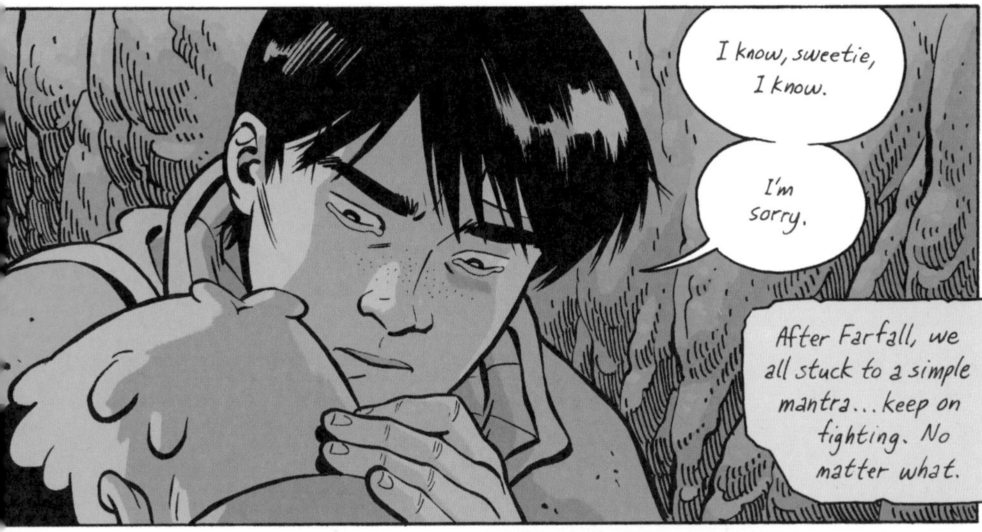
I know, sweetie, I know.
I'm sorry.
After Farfall, we all stuck to a simple mantra... keep on fighting. No matter what.

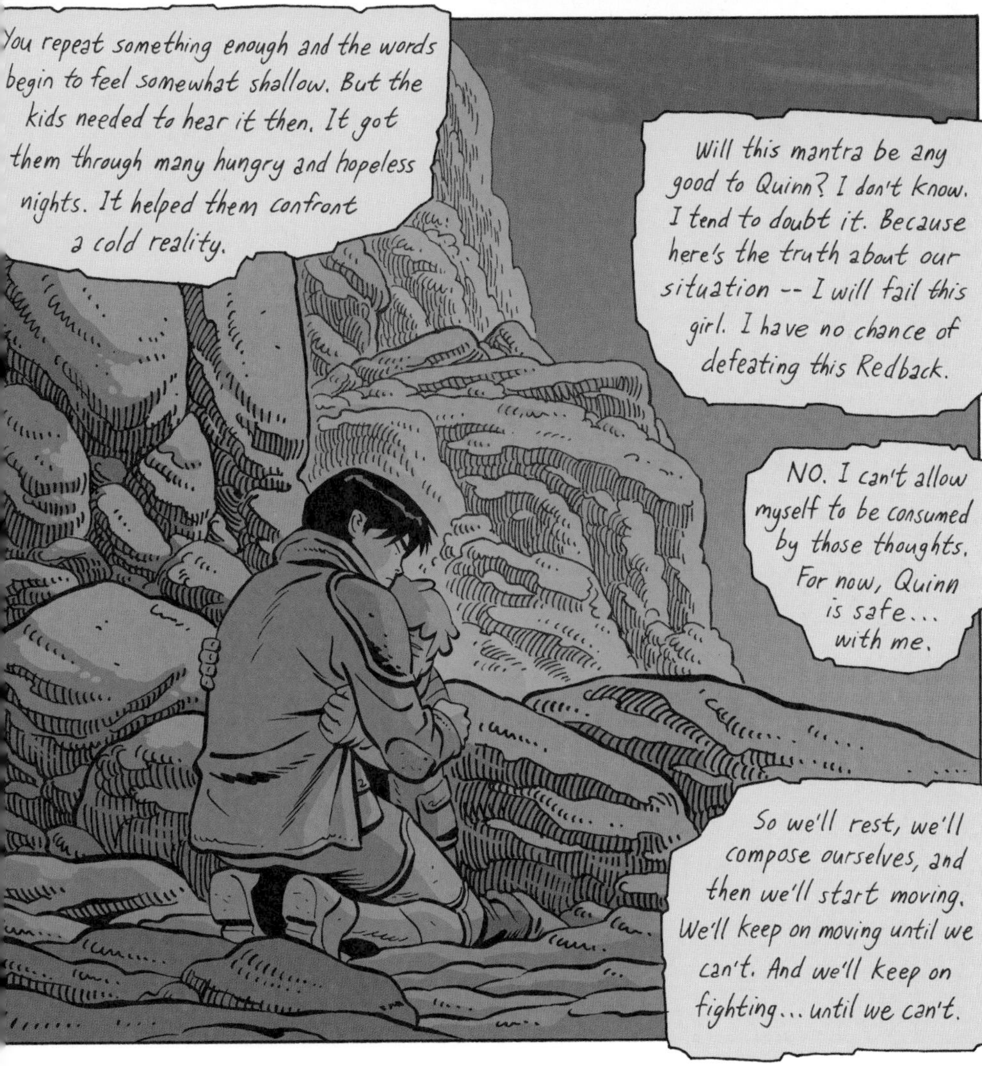
You repeat something enough and the words begin to feel somewhat shallow. But the kids needed to hear it then. It got them through many hungry and hopeless nights. It helped them confront a cold reality.
Will this mantra be any good to Quinn? I don't know. I tend to doubt it. Because here's the truth about our situation -- I will fail this girl. I have no chance of defeating this Redback.
NO. I can't allow myself to be consumed by those thoughts. For now, Quinn is safe... with me.
So we'll rest, we'll compose ourselves, and then we'll start moving. We'll keep on moving until we can't. And we'll keep on fighting... until we can't.

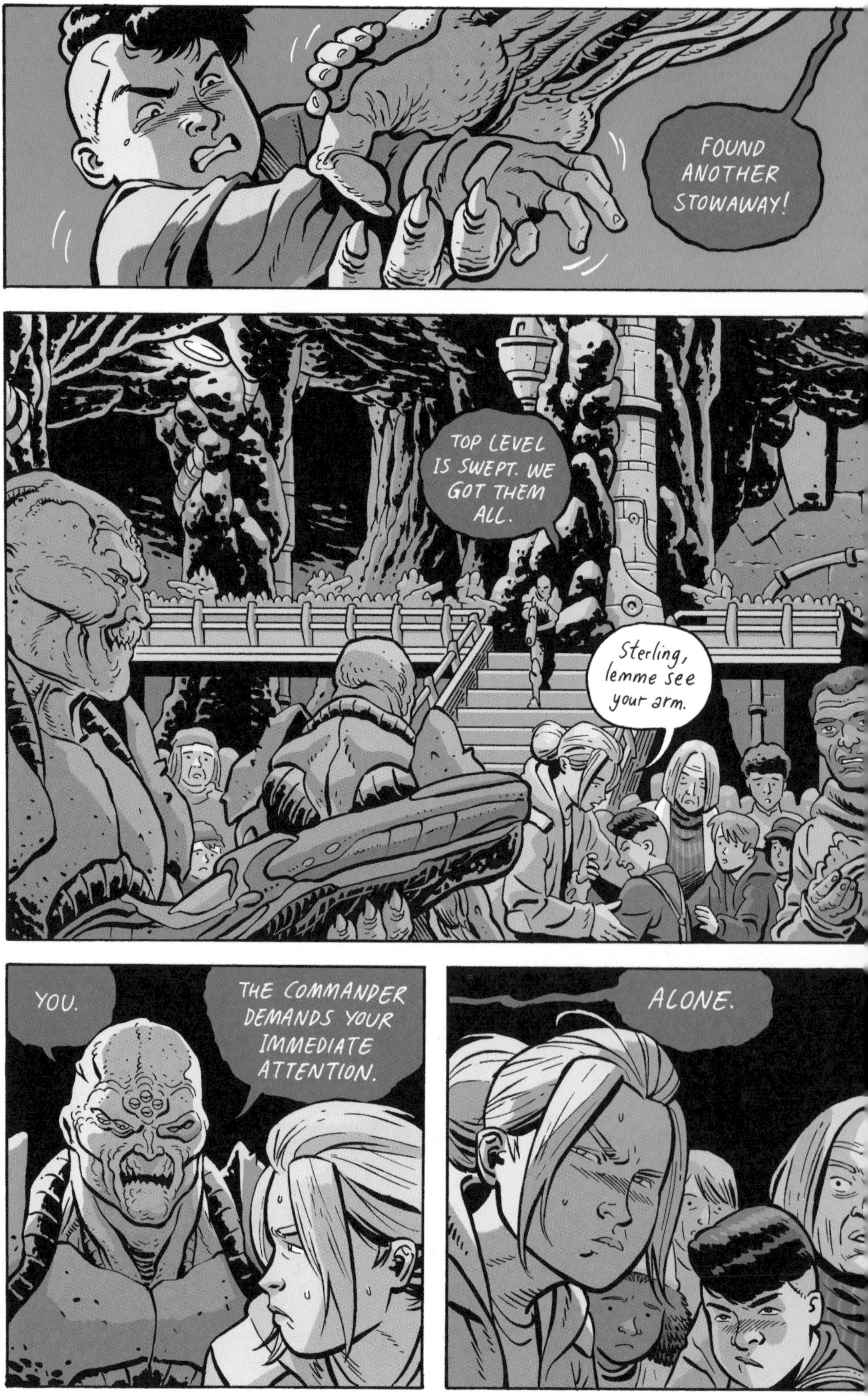
FOUND ANOTHER STOWAWAY!
TOP LEVEL IS SWEPT. WE GOT THEM ALL.
Sterling, lemme see your arm.
YOU.
THE COMMANDER DEMANDS YOUR IMMEDIATE ATTENTION.
ALONE.

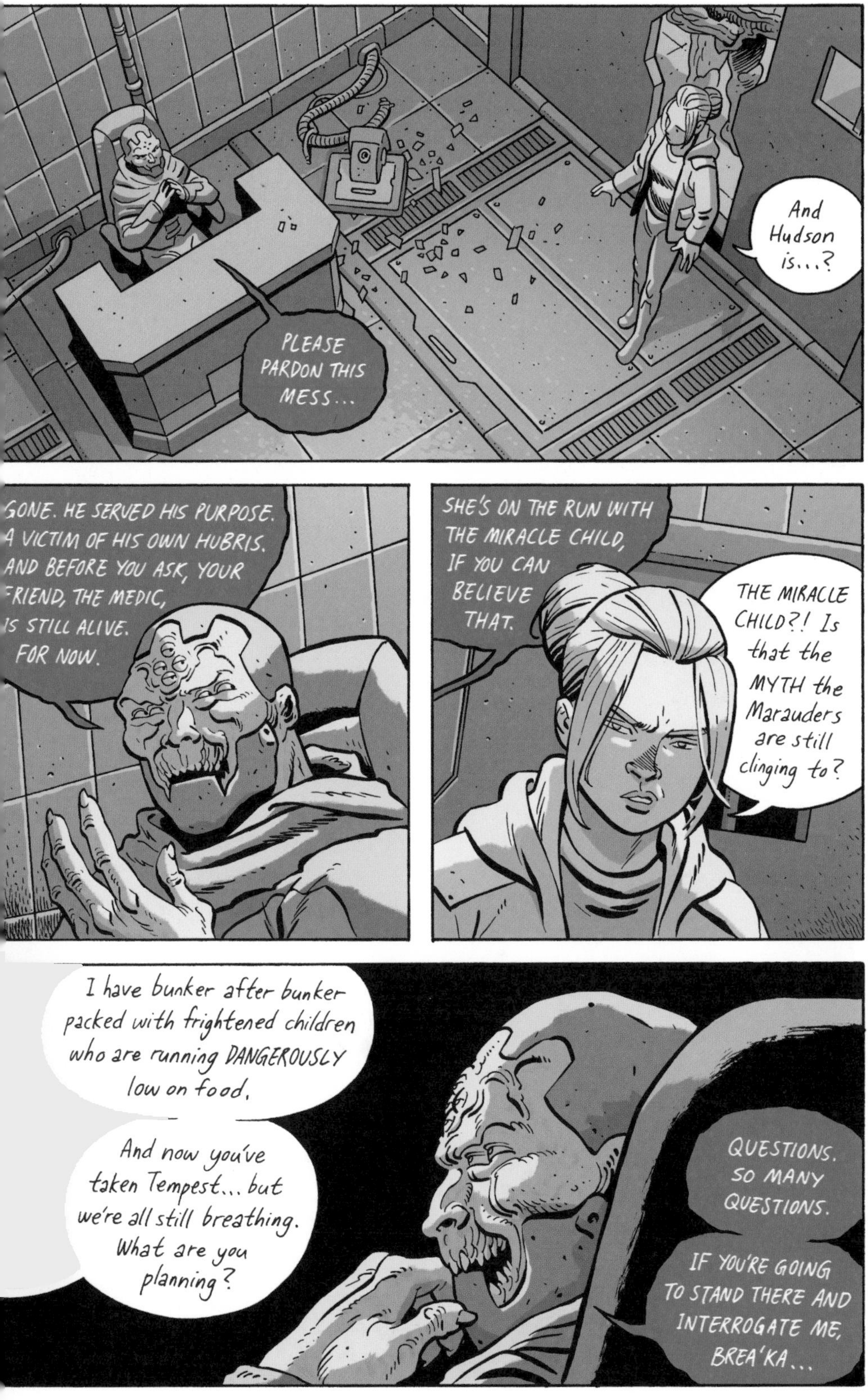
And Hudson is...?
PLEASE PARDON THIS MESS...
GONE. HE SERVED HIS PURPOSE. A VICTIM OF HIS OWN HUBRIS. AND BEFORE YOU ASK, YOUR FRIEND, THE MEDIC, IS STILL ALIVE. FOR NOW.
SHE'S ON THE RUN WITH THE MIRACLE CHILD, IF YOU CAN BELIEVE THAT.
THE MIRACLE CHILD?! Is that the MYTH the Marauders are still clinging to?
I have bunker after bunker packed with frightened children who are running DANGEROUSLY low on food.
And now you've taken Tempest... but we're all still breathing. What are you planning?
QUESTIONS. SO MANY QUESTIONS.
IF YOU'RE GOING TO STAND THERE AND INTERROGATE ME, BREA'KA...

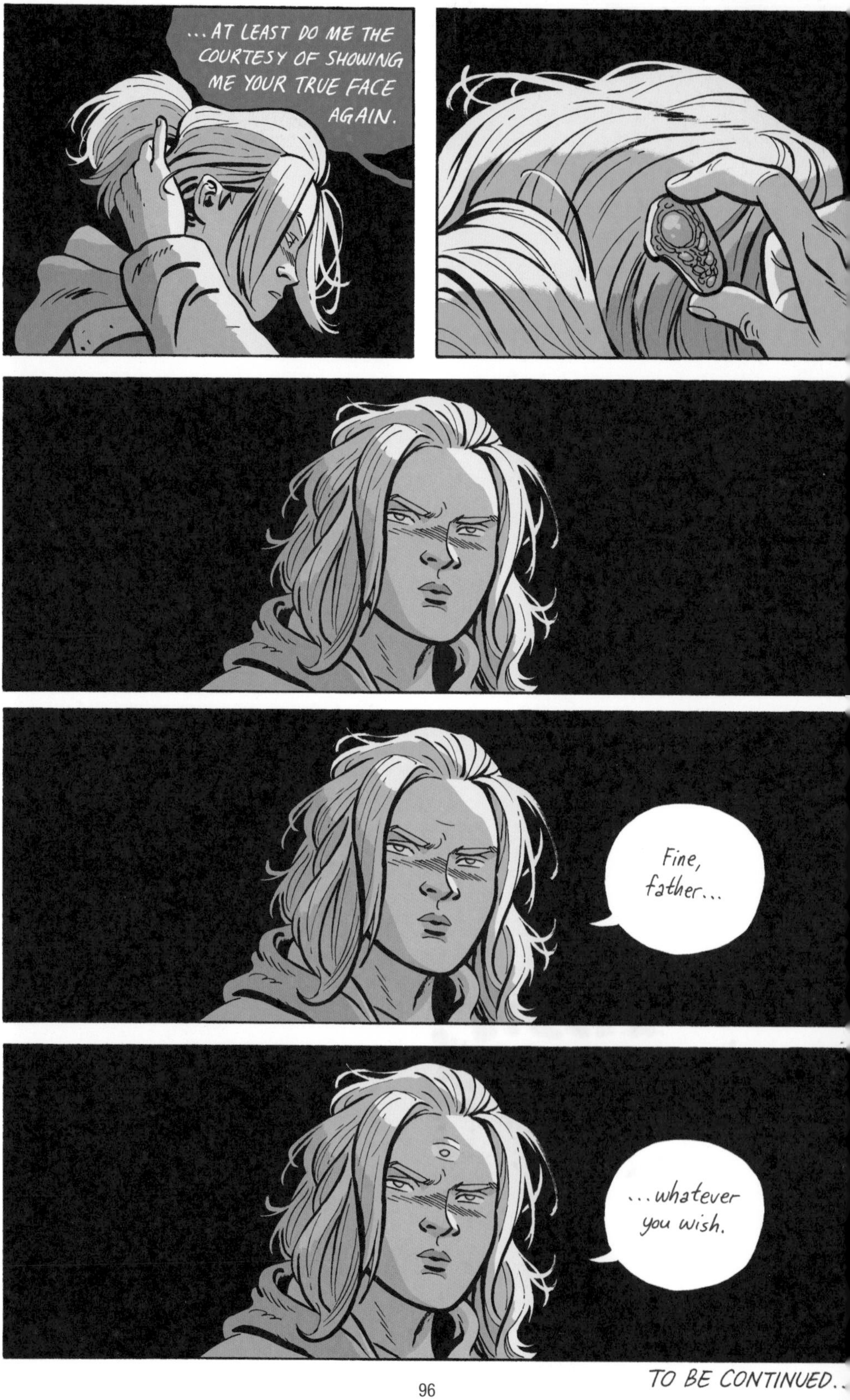
...AT LEAST DO ME THE COURTESY OF SHOWING ME YOUR TRUE FACE AGAIN.
Fine, father...
...whatever you wish.

TO BE CONTINUED...